Contents

1. Akshay

This incident occurred 5 to 6 years ago when I was working for a reputed company. Jumping back directly to the incident, the team had planned a night out and we had plans of partying really hard all night.

Our shift ended at 5 pm and we got in the cars and left for Alibag. I was in the car with my boss and 3 other team members. We played the music loud and had fun during the drive.

We had booked a nice villa that was very close to the beach. We had picked up the booze and snacks on our way. Once we reached, we quickly ordered dinner and the party started. It was a weekend the next day so we had nothing to worry about.

So, the party started, the girls changed into their party clothes and the guys got comfortable in their boxers and t-shirts. I was wearing a black V-neck top that really complimented my big bust and paired it off with some comfy shorts.

It was past midnight and half of the people had retired to their rooms, some decided to take a walk by the ocean and the rest of us (my boss, 2 friends and I stayed back to drink).

We were the only 4 in the entire villa so we turned off the lights and started dancing. We were all very high and having fun. My friends (a girl and a guy) were dancing on top of the bed in one of the rooms and I was dancing alone in the corner when I felt someone holding my hand and dancing with me.

I figured it was my friend and I didn't pay much attention. We were dancing for sometime and the music changed to something slow. The guy dancing with me wrapped his arms around my waist and started dancing very close to me.

The room was pitch dark. All we could see was a small red light beaming from the Bluetooth speaker. I closed my eyes and started dancing when I felt his lips on mine. It was so sudden and spontaneous that I didn't get much time to process.

Before I could make sense of what happened, he pinned me on the wall and slid his hand on the back of my neck. And then he slowly kissed me again and licked my lips and then he stopped. Even though the room was dark, I could feel him looking at me. Maybe he was waiting to see if I was going to give in. And I did.

I leaned up on my tippy toes to reach him and kissed him back and licked his lips just like he did to me.

"I knew it" he said softly. That was when I realised he wasn't my friend. He was my boss! But it was too late. He grabbed my face and started kissing me as if he has been starving for it. I was melting away in his arms and I couldn't stop him or even control myself.

My boss pushed his tongue inside my mouth and I felt a shiver running through my body and to my pussy. He kissed me passionately and bit my lips softly. We knew we were not alone so he stopped and went to turn on the lights.

"I am tired. I want to sleep" I told them. Akshay was looking at me but I was so shy and horny and scared that I didn't look at him once.

My friends left their rooms and since my roommates were out roaming by the beach, I was left alone. I texted them informing that I was going to sleep and they said that they will be waiting till sunrise. So I locked the door.

I cleaned the room a bit, spread out the bed sheet properly and was about to change when I heard a faint knock. I immediately knew who it was. I could have just ignored it and slept it off and acted like I didn't remember stuff in the morning but I don't know why I walked to the door and opened it.

Akshay was standing there waiting for me.

"Others?" He asked about my roommates

"They are going to stay outside. Watch the sunrise. It's almost morning, so.."

"Good for us" he was flirting.

"Yeah? How so?" I knew what I was doing was going to land me in trouble but I didn't care. I had a taste of him and now I wanted him.

He walked inside and locked the door behind him.

"Those two are outside by the pool. Drinking there."

"Okay."

"So... did you like it" he was asking about the kiss. I wanted to say that I loved it but I was in no mood of being straight forward.

"I don't know. It happened out of nowhere. You didn't give me time to process it."

"So, you don't know?"

"No. I was super high. Don't even remember most of it."

"What do you remember then?"

"Just lips. Wet lips on mine."

"What about when you kissed me back?"

"I don't think that happened." I was playing dumb but he knew I was playing with him.

He came on to me, pushed me on the bed, grabbed both my boobs and kissed me harder than the previous time. I wrapped my legs around him and grabbed his hair in my fist. I loved how he grabbed my boobs.

He sat on the bed, pulled me up and slipped his hands inside my top. He kept looking in my eyes with hunger. God! I wanted him to fuck me right then. But something told me that teasing him was going to make it fun.

He unhooked my bra and removed it and I removed his t-shirt. I ran my hands on his hairy chest. I ran my finger on his chest and his nipples. They hardened the moment I touched them. I looked up at him and smiled.

I slowly held his face and pecked on his lips. He was horny and was finding it hard to control. I could see that by the way his body was reacting to me and his breathing was heavier. Just like me, he wanted to take it slow.

I bit his lower lip gently and grabbed his nipples in between my fingers. His lips opened for a moan and I slipped my tongue inside. He grabbed my hair and we kissed for so long. Breathing heavily into each other's mouths, fondling with each other's bodies and moaning in between the passionate kiss.

We broke the kiss and he was still holding my hair in his hands and looking at my face. "I'm gonna fuck you real hard."

"We will see," I said. I knew he loved being challenged because me teasing him and being hard to get was turning him into a horny beast. And I love beasts.

"God! Those boobs are huge!" He peeked inside my top. "I swear I've never seen this big."

I pushed him away and removed my top. "Now you have" I was completely naked from the torso. My big 38D (now 42F) size boobs hanging in front of him. His eyes were glued down on them.

I kissed him on his cheek and hugged him. He grabbed me tight and squeezed my body on his. He was feeling my boobs on his chest. He didn't miss an opportunity, I was liking him.

I started kissing him on his cheek while he squeezed me in his arms, running his hands on my back like a predator getting to know his prey. I wanted him inside me. I licked his ear and moved down to his neck. "Aah" he couldn't even manage to moan and that was how I knew his seduction point.

I gave him a nice hickey and we kissed again. I got on my knees on the bed while he was still on the bed. I held my boob and brought it closer to his mouth. Like a hungry dog, he pounced on it and started sucking the life out of one and squeezing the other with his hand.

"We don't have all night," I told him reminding about our team members who might come back in a few hours.

"Who said that I'm only going to bang you tonight?" Those words turned me on to another level. I slipped my hands inside his boxers and he wasn't wearing any underwear.

He saw how horny it made me. "I never wear underwear. Not even at work. Just the jeans."

I could picture how he was going to find sneaky ways of pulling out his dick from his pants and fucking me at work. Maybe he will fuck me in the parking lot, or on the terrace. Or in his car. I knew that after today, things were going to change. I was glad I had a dick at my disposal.

I pulled out his thick fat cock and started stroking it gently. I spat on it and stroked it till the foreskin was pushed back and I could see the fat purple juicy tip.

"You like?" he asked.

"Mmhh" I wanted a taste so bad that I couldn't say a word. He took off my shorts and my panty in one pull. My pussy was leaking with juices.

"Baby!! You are juicy." he touched my wet pussy lips.

"You have no idea." I held his hand and rubbed it back and forth from my pussy to my ass. The juices were everywhere.

He couldn't take his eyes off of my pussy. "I am gonna take good care of you baby. It's a good thing you broke up last week."

"As if that would have stopped any of us from doing what we are doing right now." we both laughed and started kissing again.

He hugged me again and started licking my neck. He slowly laid me on the bed. The way he was being gentle with me was making me go crazy. He planted kisses all over my body starting from my forehead to my thighs. He lifted my arms up and I held onto the headboard.

Then he came on top of me and I could feel his cock roughing my right thigh. He kept looking into my eyes and I felt two fingers pushing my lips open. We were both breathing heavily and nobody wanted to take their eyes off of each other.

"Oh baby, if only you could see the look that you have! You can turn anyone on with that look."

"Right now, I want you!" He groaned and I felt his fingers entering my slippery hole.

"Oh fuck! Baby! It's so wet!"

"It's been this way from the moment you licked my lips."

"Good thing I came here. This needed urgent attention."

"Yes, please!"

He pushed his finger deeper and started scraping the walls of my pussy.

"Akshay!"

"Oh..." he was able to speak and neither was I. He fingered me for a few hot minutes. The entire time he held my head with his other hand so that he could look into my eyes.

"I can't" I wanted to tell him that I can't wait more.

"I know baby," he kissed me gently and got on top of me. I immediately held his dick and started rubbing my thumb on his tip.

"You are good."

"I love dicks."

"Clearly!"

He was rock hard. His cock was so thick that I knew it was going to hurt.

"Go slow," I told him knowing that it was going to hurt.

"Of course. A tight pussy should be enjoyed slowly."

I held his dick again to position it but he removed my hands.

"Let me take care of you."

I nodded because I was dying for it and didn't want to waste another second. He pushed my legs wider by sliding his legs near mine. I spread my legs as wide as I could.

"Love girls who spread their legs this way. Shows how hungry they are."

"Very!"

I could feel his cock dancing on top of my clit. I was so engrossed in waiting for him to enter that I didn't realise he was teasing me.

"Oh no! Not now. I want it."

"I know. That's why I'm gonna make you suffer."

"Baby, please. Tease me during foreplay but not now. Especially when I can feel you so close."

"So close. Right above the love hole."

"Baby, I'm so fucking wet."

"I'll like it to be more wet."

"It will be. Just put it in me."

I kept begging him but he kept kissing me and making out with me with his cock right above my hole. I tried slipping it in me with my hand but he was faster than me. He would push my hand away.

"I'll do everything you say. Just fuck me please."

"Everything? You sure?"

"Yes I am."

"I'm gonna fuck you at work. Whenever I find an opportunity, I'll call you to the place I find and you'll have to come."

"Okay, yes" I knew this was going to happen. I was already fantasizing about it.

"I'll fuck you in the parking lot after the ye dark. I'll fuck you on the emergency stairs. We'll find corners where there are no cameras and I'll screw you."

"Yes."

"And when you leave the job, we'll meet outside and I'll fuck you then."

"Yes."

"You really want it so bad."

"You saw how wet I am. I want it really really bad."

He positioned his cock on my hole and I lifted my ass up for him to get a better entry.

"Mmhh! Eager!"

He slowly pushed his cock inside me. Our eyes locked with each other. He held my face in his hands as he slowly kept entering in me. I lifted my legs up in the air and held them with both my hands.

"Oh, you are such a nice fuck."

He pushed his dick inside me with one thrust.

"Akshay!"

"Fuck! It's so hot inside," he grabbed my face and pushed it deeper in me. I could feel his balls touching my ass. He was so deep inside me that I couldn't contemplate how good it felt. I wanted that dick in me forever.

"Oh baby, that face! That wet pussy. And you are so hot inside. You have been dying to get fucked, haven't you?"

I nodded at him. "Oh baby. I'm here for you."

He started pumping his cock in and out of me. "I'm going to fuck you."

He kept pumping at a slow rhythmic pace. "I'm making you mine. You are mine."

I nodded at him looking into his eyes. Akshay increased the pace and started giving me heavy strokes. I was loving it.

"Yeah! Keep going."

He realised I was liking it. He held both my legs and started giving me heavy slow and deep strokes. I caressed his face and kissed him gently.

"Is it okay if I said I love you? You just feel so good and.."

"I love you." I cut him off. He smiled and gave me a deeper stroke.

"God! Yes!" My body was shaking up and down. He placed a pillow between my head and the pillow to make sure I don't bang my head on it.

"I'm make you mine."

"Make me yours, Akshay."

"Yes!" He started fucking me a little faster but kept giving me the heavy strokes that I was enjoying.

"I.." he was breathing heavy and couldn't speak a word.

"I know baby" I kissed him and started sucking his tongue. He groaned and started fucking me harder and faster. I grabbed him in my arms and he laid his head on top of mine and started fucking me harder. The entire time we maintained eye contact.

We loved watching each other's faces. Akshay then lifted me in his arms and pinned me on the wall.

I grabbed him from the neck and wrapped my legs around him. He pumped his cock in me while my body rubbed against the wall violently. I kept whispering in his ear telling him how good he dick felt and how I am fantasising him fucking me like this in the parking lot at the office.

He then settled me down and we walked back on the bed. He grabbed my ass and started squeezing it. I turned around, got on knees on the bed and bent down for him.

"Oh yes!" He spanked my ass hard again and again.

Akshay stood near my ass with his six rubbing against my asshole. I've never been fucked in the ass and I didn't want to. But I also wanted to feel him in my ass so I stayed there waiting for him to push it in.

"I'm gonna fuck this tight hole" he said while he spit on my asshole and rubbed it in with his thumb. "But not tonight. Tonight is for this hot pussy."

He pushed his cock back inside my pussy and this time it went deeper. I bent down further and I felt him going deeper.

I was on the bed, face down and he held my hair and started banging me.

"Look up front," he said and I did like he asked. There was a mirror in front of us and I could see him fucking me.

"Oh, yes baby. You are so deep in my womb right now."

"It's so hot in here. Nobody can last long in you."

I smiled at him and he kept fucking me while looking at me from the mirror. I adjusted myself to give him a good view of my boobs moving up and down with his rhythm.

"That's it. I'm gonna ruin you." He pulled out and pushed me on my back. It was as if someone else had taken over his body.

Akshay grabbed my legs and placed them both together in his hands and in one painful push he entered in me. He started fucking me hard with no care about the noise his strokes were making. "Akshay!!" I tried warning him but he was lost in the moment.

He opened my legs and his body fell on top of me. He held my boobs with both his hands and kept banging me. He buried his head in between my neck and his breathing got heavier and he kept fucking me.

The room was filled with the sound of our bodies slapping against each other and our hungry moans. At that moment, I didn't give a fuck about who would find out. I wanted this man to take me.

We fucked for hours, Akshay would slap my pussy in between with his dick and his hand to make me hornier. He rubbed my clit till I came on his dick but he kept going.

"Oh baby. I love you so fucking much," he said while moaning and fucking me ruthlessly.

When he was close to having an orgasm, he pulled out his dick and ate my pussy till I came on his mouth. And then he fingered me and rubbed my pussy, smeared my juices all over my boobs and nipples. He pushed his dick back in me and fucked me like his life depended on it.

When he was about to cum, I sat up on the bed and started sucking his dick. I could taste my salty pussy juices all over his dick, dripping till his balls. I grabbed his balls and smeared my juice all over it and started massaging.

Akshay was unable to stay on his knees on the bed so I laid him down and continued playing with him. He kept kicking his leg and moaned crazy. I could feel the veins on his dick pulse and I knew he was gonna cum. I grabbed his dick and took the tip in my mouth and started massaging it with my tongue.

"Baby... I'm gonna.." before he could complete, he shivered and I felt a huge load being shot in my mouth. I kept massaging his dick slowly and I felt him cumming in my mouth every time he shivered.

Once he was done, I got on top of him and swallowed his cum in front of me. He grabbed my face and kissed me so deep, we both could taste each other's and our own juices.

"I'm never going to get over this" he laid on my bed catching his breath.

I got up, changed and decided to walk outside to see where others were. I found my friends sleeping on the chairs by the pool and nobody had returned. Maybe my friends heard our noises and decided to dose off outside so that we don't find out that they knew.

The next afternoon, we checked out from the villa to go back home. Many others had their plans so they formed groups and left. Me and Akshay were with other group of friends.

Once we reached back to Mumbai, Akshay said that he had to change his route to see a friend after which he was headed to Lonavala. He told me that he was going in the direction of my home and the others got down from the car.

Once we were alone, we booked a hotel nearby and decided to spend the night there.

2. *Indrani*

I am Indrani. I am a working girl who has a crazy sex drive which has made me sleep with some sexy men. Since I am too much into sex, I can't stop any guy if he tries to seduce me. I end up getting fucked by him again and again. I keep giving him my pussy till I get bored of him or till I find someone sexier. But I don't like sending guys away empty handed. So, if you are planning on trying your luck then I'm eagerly waiting with a wet pussy for you. Anyways I am now 25 years old and I live in Mumbai from past 15 years. I am short in height with a dark skin tone and some extra fat. My boobs are 38 D (You can't hold my single boob with one hand). I have a big ass which gets touched by many men every time I travel in a bus or train (I love the male compartment for this reason).

This incident took place when I was 18 years old. I was in a BEST Bus which I had taken to go to Borivali. I wanted to take a window seat and the only window seat available was in the end row of the bus. So I took a seat by the window and later a huge man with a dark skin sat beside me. His body was sticking to mine as he was huge in size and couldn't fit in his own seat. He kept on reaching for his pockets again and again during which he managed to touch my boobs. I was too busy listening to the songs to notice his intentions. Later, when the bus started the guy beside me slept but he kept on falling over me in his sleep. Again, he touched my boobs and his legs were sticking to mine. Soon it started to get dark outside and his attempts got doubled. He was still sleeping but this time his face was facing my side.

I was wearing a tank top and a full-length skirt. Since the neck line was deep I had to pull it up to make sure my cleavage is hidden. He being tall and huge got the advantage of taking the view. After some time, he stopped troubling me to which I thought that he has given up. It was an overnight journey so I decided to take some sleep as everyone in the bus was fast asleep. While I was sleeping, I could feel pressure on my boobs again and again but I ignored. After few minutes the pressure on my boobs increased. I opened my eyes to find everyone still sleeping. Thinking that it was a dream, I tried to sleep again. And the same thing happened once again.

When I woke up, everyone was sleeping. This happened more 2 or 3 times. This time I decided to just close my eyes and pretend to sleep. And that is when I felt it again. My boob was being pressed very slowly and carefully by the man sitting beside me. For a second, I felt extremely angry and I wanted to slap him but then I decided to push away the anger. I stayed in that position for some more time giving him the opportunity to press my boob harder. This time he thought that I am in a deep sleep and he grabbed my boob and pressed it softly and waited. I was still pretending to sleep and he pressed it again. I could feel him breathing right near my face which meant he was very close to me. Slowly he ran his other hand over my skirt and grabbed my thigh. I moaned slowly giving him a positive response. He opened my thighs apart and kept his hand near my pussy.

This time I could feel him breathing so fast. He pressed my boob once again but with a lot of pressure this time. Soon he was in a rhythm and was rubbing my thighs over the skirt and pressing my boobs. Then I decided to open my eyes and act of catching him doing his thing. He was frozen with fear. With one hand in between my thighs and one hand on my boob, he looked straight at me with fear. I looked at the others were busy sleeping like the dead. I immediately kissed him on his lips and he was shocked. After few seconds he started lifting up my skirt and touched my bare skin. I kept on kissing him to contain my moans. His hand went straight inside my panty which was now wet. Realizing how wet I was he moan in between the kiss and started rubbing my pussy very hard. I was losing control and he was enjoying it. I held his hand and forced him to stop teasing me and pushed his finger inside. I broke the kiss to look at his reaction. "Ye toh bahot garam hai" (it's so warm inside) he whispered in my ear. I smiled at him and he started fingering me like an animal. I was in pain but the look of pleasure on his face was amazing. I pulled out my boob from my bra and let it hang in front of him. I could see the lust doubled in his eyes. He kept on looking at my boob and fingered me more deeply with his 3 fingers. I had to close my mouth as the pain was too much. He started sucking my nipple like a baby and never took the finger out. He made me cum 4 times mercilessly. He licked his fingers when he was done.

The rest of the journey was spent with him pressing my boobs whenever he got a chance because now people had started waking up. He kept on asking for my number but since I was no more horny, I did not give him any.

3. *Roja*

It was raining and it was perfect for sex. Roja lied at home that she had to submit a project and would be late from college. She got ready, put some make-up on, shaved down there and wore some comfortable yet fashionable-looking clothes.

She left home with a folder filled with useless papers and her handbag and did not consist of a single book. After college was over, she sat in the library for about an hour, waiting for people to leave. It was 3:30 pm students along with most of the staff left for home.

Roja made a call and asked Ritesh to meet her on the 6th-floor corridor. She went to the toilet, freshened herself, checked her make-up. She adjusted her push-up bra to reveal her cleavage.

As instructed, Ritesh reached the 6th-floor corridor. Covered in borrowed perfume, he wore a black jacket with black pants and a white shirt. 6 foot 3 inches, revealing the top of his hairy muscular chest, he looked hot.

There was nobody on this floor. It gave Ritesh a scary feeling. Yet, he patiently waited because the fruit he was getting was nothing compared to this fear. And within 2 minutes, he saw Roja in her blue jeans and long kurta with a scarf hanging from her shoulder to give Ritesh a good look at her sexy cleavage.

With the duplicate key, he opened the biology lab. He made sure he hung the lock outside so that if a by passer sees it, he would understand it was unlocked. After getting in, they carefully locked it from inside.

Standing in this empty biology lab where they could hear the swishing sounds of wind from the window. They looked at each other nervously, each one conscious about themselves. Roja's heart was beating so fast she could feel the drumming on her chest.

This was all her plan, but as a girl, she can't make the first move. She stood there waiting for Ritesh to make a move. She was a wild child, a total badass, but now she was too shy to make a move. Ritesh took a deep breath and extended his hands forward. The moment Roja held it, he took a deep breath.

He pulled her and locked his lips with her soft pink lips. He could feel the taste of mint in his mouth. The moment their lips locked; the animal Roja was hiding inside broke out. She went close enough that her tits touched Ritesh's chest.

His hands wrapped her around, one started fondling her boobs, and another one was pressing her fat round ass. She had a great body. Her bigger-than-average ass was perfectly round, and her boobs soft and smooth as butter. She was enjoying the kiss, and more than that, she was enjoying this.
Finally, they broke apart. The look in Roja's deep eyes sent a clear message that all the shyness was gone. She wanted some action, and she wanted it now. She unbuttoned her pants and started striping. Roja took off her kurta, revealing her cute boobs under it and the neon-colored push-up bra holding it.

Ritesh went hard, his cock making a huge tent in his jeans. Roja hated sucking a cock, nor she allowed to lick her pussy. In the neon bra and jeans below her knees, she opened her bag and pulled out some lubricant.

Ritesh wondered what if her dad finds it casually lying in her bag. He resisted the feeling of bringing this question up. Roja was on her pills. There was no need for a condom.

After applying the lubricant, they were ready. Roja turned around, bent on one of the big tables of this lab, and tightly held the edges. With his throbbing cock, Ritesh went forward and placed the head of his fat cock on Roja's wet pussy entrance.

Their hearts were beating crazy they were so nervous they already started sweating. Roja could feel the hot cock touching her clean-shaven pussy. She has waited for this for so long. Her mind couldn't think of anything but sex.

Right now, all she wanted was that thick hot cock touching her pussy to ram her like crazy. To make her moan and scream. She wanted all her wishes to come true – her dirty wishes.

With a push, the head of this fat cock was entered her pussy, 'Aah!' Roja sighed. Slowly it was going deeper and deeper. With her mouth wide open and her eyes closed, she was lost. Ritesh's hands were running all over her half-naked body. Her perfect ass, her boobs, were hiding behind that bra.

She pulled up her bra, and her round boobs jumped out. They were not massive. Instead, they were a little smaller as compared to the proportion of her ass. But there was still time for them to grow.

"Aaah!" Roja moaned as Ritesh cock was slowly fucking her pussy. She wanted this for so long, and she wanted it so bad. Fondling with her boobs with one hand, Ritesh held Roja's shoulder tightly with another. He was slowly going in and pulling out.

He wanted to play with her bare body. He wanted nothing to come in between this session of passionate hot sex. Snatching the unhooked bra, Ritesh threw it far away. Roja did the rest by taking her jeans off. Now that's how he liked a woman naked with his cock inside her.

He started increasing his pace and speed. Slowly the fat cock was beating her hot, smooth pussy. Faster and faster they went. His cock was fucking her like crazy, his hands playing with her boobs and naked ass while she held the table with her hands and would eventually leave it to rub her pussy.

The moment he pinched her nipples, she let out a high-pitched moan, just like anime characters. This made him even harder and hornier. "Aaah! Aaa please! Aaah aah oh oh oh..." She went on and on with every jerk.

She opened her ass cheeks so that he can go even deeper inside her. But the sad part was this was all he had. It was thick and juicy and fast, but it was just average-sized. Smaller than she had before. But it wasn't so bad.

Ritesh just kept going from behind and not stopping at all. His hands were pressing her boobs and ass harder and harder. The clapping of skin and the slapping of the ass were louder than her moans. It was time. Ritesh felt sudden energy. He went on with all his might.

The fat cock rubbing the inside of her pussy made her crazy. She wanted more and more, but his increased speed gave her the signal. She wanted his thick warm cum all over her face. But before she could instruct Ritesh to do so, he pulled his fat cock out.

"Aaah!" She moaned in pain. It was too loud, and she grabbed her mouth not to let any more of her painful screams out. Before she could turn to face Ritesh's fat cock he lost control and came all over her back and ass. The load shot as far as she got some of it in her hairs.

Covered in sweat and cum she got up happy but wanting some more. She went to look for her bra and came back to find Ritesh already in his jeans. No dialogues were shared between them. Quietly they wore clothes. They put everything back. They locked the lab from outside and went down for a smoke.

One drag, and now everything rushed to her mind. The cigarette gave her the rest of the pleasure. She wanted so much. Her body still covered in sweat and her hair smelling of cum she took a cab. Ping. She checked the message it was Ritesh, "Next?"

"Saturday," she typed and hit send.

4. Principal

This was my 2nd session. The principal already fucked me once on this very table, rested for a while. I was naked on the table. My saree was on the floor and my blouse unbuttoned while the principal was licking my naked pussy.

He was gentleman enough to ask me for water, then started again. I came here for my son's admission and was ready to for that. After the death of my husband, he was the only family I had in this city. Some people showed sympathy but most showed lust.

I can see the hunger in their eyes. Their gaze made me uncomfortable, how they looked at me first face, then my big boobs. Then my navel and then my fat ass. I was never this busty not many found me attractive.

I was never the most popular girl, but I gained a lot of weight after giving birth. Somehow, I grew from all the right place. I loved the transition, the attention from the opposite sex. I never got that, but even though I was married.

I had a fantastic sex drive I still enjoyed the attention. But that's all. I drew a line I never wanted to cheat on my husband. But things changed after his death. I realized he was the barrier between the society of some pervert hungry men who saw women as nothing but sex objects and me.

After his death, people crossed their lines many times. They came into my house uninvited, would help me carry my bag. I rub their hands on my ass and my big boobs. The teenage boys were the worst.

I was groped and spanked in crowded places with catcalling and wolf-whistling. The workplace was not safe either. I was offered to have sex on the couch to get promoted. But it never happened. No man ever got to enjoy the depth of my pussy after my husband's death until today.

The principal has now climbed upon me. He had his dick ready, and with a push, he was inside me. "Aaah!" I moaned. But he didn't stop and pushed again, thrusting the rest of his meat inside me.

"Slow, please," I said in pain, but he just smiled and started kissing me. He was too good for his age. I never fucked someone his age with his salt and pepper hairs and the wrinkles on his face. He was aged maybe 60 years old.

I wonder if he had it in him or did it come with experience, but he stayed way longer than my husband and fucked my brains out. Sex was good, but this was better than how it was 16 years ago with my husband. He must be doing it with many women.

I wonder how many married women gave him sexual pleasure and took his dick on this very table. Just like me, they must have come to him to get their sons or daughters admission to college.

He demanded money. But I explained to him my financial condition and told him that I was a single mother. Then he made me an offer. I accepted it, and here I was getting nailed.

"You are tight. Tighter than I thought. You must have not been fucked in ages," he said. With my eyes closed, I just shook my head. "Don't worry, I am going to make it worth it." He gave a strong jerk which made me moan again.

He was gaining speed in-out, in-out, in-out. I was losing it. I was loving the way he was kissing my neck. His hands pressing my fat boobs while he rammed his cock inside me. It was so fat rubbing on the walls of my pussy and long enough.

It reached the depth of my cunt. I wanted this depth to be explored by a cock. But for the past 16 years, there was no one, and today, I found the perfect cock in the most unlikely place.

He stopped and lifted my leg, and placed it on his shoulder. It was difficult to get in that position, but he was doing all the things. He once again placed his cock on my warm wet pussy. Again, he pushed hard.

"Aah!"

I did not know I was this flexible. My husband would fuck me in missionary and woman-on-top only. Never tried anything else. But this was great. For the first time, I was fucked on a table. I was enjoying this half-naked fuck.

The clapping sound of our skins echoed in the whole room. He kept kissing me at regular intervals, would pinch my nipples, and spank my fat ass. His hand was like a man who worked years on a farm, hard.

Spanking left a mark on my ass cheeks, but I liked the printed marks on his hands. This was to give him pleasure so that he would admit my son to his college in return for this sexual pleasure. One can easily say that I was enjoying it too. Maybe more than him.

He pulled his cock out. It was covered in my juices. But still, rock hard. I got up and sat on my knees. My husband never came on my face or made me swallow his cum. He would either cum inside me.

It was a completely different type of pleasure when the warm cum flows inside the body, or he would cum on my stomach and sleep. I came to know about these new things when I craved for dick. I watched porn in a closed locked door and fingered myself.

The men in these videos were so muscular. The dick size was unbelievable, not to forget how long they fucked and the way they fucked. Girls these days liked all their holes to be fucked.

If their nose and ears holes could expand, they would get them fucked too. While I sat on my knees with my mouth closed, ready for his warm sticky cum to land on my face anytime, he bent forward and kissed me.

"I thought you were a simple housewife but do have some dark fantasies. But not so soon, my dear," he said and held my shoulder. He lifted me, turned me around, and threw me on the table face down.

I could believe he was still going on. He opened my legs wide, grabbed both my shoulders. With a push, he again shoved the whole of his cock inside me. "Aah!" again. But this time, he wasn't gentle. He was fucking me like a cheap prostitute, with all his might.

"Aah aah aaah aaah, slow, slow, " he was fucking me so hard I couldn't complete a single sentence without moaning. My boobs were jiggling like jelly. My fat ass was clapping with his abdomen while my moans, along with the clapping of our skin, echoed in the room.

This room must be soundproof. Otherwise, the way I was moaning, someone must have definitely come in to see what's happening inside. Or else this was nothing new for the staff. It was not unusual to hear a woman moaning and getting banged.

The jerks were so strong the whole table was shaking along with me. Though his fat cock was making my pussy pain like hell. I was now enjoying all of it. Suddenly he pulled the clip holding my hair and threw it away. He caught a handful of my loose hairs and pulled them back.

He continued ramming his cock inside me again. "Ooh oooh aah! Yes yes... Don't stop... Aaah! Keep going... Ahh!" I was never fucked like this. I never knew deep down inside I wanted to be treated like this.

Fucked like this. Fucked like how you see cheap prostitutes are fucked. Deep down inside, I wanted to be treated like a bitch. My whole body was shaking. My eyes were blurry, and suddenly I came.

"Aaaaah!" were my last words. I was on the table like I had no life in me. My face down, my boobs and hands hanging out, and my body covered in sweat. I was thirsty. I wanted water. The principal pulled his cock out and placed the head of his cock on my lips.

The red lipstick now on the pick head of his fat and strong cock. He pushed it again inside, and I could taste my own juices. With a jerk, thick warm cum shot out of his cock and filled my mouth. Without thinking, I swallowed it all.

5. Alcohol

Dad left for his business trip today morning and would be back after a week. I knew exactly what do with all this time and how to enjoy when dad was gone. I called my friend.

"Tarak, I need some alcohol"

I went to college assured Tarak will find a way to deliver it to me. His ways were always dramatic like a secret agent delivering a confidential and important item. I was excited for tonight, couldn't wait for it. When I opened my locker, there was a brown paper bag inside with a tag on it that read: "Pay me later. Enjoy!"

My excitement was at its peak. Now all I wanted was an opportunity.

After dinner, I insisted mom to watch a movie with me. It was her favorite rom-com, she never got bored watching it. Her gaze was fixed on the screen; she was watching it very attentively. While my mind wandered elsewhere. I need to find a way and so it came to me. The bright idea.

"Mom, I am going to the kitchen for some snacks do you want something?"

"No, thank you so much, honey"

"Not even soda!"

"Alright bring some soda for me. And stop disturbing me please, it's my favorite scene."

It was the perfect moment. I had the plan and until now it was perfect. This was the final moment. I waited in the kitchen for some time and then opened the can and added in the alcohol.

"Here," I said handing her the can.

"Thanks, honey," she took a sip, "why does it taste different?"

"Maybe because it's not chilled."

She said nothing and emptied the whole can. Now all I had to do was wait. Because good thing comes to those who wait.

There were only 15 minutes left for the movie to end but when I turned to look at mom, she was fixed on her place like a manne- quin. Her eyes were still on the screen but her gaze was empty. Her pupils were dilated. I remember the first time I gave her alco- hol, I thought I killed her. I was so scared I cried all night but the next morning she was completely normal.

Her breathing was so relaxed, it was like she was sleeping. But she was not. She was completely awake. Her brain was half switched off. She can see, she can feel, and she can hear. All her senses were working but she can't understand. Her brain lost the ability to process. She can't react to anything quickly and her movements would be so slow. The next morning she will be back to normal.

I switched off the TV but she was still looking at the screen. Her hands were resting on the armrest of the couch and her legs were folded. I tapped on her shoulder – not much reaction as she was drunk. I can feel my heart coming into my mouth. Yes, I was scared and I could feel it beating so fast that I can feel its throb- bing very much. My palms started sweating, my body was heat- ing up and my cock was getting hard.

I placed my hand on her knees and started moving up. My heart was beating even faster. She was soft. My hand reached the love hole. It was so warm I can feel it from above her tights. There was no reaction to whatever I was doing on her face.

I pulled out her white t-shirt, she was not wearing her bra, and her big busts were hanging in air swinging back and forth. They were huge and I loved them. I slowly started sucking her nipples, my fear was fading away. There was confidence building up inside me. I grabbed her tits and started fondling them; her body was warm and smelled of her sweet perfume. I loved her perfume.

Well, I wanted her to react. I wanted her to play with me. I wanted her to kiss me, to suck my growing cock but that wasn't possible. And I was always jealous of dad for having a hot wife to suck and keeping her all to himself. I wanted him to share her with me.

I spent countless nights thinking about ways and techniques to get her in my bed. Hundreds of times, I jerked off imagining fuck with my own mother. She was a busty and beautiful mom. People regarded her as, "Yummy mummy".

Carefully, I laid her on the couch and pulled out her tights too. I knew she wasn't wearing any panties either. I bent down and started sucking her cunt. It tasted salty.

Suddenly, she jerked and in a very very low voice, which could not have been heard if the room would not have been so silent, she moaned. It was something like clearing her throat. For a second, I was scared but then it came to me she can feel. She cannot react very fast, she cannot process it but she still can feel it. I like that she was having fun as well.

From the shelf, I poured some oil on my thick long dick and rubbed it all over. I opened her legs wide and sat between them. I placed her legs on my shoulders and with a thrust, inserted half my cock inside her warm pussy. Another thrust and I was completely inside her.

I grabbed her boobs once again and started fucking her slowly. Her hot body thrusting against mine, I was fucking her wet cunt. Her boobs were soft as a sponge and her nipples hard; I pinched them and sucked them. My speed increased with every push and soon I was fucking with my full speed. The room echoed with the slapping of her skin.

She was still lying there. There was a slight change in her expression that proved me she could feel my cock. She too was enjoying with me. I turned her around and flipped her. She was now lying on her stomach.

I again started fucking her, spanking and kissing her and fondling her breasts. We were both sweating. She was sweating way less than me but I was covered in sweat. I could feel the heat emitting from my body. She again made that slow moaning sound. This got me even harder and I started fucking her with all my energy.

Soon I was feeling a little weak. I left her like that, naked with her legs wide open as if she was not a living thing but a man-handled sex doll. From the kitchen, I ate a sandwich and drank some soda and then more soda and sandwich. I wiped myself dry and came back to complete the fuck session and fucked her in 3 different positions for the next half an hour.

I came on her and not inside her. Then I wiped her clean, wiped my cum from her with a wet towel and the oil from her pussy. I dressed her again, which was very difficult and dragged her to her bed. I was so exhausted I couldn't lift her up but somehow she was on her bed. And then I went to my bedroom with a smile and contentment.

Like always, the next morning was normal.

"What happened last night," she asked me.

"You slept watching the movie so I have to take you to bed. You gained some weight."

She smiled and went to the kitchen.

6. Night bulb

Someone shook me and woke me up. I opened my smudgy eyes but everything was blurred. I rubbed my eyes with my hands and say mom sitting close to me. Before I could open my mouth to ask any question, she pressed her finger on my mouth and shushed me.

I sat upright and looked around, everyone was deep asleep and it was dark outside the window. All I could see was mom's face in the dim light of the night bulb. She stood up and signalled me to follow her quietly.

Carefully not to make any sound and wake someone up we both left the room and closed the door behind us. Mom was walking in front and was in charge today. She was wearing an uneasy expression on her face and was in quiet hurry. I still didn't ask her any questions and followed her quietly. We entered another room and mom switched on the light and fans. She turned around and looked at me but said nothing.

I knew why we were here; I knew why she woke me up and brought me at this hour of the night but this was not how we did it. We always played it safe. We made sure nobody would suspect us. But this was very dangerous and there were high chances we would be caught.

"Mein so nahi paa rahi hun. Bohot nasha chadaha hua hai,"(I am unable to sleep, I am feeling very horny) she finally spoke and I was right about what was happening.

"Par abhi! Koi uth gaya to?"(But now! Someone gets up then?)

"Dekh ab aur bardasht nahi ho raha. Andar se mano jee katne ko daud raha hai. Ab aur mat intezaar karwa. Jaldi se kar lenege," (See I am unable to control. Inside me it feels my life is running to bite me. Now don't make me wait. We will do it quickly.) she said desperately.

I could not resist since she was pleading and wanted it so desperately. She had never done something of this sort and it was exciting to see something like this come from her. I agreed on it. I asked her to bend instead of doing it lying on the floor.

Mom turned around and bent forward. She lifted her pink floral printed maxi above her waist and tied a knot so it won't slide down. She placed her hands on the wall for support. I removed my pajamas and out bobbed my cock. She looked back to see and a smile lit on her face. I touched down to fcel her cunt and it was already wet so I don't have to waste any time on the foreplay.

My cock soon turned rock hard and gained its full size. We both were ready and excited for a quick fuck session. She was still looking back at me with that smile on her lips and hunger in her eyes. I placed the head of my erected 8 inches cock on her shaven wet pussy and caught her by her waist. With a push the head of my thick ling cock entered her soft warm cunt. She moaned softly "ummm" and closed her eyes. With another thrust half of my cock was inside her wet pussy and slowly I started fucking her.

Her eyes were still closed and her lips pressed so she won't make any noise and wake someone up. My hands were caressing her soft ass and pressuring her big boobs. She wasn't wearing any bra and her breasts were soft and her nipples hard. Slowly with every thrust my cock would go deeper inside her. Soon the whole of it was inside her and I was no more very gentle on her.

I caught her by her waist more firmly with one hand and other was pressing her boobs and slapping her ass. She was still looking behind at me and smiling. I could see pain of her face as I fucked her and slapped her; she tried hard not to make any noise but would occasionally moan with pleasure. I was fucking her warm pussy in good speed while she bent pursing her lips and feeling my thick long cock fuck her cunt. She was waiting for it for so long. Lying on her bed she was imagining my cock fuck her like this. She wanted me so hard inside her. "ummm aah umm" she moaned.

I reached my top speed and was fucking her like an animal, just like she wanted it. Mom was enjoying it. But I was afraid if we woke someone up. Though the door was closed and we were trying to be as quite as possible, the sound of slapping of skins and mother's moans echoed in the room. "I have to make it quick. I have to make her cum soon. This can't go on for long or someone will see us," I thought.

I grabbed her arm and pulled my cock out. She thought it was over and sat on her knees with her tongue sticking out waiting for my hot cum to be smeared over her face. But she wasn't content; I could see the disappointed look on her face. She wasn't giggling like she always did when she waited for my cum to be smeared all over her face. I pulled her up and turned her around. Her face lit up again and brighter than ever with a smile wider than before. She knew she was about to be fucked really hard. It was about to get more rough.
She was on quadruped on the floor. I was kneeling behind her with the head of my cock on her cunt which was dipped in her pussy juice. I shoved the whole cock at once inside her, grabbed her boobs with both my hands and started fucking really hard with all the energy I had. She pressed her lips together and closed her eyes. The sound of fucking echoed the whole room. She moaned louder before but I was sure there was no other way to end it any sooner and I had to take the risk.

For some reason it was more fun to fuck her like this – with the fear of getting caught, with the fear of being seen. It was more fun to fuck her like this than to fuck her when no one was home and we were both alone. I fucked her in almost all the rooms, in the bathroom and the kitchen. We fucked in a rented apartment once but this was the best. The risk added an edge to it and increased the pleasure. I wasn't sure if she was feeling it as well but she was having a really good time as I could see on her face and hear her moans.

I slapped her harder and fucked her with all the energy I had. We both reached climax. "Andar hi gira de. Mu par nahi. Andar hi maal chod de apna," (Leave it inside me. Not on my mouth. Leave your load inside me.) said. She wanted the hot cum inside her wet pussy. Our body contracted and with two strokes I ejaculated thick cum inside her pussy and our body relaxed at the same time. She fell her face down on the floor with her ass still in air and my cock sticking inside her pussy. I had no energy to go any further or even pull my cock out of her. I was lying upon her back. I was very sleepy and could sleep on her. We lay there for a while. She was enjoying my cock rub the walls of her cunt even after we were done.

She shook me and got up. My cock slides out of her cunt and was no more hard. It was covered in her pussy juices and shrunk to 5 inches hanging as if there was no life in it anymore. Her pussy was dripping my cum. She ran inside the toilet and I pulled up my pajama headed back to my bed and went to a deep sleep.

7. *Fadeelah*

I am Rohan, 33 years old from Bengaluru with 5'11" in height. This incident happened around two years back.

I was staying alone in Bengaluru as my family stays at native in Tamil Nadu. I was staying with a few of my friends in South Bengaluru.

Some days ago, I gave an Ad on Locanto for a female roommate as I was in a mood to move out of my current place and just thought of giving it a try. There was no reply for almost a month.

One day I got a message in Locanto from a girl named Fadeelah. She was from Hyderabad and was traveling to Bengaluru to attend a few interviews. Post-interviews and based on the results, she wanted to settle in Bengaluru.

After having a detailed discussion about her comfort to share the room with a guy and that too in the same bed, I understood that she worked in Singapore for a few years and she was fine to share the room.

We exchanged the pictures on request over WhatsApp. She was coming from Chennai after some interviews there. I decided to pick her from the Electronic City bus stop as I stayed nearby and reaching my flat was a little difficult. The plan was to take Fadeelah to my existing flat and stay for a day or two and then look for a feasible room for both of us.

About Fadeelah, she was a 29 years old Muslim girl and divorcee (I came to know that later). She was a normal-looking girl with extraordinary assets. She was a 5 ft 11" tall girl and had a perfect body of 34 boobs and 36 butts.

The day she came, she was in a red salwar. I picked her from the bus stop. While going to home, we discussed the stay and the other plans. My roommate guys had gone to their native, so it would be just two of us for another two days.

As Fadeelah reached late, her interviews got postponed to the next day. So, we were free for the rest of the day.

After reaching home, I asked her to be comfortable and take bath if she wishes. She went to take a bath and I changed into my shorts and t-shirt. Before she came from the bath, I ordered food. She thanked me for ordering food as she took the early morning bus from Chennai and was hungry. Fadeelah was in a pink chudi without a bottom.

We both had our lunch together. We were chatting about some random stuff and passing our time. She then wanted to have a smoke and asked my permission. Then we together smoked cigarettes.

Both of us decided to take some rest. Since I had only one bed-sheet and pillow, we both were very close in the bed and covered ourselves with the same bedsheet. That was the first time our bodies were touching, and it created some erection which was visible in my boxer.

As we didn't feel sleepy, we decided to watch some movie on mobile. During that time, we were again chatting random stuff. Actually, we were very close and Fadeelah's boobs were pressed against my right arm!

As the movie was boring, we again started talking about her personal life. She was working in a firm as a marketing head in Singapore. Since her husband was jobless in Hyderabad, he had a lot of suspicion on her. So, her marriage life ended up in a divorce.

The divorced Muslim girl was feeling sad so I tried to console her. Suddenly, when she came very close to me, I hugged her! I quickly kissed her on her cheeks and smooched her which started turning her on.

Fadeelah started kissing me on my cheeks and then we were kissing on lips. It was a long lip-lock and a lot of saliva was exchanged. The kiss really made both of us so aroused. I started massaging Fadeelah's melons over her top and she was holding my cock over my boxer.

Then I removed her chudi top. She was in a beautiful laced pink bra and netted black panty now. I released the horny Muslim girl's melons by removing her bra hooks. The scene was amazing. As Fadeelah was dusky in colour, her nipples were black and she had big areolas.

Suddenly, Fadeelah pulled my t-shirt and sat on me. I was sucking for her boobs like a mad kid. She started moaning loud and that made me even more aroused. She got down and pulled my boxer. My cock was in 90 degrees and was pointed towards the roof.

Fadeelah went down and started giving me a blowjob. One thing I have experienced – married women give wonderful blowjobs!

Then I lifted her and we were in 69. Fadeelah had amazingly clean pussy, probably she must have removed her pubic hairs that day. I was giving deep kisses and deep licks on her pussy. At the same time, Fadeelah was giving me a deep-throat blowjob.

After some time, both of us reached the orgasm, almost at the same time. I filled her mouth with my semen which she drunk without wasting even a drop. Fadeelah kissed me all over my face passionately and thanked me for the orgasm.

After washing ourselves, we slept nude. When I woke up, it was around 7 pm and Fadeelah came from the washroom. Both of us were still nude and my boner was ready for another round of fun! She looked at that and laughed.

I pulled the sexy Muslim girl to the bed and started kissing her lips. My one hand was on her boob and the other hand was in her pussy. That made her also aroused and she was stroking my cock. She pushed me down and sat on my cock. Fadeelah's pussy so tight as she had last fucked a few months ago, with her colleague in Singapore.

Fadeelah started riding my dick for some time. Then I pushed her down and started fucking this horny divorced girl in doggy style. During the doggy, I was also playing with her lovely boobs. As we had fucked sometime before, it took longer to climax this time. Finally, I spilled my cum on Fadeelah's boobs which she then spread all across her body.

Then we took a bath together and fucked like mad one more time that night. It was 6 rounds of fun which we had that whole night.

As I had to leave for another town officially, I dropped her in the office for the interview. The second day, she stayed in a PG. Somehow, she couldn't settle in Bengaluru. We were in touch for a few weeks and suddenly, without any information, she stopped her communications. It is like a dream for me even now.

8. Apartment

This is Rohan from Bengaluru. I am staying alone in one of the apartments in South Bengaluru. In the recent past, the society I am staying decided to vacate all the bachelors from my apartment. As there was a change in society management, I don't have any option other than leaving the house. As I was in this apartment for almost two years, I used to the place and don't want to leave. In my adjacent flat there are 3 guys and 2 girls staying and all of them are working. As the flat is owned by one of the guys, society management can't vacate them.

I knew one of the guys there and I used to play badminton with him whenever I have time. So, I was telling him about my problem. He said he will discuss it with other guys to accommodate me. I was interested to join them as I liked the place and its nearby to my office.

A small brief about the people who are there in the flat. As I said, 3 guys and 2 girls, all of them are working in the same company. There are three rooms in the flat, one guy and girl were sharing one room. That guy is the owner of the flat and she is his girlfriend.

Another girl is a friend of her and she is in another room. Two other guys were sharing the other room. At this point, no need to have the details of those guys. Sima is sharing the room with her boyfriend.

The other girl is Anita and she is a Mallu girl. 27 years old and amazing structure. 34 C boobs and 36 butts sized typical Mallu girl.

I have seen Sima and her boyfriend Ritesh fucking in their bedroom as I could see them from my balcony. As I know all the guys there, whenever I am free, I used to go to their home and partied with them many times. So, I am very familiar with all the guys.

During weekend parties Sima used to wear very explosive dresses whereas Anita used to be a little reserved. She won't drink much that too only wine. As I also don't drink anything other than wine, we two became good friends and we used to chat a lot.

As I had enough fun with opposite flat Preeti and my office colleague Pammi, I didn't have any bad intentions on Anita. The next day, the guy confirmed no one has any objection for me sharing their flat. I was happy as I am continuing in the same apartment building.

As there are no rooms available, I used to sleep on the sofa and use the common washroom. Time passed, I and Anita became close friends. After a few months due to some work, I couldn't travel to my native on the weekend. Whereas all the three guys have got some official work and went to Delhi.

So, it's me, Sima and Anita were in the home. We were bored and decided to have some drinks. Sima had whiskey, I and Anita were having wine. Sima finished a one-half bottle of whiskey and she was full tight. I and Anita finished one bottle of wine and I was also tight.

We decided to play music and started dancing. I and Sima were dancing, she was in her sleeveless low-neck top with mini shorts. I was in my shorts and a t-shirt. As we started dancing, due to alcohol influence, both of us were started brushing each other bodies.

Anita was encouraging us to dance more and at one point, Sima started kissing on my cheeks and shoulder. I started smooching her and kissed on her lips for which Sima also well cooperated. She pulled my t-shirt and hugged me. She started playing with my nipples and kissed my nipple.

Slowly she started sucking my nipples. I got damn hot by the act of Sima. I don't know what happened with Anita. She also came towards us and hugged me from the back. She just scratched my cock on my shorts and kissed my shoulder from the back. I was like, double shocked.

I pulled Sima's t-shirt and then her shorts. She was in her pink bra and black panty. I turned and hugged Anita, stared lip kiss. My god, the way she cooperated was amazing and we exchanged our saliva. It was a long lip lock. Meantime Sima removed my shorts and started stroking my cock.

I pulled Anita's t-shirt and jeans. Now both the girls with their bra and panty, I was fully nude. Both the girls went down and started kissing my cock and balls. By now, my cock was like 90 degrees straight. Sima took into her lovely mouth and started giving deep suck. Then she gave it to Anita to taste.

Both the girls were giving blowjob one on one and I was like flying. As I had a good amount of wine, I was not leaking for a long time. At last, both the girls made me leak on their mouths, which they had without wasting a drop of it. Then I took both into Sima's bedroom.

Now, both the girls were in full mood. They removed their bra and panty. Wow, it was an awesome pussy. Both the pussies were cleanly shaved and puffy. As I have seen Sima's pussy earlier from my balcony, I know how clean it is. I was amazed to see Anita's nude body.

She has amazing assets. Nice boobs without sagging and a nice butt too. Both got into bed and started squeezing each other boobs. They were in a lip lock and started caressing each other pussy. Their hands were playing with other's pussy.

As I was seeing them, they went to 69 position and started sucking each other's pussy aggressively. By seeing that, my cock was ready for the next round. I went to bed and started sucking Anita's beautiful boobs. She started moaning loudly. Her sound made me aggressive in sucking.

As I was sucking Anita's boobs, Sima again started giving me blowjob. Meantime her fingers were into Anita's pussy and my fingers into Sima's pussy. As everyone was engaged, there was too much screaming in the room. Anita pushed me down and sat on my cock.

She started fucking me hard and meantime Sima sat on my mouth. I was giving, mouth pleasure to Sima. Everyone became aggressive with each other. First, Sima got her orgasm and then me and Anita at the same time. After I load my cum into Anita's pussy, Sima went to suck all that out.

Both the girls were exchanging with a lip lock. That night we had one more round and next day Sunday two more rounds of a hard fuck. We all were nude for the next whole day. The guys were expected in the evening. So we three took bath together in the evening and had another round of fuck. Then we dressed up.

The next day onwards, I was sharing the room with Anita and every night we used to sleep nude. Almost every other day we fuck and sometimes, Sima used to join us after making her boyfriend sleep.

9. Wicked Smile

I was home from college due to vacation and my family had to go visit some relative in another town. So, I was asked to live with my aunt(family) at her apartment which was not too far from my home.

Aunt and her kid were there because the uncle had gone out of town due to some office work.

My lust for her began a few days before this. We were on a family trip – my family and her family. Aunt and I were sitting next to each other in the car and suddenly, my arm rubbed against her arm. Contact of her skin made me feel something but I didn't know what.

During the rest of the journey, I started intentionally rubbing my arm against her and she didn't mind at all. She was very innocent and thought it was all casual.

Now back to the story. Since I was staying at her apartment, I started to feel lust toward her. It was a holiday at my college so I stayed at home all day with her. Her kid had to go to school. So, we were alone during the daytime but I could not make a move.

Then, one day we were chatting and were alone. Suddenly, we locked out eyes. I kept looking into her eyes and she also kept looking back. It got awkward and after some time, we both looked away. But things were just getting started.

Now I got some courage and the next day, I decided to make a move. The next day, as usual, her kid went to school and then I woke up. I saw my aunt working in the kitchen and I went sneak-ily behind her. She did not notice me and was busy with her work. She was wearing a nighty. I saw her sexy figure and ass.

Suddenly, I hugged her from behind, and put my arms across her belly! I placed my head on her shoulder and smelled her lovely neck. She did not mind and kept working and said, "good morn-ing" to me. But I did not stop.

I gently placed the crouch on her ass. I started to feel my penis getting hard and growing into her ass. But I had to move away before things became too awkward.

Nothing happened till afternoon when her son returned from school. Later that afternoon, I was playing with the kid (let's call him x) and he took me to the room where my aunt (let's call her Maya) was lying on the bed in her saree. She didn't mind our presence.

Her son started to play with her leg acting like a doctor. Then, he went out to play with some other toy. My aunt then asked me to massage her legs. I started massaging her legs and started to get a hard-on just after touching her.

Then I lifted my aunt's saree to her thighs and started massaging her legs till the knee. My cock was throbbing. She was half asleep but she was innocent and she let me continue.

I slowly went upwards for her thighs and massaged them very softly, taking full pleasure. But still, I couldn't make a further move and stepped away in fear of going too far.

Now my confidence was high and I started flirting with her. The next day in the afternoon 1 hour before my aunt's kid came from school, I went into her room. She used to sleep in the afternoon and only wake up when her son came home. But she was awake that time.

I asked her if she was alright. She replied that her back was ach-ing and so I offered to massage her. She lied down on her stom-ach. I took some oil and started massaging over her back.

I started to get a hard-on. So, I decided that instead of sitting on her side, I sat on her thighs just so that my penis was aiming into my aunt's ass. I massage her waist and shoulders. She was wearing a blouse which was stopping me from feeling her whole back. But I continued. She started making noises and was moaning.

Now my cock was fully hard. I put more pressure on her shoulders and slid my hands to the sides of her waist. It was giving me so much pleasure. Then I intentionally spilled some oil on her blouse. I told her that she should unhook the blouse so I can massage the excess oil on her back. She did not suspect me and did as I said.

Now I started to feel my aunt's whole back. Then I slightly slipped my hands below her waist into her saree. I also felt the sides of her bra. My penis was pushing hard against her ass but she did not take any notice.

Now every day I used to walk up to her in the kitchen and push my penis against her ass while hugging her from behind. This became a routine and now it was time for my next move.

One day while my aunt's kid was going to bed at night, she gave him a goodnight kiss. I was there. So the kid asked her to give a kiss me too. She kissed me on my cheeks. Then the kid asked me to kiss her back and I took that chance and kissed her cheeks. I rested my lips for longer than they were supposed to. My dick started to grow.

After the kid slept, I went to my aunt's room and told her that I could not sleep in my room so I wanted to sleep in her room. She allowed me. She looked gorgeous in her sleep and her figure was glowing in the night.

We were on the same bed and she had her back towards me. So I went ahead and slowly, placed my hand on her bare waist. I moved closer and spooned my aunt. My erection was pushing into her ass. I was enjoying her sweet smell. Then she turned towards me. I put my one arm and leg over her. Our faces were too close, almost kissing.

My aunt's breasts were touching my chest. I could see her boobs as her saree was not covering her blouse.

The next morning, we woke up and it was my last day of stay. That day, I went to take bath before her and brought all her clothes out of the bathroom, leaving only the towel. When she went to take bath, she did not have clothes to wear before coming out. So she called me to bring her clothes inside as she was wrapped in a towel.

I went inside and hugged her tightly! She was surprised and asked why. So I answered I was feeling thankful to her for caring for me for the past few days. She smiled and said that I can show my thankfulness later also and asked for her clothes.

I purposely hugged my aunt in such a way that when I moved away, her towel slipped! And wow, she was fully naked. I acted to not look at her but checked her out from all the angles while giving her clothes. But nothing much happened after that.

I came back to my house but the story doesn't end here. A twist is yet to come.

After a few days, my mom asked me to deliver some pickles to my aunt's house in the morning. I went there and saw her alone in the house as usual. I was so excited to see her after so long. I was dying to feel her touch and warmth.

I gave her the pickle she kept it on the table. And suddenly, my aunt fainted and was about to fall. I caught her in my arms. She was wearing a beautiful saree that day. Even at such a moment, my mind went dirty. I had her back resting on my right arm. So I pushed her with my right arm to catch her with my left arm.

I grabbed her boob with my left hand to catch her from falling and put my other arm on her milky smooth waist. I could feel her soft breast and its warmth. I was squeezing it with my fingers. I was rubbing my hands on her waist roughly.

I wanted that moment to last an eternity but I knew I should call a doctor. I rested her on the sofa and start scrolling my phone to see whom to call.

But the story had a twist.

Suddenly, my aunt started laughing with a wicked smile on her face. She looked at me with lust and biting her lips. I was confused and didn't know how to react. Then she asked me, "If I faint again, will you catch me the same way?"

Now I knew that she was willing and I smiled back. She came up to me and kissed me on my lips. I put my hands on her ass, brought her closer, lifted her and kissed her passionately.

This was the beginning of my sexual relationship with my aunt.

10. Sefa

My name's Raees. I live in Kashmir and am going to tell you about a Kashmiri wedding. I'm 21 currently doing my graduation in Computer Sciences. I have a light brown complexion, an average build with a height of 5'9 and my size is 7.2.

It happened in February last year at a family wedding before the pandemic struck.

Her name is Sefa, and she is a relative of mine. She was 25 at that time. Let me tell you about her. She has a height of 5'8", a fair complexion, and a body that would make a dead man wish he could be alive to see that beauty. If I had to guess, I'd say that her body assets are 34-26-34.

Getting back to the story, in Feb last year, one of my cousins was getting married. That's where I saw her for the first time. She was wearing a black lehenga with a blue top and a white scarf. I have dated quite a few girls till now. But she undoubtedly was one of the most beautiful and sexiest.

But as family weddings in Kashmir go, I was busy doing the chores and helping others. At around 7 PM, I got tired and sat in the guest area when my cousin Raahi came with Sefa. That's where we got introduced to each other. Raahi told her that if she needs any help, she should ask me.

Then Raahi got a call and had to leave for some time, and Sefa and I got to talking,

"So, you are the one who is going to take care of me?"

"Well, it's not like Raahi gave me much of choice now. Is it?"

And we both laughed a little.

"To Raees, kya karte ho aap?" (So Raees, what do you do)

"Well, currently I'm doing my graduation in Computer sciences. What about you?"

"I just completed my M.A in literature, thinking about Ph.D. now."

"That's cool."

We talked for a while and got to know each other. Then I got called by my cousins as I had to help them with some stuff. The night passed, and the next day was hectic too. I saw Sefa quite a few times, and we used to pass smiles at each other every time our eyes met.

It was around 9 PM now, and the Barat had just left. I wanted a break. So I went to the 2nd floor, which was empty for sleeping arrangements. I went to the room where the cousins slept. I opened the window, lit up a cigarette and put on some music.

After a couple of minutes, I suddenly heard the door opening sound. I didn't even bother to turn back as I thought it might be one of my cousins. But suddenly I heard a girl's voice.

"What are you doing?" It was Sefa.

"Nothing just wanted to take a break, so came up."

She asked me why I was smoking. I told her that I smoke occasionally and she was cool about it.

"By the way, what are you doing here?"

"Actually, I wanted to use the washroom. All the ones' downstairs are occupied."

"Go ahead then. It's not like I'm holding you or anything, haha!"

She winked at me and said, "Yeah, you wish."

She went to the restroom and came back after a few minutes. That's when I noticed it, man, she was looking gorgeous. She was wearing a maroon dress with a golden scarf. For a few seconds, I got awestruck. She snapped her fingers in front of my eyes and spoke

"Yaar itni bhi achi nahi dikhti main," (Friend I don't even look that good) we both laughed at that. "By the way, do you mind if I stay here? It's boring downstairs."

"Sure, even I'd get bored if I stay here alone."

We sat on the couch and started talking about our interests and hobbies, and it was going well.

"You seem to be a really good guy."

I don't know what got into me. I went a little close to her and whispered in her left ear, "Trust me, a good guy is the last thing I am."

Then I slowly kissed her cheek. Both of us were silent after that for a minute. She suddenly got up and left. I felt like I screwed this up and got angry at myself. But after a few minutes, she came back.

I thought I should apologize. But before I could say anything, she locked the door and came towards me. I didn't know what was happening. She pushed me on the couch and came on top of me, and said,

"Just went downstairs to make sure no one disturbs us. Show me then. How bad are you? "

That was all I needed to hear. I kissed her wet lips hard, and in no time, we were making out passionately. She slid her tongue inside my mouth and started licking mine. I slowly unlaced her top and took it off.

I came on top of her with her face downwards and started sucking her naked back, and a moan escaped her lips, "Ah, baby! I love what you are doing there."

I unhooked her bra and slid it off her body while holding it with my teeth. I swear to God, just touching that skin was more than enough to make any man cum. She took off my t-shirt.

I got on top of her and slowly started sucking her neck while my hands were playing with her boobs. And then, all of a sudden, I sucked her neck hard while both of her nipples hard with my fingers. She started moaning again,

"Ouch! Aaah Raees! I love what you are doing to me. Just don't stop, babe. I love your lips! "

Then I went down and started to suck her nipples. The taste of them was driving me crazy, and I kept on sucking them hard. I could sense that it was hurting her, but lust had taken over her so bad that she didn't want me to stop.

"Aaah. Suck them harder. Bite me. I'm all yours. Bite my nipples harder, you asshole."

After a few more minutes, I went down and kissed her navel. I took off her lehnga now she was wearing just her panty. I picked her up, and she locked me with her legs. We were kissing, and I took her to the bed. The moment I laid her down on the bed, she pushed me down, rolled over, and got on top of me.

She started kissing me hard. Then she went down and started licking my body, sucking my nipples, just thinking about all that turns me on even now. Then she kissed my jeans near my dick. She took my jeans and underwear off.

She held my dick in her hand, kissed it, and said, "I'm so tired of being perfect all the time, with my family, my friends, my boyfriend. Just for this one night, I want to be bad. I want to be a slut who just wants to get fucked."

I was shocked she had a boyfriend, and here she was acting like a complete slut. But it was too late to turn back now. She opened her mouth and took my entire dick inside it. It felt like heaven. She kept on sucking my dick, spitting on it and licking it for 10 minutes straight,

"Aah, Sefa, it feels so good, but stop. I'll cum in no time like this."

She took my dick out of her mouth and was her breaths were heavy

"Haah. I'm not going to stop until you put that thick cum inside my mouth."

At the moment she said that, she got on her knees and brought my dick near her mouth. As soon as he opened her mouth, I pushed my dick in her mouth so hard that she almost choked. I held her hair and started to fuck her mouth as hard as I could.

After 10 minutes or so, I was about to cum. I shot my cum inside her mouth, and she drank it. She had a slutty look on her face. We made out for some time after that. I slowly slid my fingers inside her panty and started to rub her wet pussy.

Her breaths were getting heavier with every passing second after a couple of minutes. Her panty was completely soaked, and in a breathless voice, she said, " Raees, I can't take it anymore, take it off, please."

I went down and took off her panty. The moment I saw her pussy, I was amazed. She had a clean-shaven pussy. That pink wet pussy could make anyone go mad. I spread her legs and slowly started licking the edges of her pussy.

It tasted like heaven. Her moans were driving me crazy. I slid a finger inside her pussy and started licking it hard. She held my head and pushed it hard on her pussy,

"Oh baby, that feels amazing. My boyfriend never does that. I love it. Aah, lick me like a dirty whore. "

At that point, we both were acting like animals. I slid another finger inside her pussy and moved my fingers away from each other. Her pussy was being stretched from the inside, and her fluids were running down my fingers.

I slid my tongue deep inside her pussy and started licking it like a wild dog. Within a few minutes, her body started shivering top to bottom,

"Aah, Raees, you're so good at this. I'm cumming, baby, I'm cumming. Haaa."

Saying this, she came all over my face. She then held my hair and pulled me up, and we started kissing vigorously. She was sucking her juices off my lips like a wild animal. She spread her legs wide open. I slowly started rubbing my dick over her pussy and slid the head inside her pussy.

I was moving it up and down. I could see it on her face how badly she wanted it. But I wanted to tease her a little first. I could see it she was getting pissed, "Raees, just stop teasing me and put it in, just fuck me."

Before she could complete that sentence, I pushed my dick inside her pussy hard. I was so wild that I didn't go slow at all. I started ramming her pussy like a dog.

It was so tight it felt like her pussy was sucking my dick harder and harder with each passing stroke. I started sucking her neck hard while I was fucking her like a maniac.

"Oh yeah, aah. Fuck me, fuck me harder. Make me your freaking slut tonight."

Her words were driving me crazy. I got up and pulled her hair, and kept her on her knees. Without waiting for even a second, I pushed my dick inside her pussy hard. I was fucking her from behind and spanking her ass at the same time.

"Oh yes, daddy, fuck me harder, spank that ass. Make me your bitch tonight."

We fucked in that position for around 10 minutes, during which she came again. After that, we changed the position again. I brought her to the edge of the bed, and she kept her legs on my shoulder. I started fucking her as hard as I could. My hands were on her boobs and ramming that pussy at the same time.

"Aaah yeah, harder Baby, you fucking own that pussy tonight.

Chod mujhe."(fuck me)

Her moans were so loud that I was afraid that someone might hear us. But it was turning me on even more. I went all out. Her hands were on my chest. She started scratching it with her nails while asking me to go harder and harder. After another 15 minutes, I was about to cum, "Sefa, I'm cumming."

"Aaah, me too. Just don't stop. Put it inside my pussy. I want to feel your warm cum inside me. Aaah."

I started giving her deep hard pushes, and in a few seconds, I came inside her. We both were exhausted and stayed there on top of each other for a few minutes. After that, we got dressed, and before we left the room, we kissed again.

I said, "That was amazing."

"Yeah, it was. I have never been this wild with anyone before. Who knows, maybe someday we'll get another chance."

Saying this, she winked at me, and we left the room.

The next day we all had to go back to our homes. But before that, I did manage to get her an I-pill, so we were good. We did have sex once more after that, but that's a story for another time.

11. Dance Partner

I was always interested in extracurricular activities and dancing was one of my biggest passions growing up. I represented my school at many platforms and now, I was representing my college as well.

I was among the 6 people chosen to represent our college in a competition at the national level. I was selected for dance and there were others selected for either sports or other activities. Even though dance was my passion, I was excited to represent my college. I was also excited about traveling alone.

Away from all the eyes, expecting for some action with a hot and handsome stranger. It had been a long time since I had a dick drill me. But I was not ready for a fuck with just anyone. This was the best opportunity as there would be a lot of young blood attending this event.

I wanted to choose the best one for some fun. When we reached there, I got to know that they had organized the dance competition in a unique manner. They had paired students from different colleges together. So, I would be performing a prepared solo dance and another dance with a student from another college.

I found it interesting. this would clearly showcase one's dancing talent and how quickly one could prepare a dance with a complete stranger. I was tensed as to who my partner would be and how skilled he would be performing at the same level as me.

I was here to win the competition at any event and wanted to have a good partner. I got a message from the organizers that I was paired with Akshay Kapoor. Hearing his name itself, I had a tingling sensation in my pussy. But I really hoped that the guy lived up to his name.

I was with my college guys when a 6 feet tall guy with an open hoodie walked in and asked, "Who is Charmy Kaur?" I looked at him directly and said, "It's me." I was able to see his face clearly now. He looked smart with a chiselled jawline, well-kept hair and deep brown eyes looking at me.

He extended his hand for a formal handshake. I shook hands with him and he held my hand firmly. I could feel his confidence and was much impressed. He asked if we could discuss the dance event separately. We moved away from my group.

He introduced himself and asked if I wanted to have something to eat before we started. I was impressed with his gentleman-like behaviour and was impressed with his physique as well. He was tall, handsome, had strong hands and seemed to be an active gym-goer.

We sat in a coffee shop and discussed the event. He spoke about himself and his style of dance. He was not awkward at all and we got friendly soon. He complimented me on my physique. He said that he was happy that I was his partner. It won't be difficult to perform lifts in the dance with me.

He seemed to be a charmer as he was flirting with me and also complimenting on my figure so casually. I was listening most of the time. But soon realized that we were there for the competition. I asked him what the plan was for the competition.

The performance was supposed to be in the evening. So, we had only the afternoon for the choreography and practice. After a lot of deliberation, we decided to dance on the song 'Bang Bang' from the movie 'Bang Bang'. We both went to the practice room given to us.

It was a room with a music player and a huge mirror. The

choreography had a lot of lifts and I had not done lifts before. So, it was new to me. Akshay was an expert and he taught me some basics and I started following him. The choreography of the original song was very sexy.

We also wanted to retain the oomph and Akshay had choreographed a lot of sexy moves. He seemed very cool about everything. But I started feeling like the choreo would be rejected as the judges might find it vulgar. Akshay laughed at it and said confidently that the judges would love this.

He was there the last year too and had seen many dancers literally strip in the dance. He convinced me that it would be sexy and not vulgar. He said that I had a figure to die for and that my expressions were so graceful that people would just fall for our moves.

Akshay was a smooth talker. I felt very comfortable with him and did not realize that I met him just a few hours before. We started dancing. Akshay did his song intro in one and signalled me to start. I was performing my steps when he stopped me. He asked me to feel the dance and not to hold myself.

While saying this, he unzipped his hoodie and dropped it on a chair lying nearby. As he did that, I could see his well-toned back that was so far covered by the hoodie. He had slotted cuts at his back and wide shoulders. He turned and I could see his big biceps and flat abs.

I guessed they were more than six-packs for sure. All of a sudden, all my inhibitions were gone and I started opening up. He looked at me and signaled me to start again. I also unzipped my training jacket and revealed my flat tummy.

I could see his eyes move down as I unzipped from my neck all the way to my abs. When I opened the jacket, he looked at my flat tummy and realized that he was staring. I looked at him and said, "Mister! look at me." I was enjoying the attention. But wanted to show as if I was not interested.

He didn't mind my comment. He smiled to say that I had taken good care of my body and that he respected it. I also complimented him for maintaining his body. We resumed our practice and I finished my intro. Now, we had to complete the steps where we both were dancing together.

Akshay stopped the music and came close to me. He said that the following choreo was gonna be sexy. So, I should be ready for him to touch me and then he held me by my waist and pulled me close. I loved his touch and immediately felt the passion in his pull.

I fell on his body with my boobs crushing his chest. I slid my hand on the side of his back intuitively. He lifted me in the air with one hand cupping my butt. I was in the air and he was turning around. Then placed me on the ground again. I felt a rush of blood and was excited by this.

As he landed me down, he said excitedly that I was a natural dancer and that his job was easy now. I understood that he did this all of a sudden to check my natural instincts. But also got his signal that he would be using this dance to feel me and take advantage of the situation.

I was okay with it as he was harmless and also because I enjoyed his company. We started practicing the choreo and slowly, he got bold with me. He would lift me up and then slowly bring me down as our bodies would touch each other and feel each other.

My thighs would slide across his face, strong chest, feel his abs and sometimes also feel his cock getting harder. As my thighs rubbed it while he would feast on my round boobs in front of his face. He made sure that he felt them with his face and chest.

On occasions, he would go behind me and stick his pelvis region on my butt and groove to the music. I could feel his hard dick against my ass. I didn't say anything as I started enjoying it too. Our choreo was good and we were getting along good with the practice as well.

I thought we were doing really good when Akshay mentioned that we need to add some more oomph. He said that we would adapt the movie step where he would pat my ass and I would slide my hand over his thighs. I was not sure about it. But the smooth talker he was, he convinced me and we started practicing it.

He patted my ass softly and felt it too. Then I slid my hands over his thighs looking in front. As a final position, he would position himself behind me and gave a finishing pose. The dance was prepared and we were happy with what we had done.

We decided on our clothes. I was going to wear a short black skirt and shiny blacktop. The outfit was sexy with my abs on the show and milky thighs tempting the audience to go under. Akshay was wearing open black shirt and matching trousers.

When we both got ready and looked at each other, we both were blown. I could see Akshay ogling at my milky thighs and abs. While I was shell shocked looking at his abs. Until now he was wearing a vest which covered his abs. But now with the open shirt, I saw his washboard abs which had small cuts everywhere.

Strong arms and abs are my weakness and seeing his abs, I was literally biting my lips. We were both so lost in each other that we didn't realize when our names were called for the performance. We both wished each other luck and instinctively hugged each other.

I hugged him tight feeling his abs and by now. His dick was also rock hard and I felt that as well. I was extremely horny now and I assumed he was too sending the hardness of his dick. We both went on the stage and did our solo part one by one. When we got to our duet portions, we felt each other's body with a lot of passion.

He caressed my abs and held me close to him crushing my boobs. He lifted and brought me down extremely close feeling each and every part of my body. I could also feel his hardness every time he went behind me or was close to me. During our final step, he literally spanked and grabbed my ass.

And accidentally, I slid my hand over his dick instead of his thigh. As I slid my hand over his dick, I grabbed it as it was tearing his pants open. But soon realized that I was on the stage and left it. As the last step, he positioned himself behind me so close that his dick was poking into my ass.

We quickly emptied the stage and as we moved out, we heard people whistling and clapping. It sure seemed like everyone enjoyed. But more than anyone else, it was both of us who enjoyed the most. As we got off the stage, I could see Akshay adjusting his pants.

I looked into his eyes and told him that this was the best dance I had ever done. He felt the same way and silently smiled. I looked at his pants and said that he probably needed a bigger size. He looked at me, came close to me and whispered, "Probably I don't need pants!"

He was now openly flirting with me and I knew that this night was going to be memorable. As soon as we finished our dance, I knew that I wanted to fuck this dude. I was sure he too would be itching to lay his hands on my body. I was excited to discover as to how he would approach me and eventually fuck me.

So, I asked him what plans he had till the announcement of the result. He said that he would change into something more comfortable. He asked me to wear something nice as he wanted to take me out to a club nearby to celebrate our win. He was extremely confident that we would be winning (and we did win eventually).

I decided to wear a short flowy skirt and a low-cut tee showing just a little cleavage. I purposely decided to wear a skirt so that I was accessible to him in public. All these thoughts were already making me wet. I was just so ready to be fucked.

I got ready and went to the parking lot where Akshay was waiting in his car. He had a Ford Explorer. I knew that he purposely got a big car to be able to get naughty inside. He wore a nice black shirt with top 2 buttons open showing his sculpted chest.

Below he had worn casual blue jeans which I was hoping to remove as soon as possible. He looked at me from bottom to top as I entered and admired my shapely calves. I looked at him and again pointed him to look at my face. He complimented me by saying, "You have a great face. But this skirt is doing complete justice to your toned legs."

As he started driving, he told me that none could stop us from winning. We would definitely win the competition. I told him that I didn't care about it. I enjoyed the dance and that was what mattered the most to me. He looked at me and said, "You must have not enjoyed as much as me," and winked at me.

He then made a tongue in cheek comment by saying, "You must have already experienced how much I enjoyed." I replied to him saying, "I have experienced much more than what you have enjoyed so far," to which he gave a slight smile and just raced the car.

We reached the club and like a true gentleman, he opened the door for me. He helped me get down and at the same time caressed my waist. We got inside and the place had loud music and a lot of people inside already dancing and grooving. He directly escorted me to the bar.

We gulped some shots and then he grabbed me by my waist to the dance floor. The dance floor was already crowded. I felt many hands on my body all of a sudden. I looked at him and gave him an uncomfortable look. He quickly understood and made some room around us. But still, it was crowded.

Now came the moment I was waiting for. He grabbed me and pulled me close to him. He put his arms around me to distance me from others. Now my boobs were crushing in his chest and his dick crushing on my cunt. I skipped a heartbeat and let out a soft moan.

I couldn't believe he just grabbed me with such confidence. I literally surrendered to his move without making any fuss. I was just ready to experience him inside me. He slowly escorted me to a corner less crowded and pushed me against the wall.

He came close to me and whispered in my ears, "Its time to give you an experience of a lifetime." He gave a pelvic thrust to my ass pushing me further against the wall (Luckily the walls were not dirty). He put one of his hands on my thighs and slowly caressed them.

I was moaning softly and breathing heavily. His fingers reached under my skirt already and played with my panty line. I was so excited but at the same time, I was thinking about what others might be thinking about us. He just didn't leave me any options or chances and started feeling my pussy under the panty.

I was breathing heavily and out of reflexes, put my hand on his hand and stopped him. He grabbed my hand and put it on his dick and continued exploring my clit. I could feel his bulge and dick throbbing in my hand. He was going commando that night.

I could make out he was not wearing any underwear. Then he slowly rubbed my clit and I could feel his finger slowly entering me. My nipples were getting hard and I was surprised he didn't knead my boobs yet. His bold approach to play with my pussy was so enticing that I used my other hand on my nipples.

Now I had his dick in one hand and my boobs in the other while he continued to play with my pussy. His other hand was exploring my belly button. While his lips were moving on my neck under hair and in between biting my ears. I was experiencing a pleasure like I never had.

He had not even entered my pussy yet. Then I felt more fingers as he entered them slowly in my pussy. He lined his fingers inside my pussy one after the other. I could clearly feel his fingers going inside and opening my clit. While I was feeling that, I felt his other hand on my boobs as he cupped them and grabbed them.

He felt the nipples hardening further and pinched them softly. Now I let out a loud moan losing control and awareness. He bit me harder on my neck now and I grabbed his hard-on over his jeans. I wanted it out and inside me but he didn't give me any room to unzip him.

He used his fingers faster now. I felt like I was going to cum and he sensed it. All of a sudden, he removed his fingers from my pussy and grabbed my hand and pulled me towards him as he walked. He barged in the room marked 'Employees Only' slamming the door behind him.

It was a washroom for the employees and looked empty. He locked it from the inside and pushed me against the door and undid his jeans. I saw his hard dick come out and instantly grabbed it and knelt down on my knees. I looked into his eyes and stroked his dick hard before putting my mouth on it and sucking it.

I loved the taste of it and used my tongue on his dickhead and sucked it again. He held my hair and didn't let them disturb me eating his dick. He pushed my head further inside reaching the end of my throat and briefly gagging me. He lifted my shirt and bra, grabbed my bare breast and played with my nipples.

I kept sucking him hard while he caressed my boobs. Then he lifted me up and spread my hands and put his face on my breasts and sucked them wet. I felt his tongue all over my nipples and he made them wet completely. His hands were in my hair massaging my neck and taking me to a completely different world.

I was at his mercy and my pussy was dripping wet now. He did not waste any time. He pulled my panty down in one go leaving me just in the tiny skirt and fingered my pussy with his right hand. I was moaning loudly. I let out a batch of cum on his hand. I was all wet and begged him to do me.

He turned me around and inserted his hard dick in my pussy. He expertly guided himself inside me and stroked me slowly. I was feeling so horny and his dick just gave me a sense of myself as I started feeling his dick inside me. He stroked harder now and I started moving at his pace.

He started fucking me hard and I was moaning in ecstasy now. He kept thrusting me and I kept enjoying and moaning. He fucked me with my skirt on which made me feel happy as I wanted him to do it. Then he bent me and went full doggy caressing my boobs simultaneously.

I was now being fucked vigorously by his hard dick and was enjoying each and every second of it. Slowly his thrusts were getting faster and stronger. I felt that he was going to cum. As I could think of it, he pulled his cock out and made me kneel on my knees and asked me if I would take it in.

I refused and asked him to instead spray it on my boobs. He cummed all over my chest and his cum flowed onto my boobs. I teased him by using my finger to taste his cum. We fucked for almost 30 minutes and were sweating. We both sat on the floor side by side happy and satisfied.

But this story doesn't end here. This was just one part of the story. We did explore many things later on about which I will tell you some other time.

12. *Stranger*

This incident happened at the beginning of this year when I was tired of my job and went for a vacation alone to Goa to have some fun. I was staying in a resort. From Akshay's point of view...

As soon as I entered the resort, I saw an utterly gorgeous face. There she was, Charmy, standing and talking to the receptionist. I thought that it could be the best possible start to my vacation. So, I approached the desk and asked for my room as I had made my reservation about two days back.

As the receptionist was giving me the keys, I was just having a look at Charmy. To be honest, until that whole time, I hadn't had a look at her assets because I couldn't take my eyes off her beautiful face. She saw me staring at her face. But then I moved my hand forward and introduced myself.

She shook hands with me and replied with a big smile on her face. I don't know if it was a coincidence or something but our suites were side by side. We went in the lift and till reaching out respective suites, we both were talking continuously. We bid farewell and I entered my room.

Damn, it was so beautiful. It had a sea view as the resort had its own private beach. I was really happy seeing that suite and on the top of that, I met a beautiful girl a few moments back. I was hoping for a decent nice vacation and in the midst of thinking all this, I slept.

When I woke up, it was pretty dark and when I checked the time, it was 8 pm. I took a bath, wore shorts and a vest and went out for dinner. To my surprise, I saw her there. She was standing in the queue and was wearing a knee-length black dress. It was showing her sexy curvy body.

I joined her in the queue and she was happy to see me. I complimented her on her looks and she replied with a big smile. We sat on a table and started having our dinner. I could clearly notice her staring at me from the corner of her eyes. I was looking good (hot I guess) in just a vest showing my impressive upper body.

The dinner was amazing with different varieties of food. We ended up eating stomach full and decided to go for a walk. The moon was shining brightly and it was a great night to walk around the beach. As we were walking, we were continuously talking about our jobs, hobbies, etc.

I came to know that she was an engineer. And while working, she was also preparing for IAS and came there to take a break from her monotonous and tiresome schedule. I also had the same reason. I was feeling good that I had someone with whom I could spend some part of my vacation.

We walked for quite a good time and then we settled on one of the benches near the beach. We were just sitting and chilling enjoying the cool breeze. In that moonlight, she was looking absolutely amazing. So beautiful that I wanted to just kiss her there and then. But I was a little frightened to do so.

We kept talking for some time. Then, she just kept her head on my shoulder and continued talking. Time passed and soon it was 1 am. We decided to go to our rooms and sleep since the next day we had to go out. I said 'Bye' and 'Goodnight' even though I wanted her to sit beside me and wanted so many other things.

As soon as I went to my bed, I slept like a child as I was pretty tired. The next morning, instead of going out, we both decided to explore the beach. The resort had a huge beautiful beach and very few people. We thought it would be better there. I knocked on her door and there she came out.

She was wearing a crop top which ended 2 inches above her navel and shorts which were just enough to cover that sexy ass of hers. She was looking like a bombshell. I was wearing another of my vests and shorts and I had a backpack. I again, literally ogled at her and complimented her on her beauty and sexiness.

For the first time, she complimented me in return. I was on cloud nine. We went to the beach and there were only a few people there. So, we started walking around the shore. I was stealing glances at her body. She made sure that plenty amount of her cleavage, navel, and waist and her ass were visible in her outfit.

We both were stealing some glances at each other. We reached a place which had a shallow water. I directly dived in but she didn't join me as she did not know how to swim. So, she just sat there in the sand watching me. I had a good dive of around 15 minutes.

Then I came back, removed my vest and sat beside her. As soon as I removed my vest, she started looking at me and smiled. I smiled back. We talked for a bit. I saw she was facing some problem due to the sun and the heat. I asked her and she said that she forgot to apply lotion on her body before coming there.

It was kind of burning. I said that we could go back if she wanted but she wanted to do the sport rides. So, I asked her if she minded if I applied lotion on her body. She was a little shocked to hear this as she was not expecting this. To my surprise, she agreed.

I was very happy and I took a lotion bottle out of my backpack. She was happy to see that I had come prepared. I asked her to lie down on the towel on her stomach. I just had a look of her backside. She was looking so so sexy in that crop top and shorts that I couldn't wait.

I took some lotion and started applying on her lower back which was not covered by the top. I started with slow and controlled movements touching her smooth sexy white skin. "Your skin is so smooth, Charmy," I told her to which she blushed a little.

I asked her to remove the crop top since it could get dirty with the lotion. She was a little hesitant to do that. But I requested and also the fact that there were almost no people on that side of the beach. she removed her crop top but still, I was not able to see her from the front.

She was wearing a red lacy bra with just a knot at the back. It was complimenting her white skin. I started applying lotion on her upper back. I was literally massaging her with my warm tough hands. She was enjoying my touch and small moans were escaping from her mouth in between.

I could feel the goosebumps on her smooth skin as I was touching her body. While rubbing her back, I accidentally removed the knot of her bra. She just turned a little and asked me what I was doing. I told her that it happened by mistake and that I would tie that again.

But to my surprise again, she said, "No! Let it be." And on the top of that, she asked me to massage her front side. She said that she was enjoying my touch on her body. I asked her to turn around. Before she turned around, I tied the knot of her bra. It was the only thing covering those massive beautiful tits.

She was very happy to see how gentleman kind of a person I was. But I was able to see her side boobs which gave me a hard-on and a pretty big boner. She must have seen that as I saw her smiling secretly. I started massaging her shoulders and her stomach.

Her navel was so beautiful that I wanted to play with it and suck it even though I am not a navel kind of a man. I could hear her moans even though they were low. After massaging her shoulders and stomach for some time, I moved to her legs. She said that I had missed some part over there.

I was sure that I did cover every inch of that body except what was covered by her bra. I told her the same. She said she wanted me to give massage to her tits as well. They were badly aching for a manly touch. I was happy and shocked but I asked her if she was sure, she wanted that.

She said, "Yes." OMG! as soon as she said this, my manhood rose higher and higher and it was saluting those magnificent tits. I started massaging them slowly together. I could see that she was very horny as her nipples were hard. I was able to see those hard nipples over her bra.

I was just staring at them as I was massaging her. She was moaning a little louder than earlier. After massaging her 34 sized tits for some time, I couldn't control anymore. I planted a kiss on her lips while massaging. She did not know as her eyes were closed.

But man, she responded in full flight as if she was expecting it. We were kissing like hungry wild animals. I started involving my tongue while I was massaging her as well. Her hands reached my shorts and she started massaging my cock over the shorts.

I moved one of my hands from her tits to her thighs and pussy and started rubbing it over her shorts. Her panties were already wet. We were madly kissing each other and playing with each other's body. After some time, we gasped for air and had a look around us. But to our luck, nobody was there.

So, I asked her to wear the top without that bra and asked her to come to my room. But she refused and wore the crop top and started walking. But when I saw her ass, I couldn't control. I again grabbed her, pushed her towards the side tree and started kissing again.

But this time, my hands were on her ass. She was responding in the same way as I was. I was playing with her ass smacking and groping those ass cheeks. She said she wanted me inside her and then we walked to my room.

The next part is from Charmy's point of view.

All that kissing and playing with each other's body made me very wet. My panties were fully drenched with my juices. As soon as we entered Akshay's room, he locked it and we pounced on each other like hungry wild animals. We started kissing each other in a wild manner.

He pinned me against a wall and continued kissing me. While he was kissing me, I could feel his hands roaming all over my body exploring it in a very sexy manner. I was loving his manly touch all over my body. He kissed me on my neck and shoulders and started exploring my tits and my wet pussy.

One of his hands was busy playing with my tits over the bra while the other one started playing with my pussy over those tiny shorts. I was really enjoying this and moaning loudly. All of a sudden, he turned me around, slapped my ass and started removing my tiny shorts.

As he removed them, he made me align my ass crack over his hard big cock while he started playing with my body. We were moving in rhythm as his hard cock was being brushed against my ass. At the same time, he was busy playing with those massive tits of mine.

He did not remove my bra. Instead, he put his hands inside and then he started fondling them. As I was moaning, he put one of his hands over my pussy over the panties and started rubbing it. He started giving me love bites on my neck while his hard cock was grinding against my ass crack.

He slowly inserted one of his hands inside my panties and started rubbing the clean shaved pussy. I was very turned on by this gesture of Akshay. I was near to exploding and nobody had made me feel like Akshay did. I was feeling great being with him. He continued playing with my pussy with his fingers.

He was busy fondling my tits as well with his other hand and at the same time, kissing and biting all over my neck and shoulders. His hard cock was feeling so good against my ass. I told him that I was about to explode but he did not listen and continued each and every action of his.

After about 15 minutes of this dirty playing, I cummed and he licked it all clean. I took charge afterward kissed him from his mouth till his cock. I removed his shorts and boxers and began to suck his cock. I kissed and licked and sucked his biceps, triceps and chest and nipples and six-pack abs.

After I was done sucking his cock, he came like a fountain, cumming all over my tits. After this, we took a break and cleaned ourselves with tissues. He ordered juice and some food for us. Until the room service came, we were sitting just like that on the couch talking and cuddling, playing with each other.

As the room bell rang, I put on a robe and went to open the door. I was taking the tray from the waiter. He couldn't take his eyes off my tits which were partially covered with that robe. It must have given him such a hard-on. I was feeling sexier and sluttier from inside. I was wearing just panties.

I locked the door and threw my robe on the couch where Akshay was sitting. He was looking at me like a hungry tiger. We ate some food and drank some juice as well as we were pretty thirsty with all that erotic action. There were some grapes as well.

I was eating one when Akshay came near me and asked me to share that grape. I readily agreed and we started kissing over that grape. Soon it went to his stomach, I guess, I don't remember to be honest. We started kissing again as we laid down on the couch kissing each other madly all over the body.

He started playing with my tits again. Looked like he had grown very fond of them. He started caressing and groping them, pinching the hard nipples in between which was driving me crazy. I wanted his hard dick inside me at that moment. I asked him to fuck me like anything.

His dick was hard as a rock. So, he lifted me, made me lie down on the bed and started fucking in the missionary position. I was waiting for him to enter me. But he kept teasing me, keeping his cock at the entrance of my pussy. I was getting angry now. So, I took his cock and made it enter me.

As soon as he entered my pussy, I let out a loud moan. He was having a monster cock, not in length but in girth. In the beginning, he was slow with his movements as he was a little caring towards me. But after a few strokes, I started to enjoy that cock and asked him to increase the pace.

He started fucking me giving me consistent thrusts. The sound our bodies were making was making the whole scene very very erotic. He was pressing my tits as he was fucking me. I was moaning and shouting his name, "Akshay! Akshay! Fuck me harder. Make me your bitch. Fuck me harder."

He got excited about hearing this and started fucking me faster. His movements were so fast that I could feel the tip of his cock hitting the end of my pussy. It was feeling so so good. I knew that he would cum soon if he went like that. But I didn't stop him since his cock was feeling so good inside me.

I was totally enjoying the fuck and moaning a lot. He told me that he was near cumming. I didn't listen to him and asked him to fuck me fast. After a few strokes, he cummed in loads inside me. What a feeling it was! It is very difficult to describe it in words.

But I hadn't cummed yet. So, I asked him to lick me until I cum. He went down and started licking me. He was very good at that too. He was playing with my pussy with his hands and his mouth rubbing and licking it. He was driving me crazy. He started fingering me.

With time he increased the number of fingers going inside my pussy. He continued to finger fuck me until I came and released a lot of juices. He drank it all like a good little boy and licked my pussy clean. We were so drained that we slept there on the bed itself and that too naked.

When I woke up, it was evening already. When I saw to my left, there he was, Akshay, lying with his hard cock. I couldn't control myself and I started playing with his cock giving him a handjob. I think he woke up because of that and he was very happy to see my hands wrapped around his cock.

He laid back and didn't disturb me playing with his cock. In no time, his cock was rock hard and he stopped me in between. He picked me up in his strong build arms (both of us were naked) and we went into the bathroom. It had a jacuzzi as well but he said that he wanted to clean me and then fuck me.

I readily agreed to that and we kissed again under the shower. He took soap and started applying to my body. He was applying it very passionately on my tits and my ass. I was wet seeing him do all that to me. He continued to play with my tits and started rubbing my pussy.

I was very wet with my juices flowing and the water, of course! He asked me for a tit fuck in between. I couldn't say no to him as he cleaned my body so lovingly. I placed his cock in between my big tits and started to give him a tit fuck. I was licking his tip as well between the tit fuck.

He was moaning and slapping my tits in between. I was enjoying his hard big cock between my tits. I really wanted to get fucked again by that cock. I asked him to fuck me again under the shower. He made me turn towards the wall, bent me and slowly entered my wet pussy from behind.

It was such a heavenly feeling to get fucked by that cock under the shower. This time he did not start with slow movements. Instead, he went with full speed and was fucking me harder than before. He started pressing my tits which were hanging as he fucked me from behind.

His thrusts were increasing and the speed as well. He started slapping my ass making it tomato red. I really got excited by this and asked him to fuck me harder. I was moaning his name very loudly as he was fucking me with his hard cock entering my pussy.

We both were so close to cumming and this time, we wanted to do it together. I asked him to hold it as I was also near cumming.

After a few strokes, with lots of moaning and shouting, we both came together under the shower. It was one of the best sexual encounters of my life.

I enjoyed that vacation and we fucked like anything at all the places in that resort. It became one of the best vacations of my life.

13. *Lockdown*

Three weeks had passed since the nationwide lockdown was announced. Almost all of my friends had left for their hometown. I had to stay in the city as I couldn't leave in time because of my prior work commitments. Then all airlines and rails came to a halt.

Eventually, I was extremely bored, alone and horny. So, I thought of giving Tinder a try to pass some time with hot guys. I installed the Tinder application on my phone on a Tuesday afternoon

I added some sizzling hot pics of mine with a bio 'Waiting to be locked in together with someone in this lockdown. Are you up for this challenge?'

I then got engrossed in work for an hour or so. Later, when I checked my Tinder, it had more than 73 likes and some messages on Tinder Gold. I was taken aback by the response. I figured out that half of them would be fake profiles.

I started browsing the profiles and almost left swiped everyone. Then, I came across the profile of Neil, who had uploaded some shirtless pictures on the app. The man in the pics had a perfect chiselled body with sexy six-pack abs, biceps, and triceps, and a sharp jawline.

As much as I liked the pics, I was sure that that must be another fake profile. He had the bio Coffee | Travel Enthusiast | 6 feet | Would love to talk about how badly the lockdown needs to end. I got interested and swiped right, and it was an instant match.

Then, the real fun began.

I was damn sure that he would send the first message, and so I waited for some time. In half an hour or so, I got a ping from him. I liked the body of the person displayed in the pics. But I still had my doubts. I knew that I would proceed forward only after thoroughly verifying the full credentials of the person.

Neil: I am up for any challenge in the locked room with you. (He said, referring to my bio.)

Me: Oh! Straight to that? I like your attitude. But how do I believe you are the same person as in the pics?

He: You want to see me live then? Your place or mine?

Me: Not so fast, Mr. Neil. Hold your horses. How about some more pics?

He: I'll show you mine if you show me yours. It's 'give and take.'

He sent me a few more pics. But this time, he sent me his pics in full clothes. I still was doubtful if he was the same guy in the pics. So I thought of taking things a notch higher.

Me: I still can't believe you are the same person as in the shirtless pics. How about my name written on your torso?

He: Oh! So we are going there, aren't we? Cool! Give me a minute.

After a few minutes, he sent me a picture with my name CHARMY written on his wide chest between his nipples with red lipstick. I scanned it carefully and finally believed it was him, actually.

Me: Alright, you are the guy then.

He: It's your turn now, Charmy.

Casually, I sent him a picture of my arm and hand with my name CHARMY written on it.

He: That's way too 1940s and unjustified.

Me: Then? What do you want?

He: Be a sport and send me a bolder picture. Write my name across your cleavage.

Me: If we gel well, I might. Come on, impress me.

He: Oh! Another challenge, then? Not yet impressed with my gym physique? That usually does the trick.

Me: I loved your physique. In fact, that's the only reason I right-swiped you.

He: Oh! Thank God. I put my shirtless pics, or this would never have started.

Me: That's right.

He: How about you showing me something now? Just to keep the game hot.

Me: Feast yourself with a little cleavage pic of mine.

I searched my gallery and sent him an old cleavage pic.

He: I can't see my name. Why don't you write it between your boobs? Or is it too early? Come on, I thought you are much bolder and sexier. Show me something more.

Me: Just shut up and have some more.

I surfed my gallery and sent him some pictures of my sexy bareback.

He: Oh! I love the view from here. It would be better with me in the picture, though. Look what you are making me do.

And he sent me a picture of his huge bulge in his shorts. I must say these guys are really quick. Not even once did he try to know if I am actually the girl in the pics. He was ready to bare it all before me. I then asked him to take it easy and take things slow.

I explained that we need to develop mutual trust and understanding before we actually take things ahead. Gladly, he too understood my point of view. Over the next couple of weeks, we talked and chatted a lot on WhatsApp after exchanging numbers.

We sex chatted and also did some great phone sex. We had many sexy roleplays, which would lead us to multiple orgasms. He kept on persuading me to video call and all, but I always ignored him. He would frequently send me his workout videos and pics of his abs and muscles.

After watching those videos and pics, I would finger my pussy. But a finger can't do what a cock can. I was alone and craved for some really good sex.

One day while chatting, Neil again sent me the pic of his bulge in his shorts and began persuading me to come out of the closet. I was also horny and decided to play along.

Me: The view of the bulge would be better without the shorts, isn't it?

He: The view can even be bigger and better with the help of your sexy boobs without a bra.

Me: Someone's getting too needy.

He: With a girl like you, it's a crime to not be needy.

Me: Okay then! Let's start with the neediness. I want the perfect view.

After a minute or so, he sent me a picture of his large and thick dick. I have to admit that it was meaty and veiny and just the pic of it made me wet. I kept looking at the pic for some time.

Me: Umm! Looking at its hardness, I can definitely say someone's definitely horny about me.

He: It's your turn, babe. I kept my promise.

I, too, let go of all my inhibitions. I unhooked and removed my bra immediately. I clicked a pic of my perfect 34 sized boobs and sent it to him.

He: What sexiness! You know what I am thinking?

Me: What?

He: That I suck those melons dry and bite your nipples while you moan in pleasure.

Me: And can you guess my thoughts?

He: Shoot!

Me: That I suck the juices out of that meaty dick of yours again and again.

He: Just the meat? Are you sure you don't wanna suck anything else?

He again sent me a few pics of his gym build body – front and back.

Me: Sure! I wanna kiss all over your washboard abs, chest, shoulders, and bite your neck and earlobes. Give hickeys and love bites all over your body. Scratch your muscled back as you make wild love to me. Kiss your lips passionately as well as bite them – love-making at its best.

He: Spicy! I like it. In fact, I love it. I am already imagining the things I'm gonna do to you once we meet.

Me: And what things are those?

He: Licking your clitoris hard, fingering your love hole, and inserting my tongue deep inside your pussy. Licking your pussy until you cum. And this will just be the trailer before the actual film and its climax. Charmy, come to my bed. I will make wild love to you all night. I will fill all your love holes.

He started singing the song 'Bheege Honth Tere.' I started getting aroused with his talking and singing. I don't know when but I got rid of my night shorts and was only left in my black panties.

I put my hand inside my panties and started rubbing my pussy gently. My naughty pussy had already started flowing its love juices. We were both calm for some time when suddenly he asked me if I was fingering.

He: Naughty girl! Fingering your pussy?

Me: Nope! Don't be overconfident. I am not desperate.

He: But I am damn sure you have one of your hands over the pussy. Come on, tell me. Don't be shy.

Me: Oh, please! My hand can be over the pussy once I see the full movie. I am sure you have your dick in your hand. Right?

He: Absolutely right. I don't hide things like you. But the full movie telecast is only possible live on a video call, and that too a nude video call.

Me: Want everything in just one movie? I don't know about a nude video call but let us begin with a normal video call.

He: I am up for anything. So, today's the day then when I will see the hotness live. Can't wait. Hurry up.

I made sure I wore my black padded bra and sexy black panties to tease him all the more. Then, I video-called him and kept the video feed focussed on my face.

He: Wow! You are prettier than your pics! I guess I will die seeing your beauty. Your pics don't do you justice, Charmy (He said, winking.)

Me: There's absolutely no need to overdo it. And tell me something I don't know. I know where your interests lie. Not in my face but everything that lies below it.

He: You are right, but I only told the truth. Let it be, what were we sucking for each other? Come on now and don't be shy and show me your boobs, babe.

I directed the camera towards my bra caged boobs.

He: What the fuck! Don't tease me further, babe. I'm already hot. Look what your face did to my mate.

(He directed the camera towards his cock caged in shorts. Since the shorts were loose, it was standing erect like a tower. My eyes glued there, and he saw that.)

He: You will see more of it once you show me your valleys.

Me: What should I do, darling? Your tool has made me very

horny.

He: Let's start by taking off that bra first. It's hiding your beautiful jewels. Come on, Charmy, my balls will explode. My tool's very hard. It badly needs a mouth or a pussy.

I supported my phone at the bedpost. I slowly and sexily unhooked the bra from behind, removed the straps but didn't let it fall down.)

He: Charmy, you are such a tease. Come on. I have waited enough. Show me those assets.

I continued teasing him by slowly getting rid of the bra, but then I kept my hands on my boobs.

He: Fuck Charmy! Come on. Remove your hands. Let me see your beauty.

I finally showed him my right boob.

He: Sexy! Nice! Show me both of them, babe. Can't wait anymore.

I then displayed both my boobs to him, and he acted like getting the shock of his life.

He: Fuck Charmy! A lovely pair of big melons you have been blessed with. I am sure a lot many men worked on them to get the desired results.

I just blushed and started playing with my boobs with my hands.

Me: What are you gonna do with them, Neil, once you get hold of them?

He: I will suck these milky boobs of yours. Bite these nipples to my satisfaction. Suck and press them so hard that I can make you moan at the top of your voice. Such wild love, I will make to your boobs, baby.

I could sense from his tone that he was stroking his dick.

Me: Oh yeah! I would love it. And then what are you gonna do? (I asked in a seductive tone.)

He: I will tell that only if you take off those sexy panties hiding your love holes.

Me: Oooh! Someone's in a hurry. What's the rush, cowboy? And how do you even know I am wearing something downside? Possible that I am already naked.

He: When you're on the other end, can't go slow, darling. And I know you are wearing panties there to tease me. I have known that much about you.

Me: Tell me, why do you want my pussy?

He: So I can make passionate love to it with my fingers and my throbbing dick.

Saying that, he also placed his phone on his bedpost and removed his shorts in front of me in one go. He started stroking his dick. I also started continuously looking at that veiny meaty dick. He was stroking it in front of me, and I was looking at its big pink thick head.

I was extremely excited. I sexily took off my panties in front of him, spread my legs wide to show him my love holes, and started rubbing my pussy. He stopped stroking his dick and intently kept on looking at my clean-shaven pussy.

Me: What happened? Never seen a pussy before?

He: Seen dozens of them, but yours is extremely beautiful. Seems very tight to me. I am sure I will enjoy ramming that tight pussy. Come to me, Charmy. I will make it a memorable night.

Me: Cut the crap. Now, tell me, what are you gonna do with my pussy?

He: Why don't you rub your pussy hard while I describe what I am gonna do to your love hole once I get you in my arms.

And I started rubbing my pussy.

He: I will spread your legs wide and lick your clitoris with my tongue slowly. Then, I will increase my speed while you keep moaning. Afterward, I will insert one finger inside your vagina while I lick and gently bite your pussy. Then, I will enter another finger in your pussy.

His words were making me extremely excited. I pushed my index finger inside my pussy and started moaning lightly.

He: I will continue stroking my fingers inside your pussy while I bite your clitoris. Come on, Charmy, one more finger.

I then penetrated two fingers inside my vagina and started stroking swiftly.

He: Think of your fingers as my dick, baby. I am fucking your pussy hard. Come on now, insert another finger, babe. Three fingers will provide you with much more pleasure.

I could see him holding his dick and masturbating while pleasuring me with his words. I didn't insert the third finger but continued fingering my pussy. My other hand was mauling my own boobs.

He: Think that I am vigorously fucking your pussy, babe. Quickly pounding my dick in and out and as deep as possible with my thrusts.

I started moaning loudly and was almost on the verge of cumming. He was very good, just with his words making me wonder how good he must be in real.

He: I know you're feeling great, baby. Feel my hard dick inside your pussy as I am fucking you with my full capacity.

His words were seductive enough that I had a huge orgasm with a loud moan. My body was shivering with the orgasm. I looked at Neil, and my eyes were filled with nothing but pleasure and immense satisfaction. I could see him stroking his dick fast. I also decided to get into the act to make him cum fast.)

Me: Yes, baby, keep stroking that big thick dick of yours. Think as if your long dick is inside my mouth and reaching till my throat feeling the fluids and the warmth of my mouth.

He: Oh yes! Keep it going, baby. I so wanna fuck your mouth hard and penetrate my full dick deep inside your throat.

Me: Yes, darling! You're holding my head and very swiftly pushing your penis deep inside my mouth in and out, making me gag. My mouth is oozing oodles of saliva and your pre-cum on your dick. Fuck my mouth harder, baby.

He: Oh yes, baby! I am fucking your mouth very hard and fast. I can feel the insides of your mouth and throat. It's fluid and very warm. I love it. I am fucking your mouth as if it's your vagina.

I sensed that he was closing in on his orgasm.

She: Come on, baby, push your dick further inside my mouth. Choke me, baby. Choke me.

He let out a loud moan and finally cummed a lot. And by lot, I mean a lot.

He: You were sensational, babe. I can't wait to meet you and lick you all over your body. Damn this lockdown.

She: You were great as well. Skilled with your words. It was an amazing orgasm that we had together.

We continued those erotic chats and video calls over the days. Due to lockdown, everything was closed, and there was no place to meet. We were getting hornier every passing day – a feeling we had to live with.

As the lockdown restrictions started lifting slowly, a few coffee shops opened up. We finally decided to meet over coffee. I was very excited and decided to dress accordingly. I wore a sexy yellow crop top revealing my belly button and paired it with Zara white shorts.

When I reached the coffee shop, I found him waiting already. He was 6 feet tall, dressed in a white tee, an open striped red shirt paired with faded blue denim, and white sneakers. He was just as handsome in real life as I had witnessed over video calls.

We met and hugged. We ordered some light food and cappuccino in the coffee shop in our first official meeting. He was a fun-loving smart guy, exactly the way I thought about him. We talked about what transpired between us in the past few days.

We discussed how eager we both were to meet and fuck each other. I had no plans to fuck him that day. After our coffee date later that night, he dropped me in the parking of my society building. Before getting off of the car, we bid goodbyes.

As we looked at each other, it was very evident what both of us wanted. Our sex hormones were driving us crazy to devour each other. He brought his face closer to mine, pulled my face towards his, and started kissing me on the lips. We both then indulged in a passionate French kiss with continuous drooling.

We were vigorously kissing and biting each other's lips. We then stopped for a while.

He: I was waiting for this moment, Charmy. Kissing and biting your cherry lips.

Me: So what are you waiting for, now? Kiss me again (I said seductively.) I have been longing for it since the time I saw you.

He then again started kissing me passionately with me cooperating with him. We opened our mouths wide, so we could feel each other's tongues. We kept on kissing for some time. While kissing, he was also fondling my boobs with pressing and mauling them, and rubbing my pussy.

I didn't stop him at all. Even if he had rendered me naked in the car and fucked me then and there, I would have been okay with it. I also didn't shy away from feeling his cock over his denim. Also, I lifted his tee and felt his washboard abs. It took my excitement to another level.

I kept my hands over his crotch and felt, to my satisfaction, the size of his dick. He also moved his hand inside my crop top and pressed my melons and my nipples. We could no longer control our urges. After much thinking, I invited him to come to my abode and fuck my brains out.

He was waiting for it and immediately agreed. We soon parked his car and reached my place. Crazy and wild lovemaking happened between the two of us at my place. But I will write that in a completely new story.

14. Airport Hunk

It so happened that I had to travel from Delhi to Chandigarh for professional reasons. My flight was scheduled at 11:35 pm, and I reached the airport well in time at about 09:30 pm. Once all the security checks were over, I hopped over to the airport lounge for dinner since I was famished.

I made myself comfortable with my pasta and started scrolling my Insta to kill some time. During this time, my eyes locked with a guy who was constantly staring at me. I chose to ignore it first. But when I gazed upon him carefully, I found out that he was no ordinary pervert.

He was a 6 feet tall guy with a hunky body, fair-complexioned with a French beard, and having a toned body. It was evident from his muscular arms, exactly the kind of guy I like. He was wearing a sleeveless tee and ripped jeans with loafers.

I also started exchanging glances with him and couldn't take my eyes off him. At the end of a stressful day, I just wanted someone like him to devour me and set my loins on fire. It had been a couple of weeks since I last had sex.

I was not much into relationships but into hot and sexy men who could take control and drive me into oblivion. I measured 5'10" when on heels with a busty ass and luscious boobs measuring 34.

No man could ever ignore me, and no man could be done with me just in a single night. I was the perfect embodiment of a man's desires from a woman with the perfect body.

I didn't want to let go of that opportunity. I also started looking at him from time to time, knowing fully well that our eyes would lock at some point. I was eating my pasta, and he had his drink. We were both looking at each other. He smiled at me with a smirk, and I responded back with a wry smile.

I thought of making a move and moved my purse from the other chair of my table, indicating that the chair was available for him. He understood my signal and moved with his drink towards my table.

Akshay: Hi!

Charmy : Hey!

Akshay (smiling): I notice you have a little crush on me.

Charmy (surprised): What? I have a crush on you. Please spare me. It is you who's looking at me since the time I sat here.

Akshay(drinking): Then I guess you catch on to the little hints.

Charmy : I am good at that. Anyway, where are you headed to?

Akshay: Chandigarh. And you?

Charmy : Chandigarh too for me.

Akshay: Looks like fate has brought us together. Indigo 11:30 flight?

Charmy : Yes! OMG! Are you sure you aren't stalking me, handsome?

I said as I crossed my right leg on the top of the left one. Thereby exposing my toned sexy long legs over the one-piece red dress, I wore. It barely reached my knees.

Akshay(zooming his eyes over my dreamy legs): I wouldn't mind stalking you, Miss...

Charmy : Charmy ! You can call me Charmy .

Akshay: No wonder you are!

Charmy : And what should I call you, Mr...

Akshay: Akshay is the name.

Charmy : So, Akshay, how long will you be in Chandigarh?

Akshay: I expect it will be a fortnight. You? Business or Personal?

He asked while he indicated the server to get us some fresh juice.

Charmy : Business, sadly. But I will be there for about a week.

Our conversation then continued over juice. It was announced that due to some unforeseen circumstances, the flight to Chandigarh had been canceled by the airlines. The officials maintained that they were arranging for an alternate flight at the earliest. But that would only be possible the next day after 9 am.

Akshay: Charmy , there is a hotel nearby and I will be checking myself in. You, too, can take refuge over there for the night. Shall I call a cab?

Charmy : There's no other thing to do, right? Let's proceed, shall we?

I was very excited, which was evident from the spring in my step. I could already feel my pussy getting wet in anticipation. But I tried to control my urges. He then called a cab.

As we sat in the backseat of the dimly lit car, I could feel the sexual tension rising between us over the few kilometres distance from the airport to the hotel. He kept his right hand on my left thigh. I froze then and there. He kept on measuring my voluptuous body with his lusty eyes resulting in a boner.

I also could feel my pussy getting wetter slowly. The heat was on, and the night was young with two burning souls. Finally, the hotel arrived. On the way to the reception, Akshay said, "I will be booking two separate rooms for the night. Is that okay with you?"

I said, stuttering a bit, "Yeah. Sure!" clearly sounding a bit disappointed.

We checked in at the reception and headed towards the lift. Our rooms were on the 15th floor. Only the two of us in the lift and the sexual tension between us hit the reef. My heartbeats increased as I was ready for him to take me apart. Akshay looked at me and smiled as the lift started ascending.

Our eyes locked as we both couldn't control any further. He held my waist with both his hands and pulled me closer to him. He placed his lips over mine and started kissing me passionately. I also reciprocated back, and we continued kissing as the temperature of the lift increased manifold.

The lift stopped on the 15th floor, and we stopped kissing immediately after the doors opened. We quickly walked towards his room. As soon as he punched his card and opened the door, we quickly went in and began kissing intensely. He pushed me against a wall while still holding my waist.

He started kissing me on the lips with our tongues exchanging saliva. A passionate smooch was going on with our tongues exploring each other's mouths. He made me face the wall and started kissing me from behind. He held me in that position and started unzipping my dress from behind.

He soon slid the dress below my boobies. He started kissing my back, shoulders, neck, and ear lobes. My excitement knew no bounds, and all that made me hornier than ever. I was wearing a red-coloured push-up bra and lacy red-coloured panties.

He unhooked my bra from behind and removed the straps, and rendered me topless. He twirled me around and started sucking my boob while mauling the other with his hand. I began moaning at the treatment being meted out to my boobs.

He kept on sucking my boobs and biting my nipples as he stretched out and held my arms tightly against the wall. In a moment of passion, he picked me up and made me sit on a table nearby. He started vehemently sucking and biting my tits. My milky white boobs turned red as I kept moaning in pleasure.

All this while, I was constantly pushing his mouth more into my boobs as I couldn't contain the excitement. As soon as he stopped ravaging my tits and again started smooching me, I knew it was my turn to return the pleasure and take control.

In the same position, I removed his tee and immediately started kissing his neck and broad shoulders. The position was not very comfortable. So, Akshay picked me up in his strong arms, placed me on the king-size bed. Then removed my dress completely from my legs.

He also removed his denim, and I could see a huge tent in his underwear. But it was my turn to feast on him. I laid on him on the bed and started kissing his strong muscular veiny arms. He tried to dominate me by coming on top of me, but I resisted him.

I then began kissing his shoulders, chest, and nipples to arouse him further. I started kissing him madly on the lips as he was just a fantastic kisser. Once I satisfied my desire to kiss his lips, I went down on him to kiss, lick, and suck his washboard abs and navel.

I went further down on him to take a peek of his large throbbing dick. I pulled his underwear down, and a dick that seemed quite long and thick sprung up. I knew it would lead to a satisfying penetration. I wasted no time and began to lick his dick with my tongue.

He kept on setting my hair so that he could see his dick entering my mouth. I was gently swallowing his dick and smothering it with my tongue. I was enjoying sucking the veiny piece of meat. I lubricated the shaft with my saliva and even gave his balls a taste of my mouth.

He was moaning gently with pleasure as he was pressing my mouth over his dick so that his penis could get deep inside my throat. He started thrusting my mouth with his dick while tightly holding my head. Saliva mixed with his pre-cum started oozing out of my mouth.

He couldn't take it anymore and soon overpowered me and came on top of me. He advanced down my body and removed and threw my lacy panties in one of the corners of the room. He swiftly moved his mouth towards my clean shaved pussy and started licking my vagina with his tongue.

He held my thighs with his hands and kept on licking my clitoris very fast. He was very experienced in eating a pussy. I was moaning at the top of my voice, and my pussy was wet as hell. He soon fingered me by first inserting the middle finger in my pussy while simultaneously licking and gently biting my clitoris.

Soon after, he inserted another finger in my pussy and started stroking both the fingers as fast as he could while kissing, licking, and biting my clitoris. My body was shaking at the violent love being made to my pussy by this hunky monster.

I was in another world with my entire body shaking with excitement as I raised my hips in one final loud moan. I cummed hard on his face with deep long breaths and a sense of immense satisfaction. Even before I could recover from my first cum.

He soon completely removed and threw away his underwear and brought his dick in front of my mouth. He pulled my hair to open my mouth and stuffed his long shaft inside my mouth. He knew how to dominate and pleasure a girl to the fullest.

He held my face with his hands and started stroking his dick inside my throat like it was a vagina. He was very rough, and I loved every moment of it. I was gasping for breath. He pulled out his dick and made me sit on the bed so that he could stand on the bed and shove his dick even deep inside my throat to gag me.

While gagging me, he held my head and let out a deep, moaning voice. He kept on stroking his dick swiftly in and out of the throat. He really liked doing it. He kept on gagging me multiple times, and I spit out oodles of saliva. His dick was dripping with my saliva and his pre-cum.

After a few minutes of fucking my mouth vigorously, he made

me lie on my back while my head was dangling out of bed. I just knew what he was about to do. I was lying upside down on the bed. He climbed down and held my neck, opened my mouth.

He inserted his dick to directly enter my throat while he could see how deep he could push his penis inside my throat. He absolutely loved doing that to me, as was evident from the glow in his eyes. He was moaning loudly. He could feel the warmth of my throat while shoving his penis as deep inside as he could.

I could barely breathe, and my face was turning pale. He knew exactly when to remove his dick so I could breathe, and he would again push it deep inside. He kept doing those multiple times. I could not do anything else while he would repeatedly choke my throat with his large and thick penis.

I loved what he did as I had never been handled so roughly in my previous sessions with my lovers. After some time, he freed my mouth and throat of his dick and climbed on the bed. He came on top of me, held me as tightly as he could from my shoulders, and positioned his penis at the entrance of my vagina.

In one shot, he pushed his penis deep inside my vagina. Initially, he did it slowly and gently. But later on, he picked up the pace and started ramming my pussy with his dick. While fucking my vagina, he constantly biting and licking and sucking my boobs which were already sore.

I was moaning with both pain and pleasure. He kept on vehemently stroking his dick deep inside my pussy. He had amazing stamina. At some moments, he would keep on sucking my boobs as hard as he could while fucking my pussy. At other moments, he would kiss my lips and bite them to his pleasure.

He would also lick, kiss, and bite my neck, which made my neck region red as well. It seemed like he intended to bite every inch of my body. He kept on letting out moans of pleasure while stroking his dick in my pussy. I cummed a second time.

After a few minutes, he changed the sex position. He made me lie down on my belly on the bed and came on top of me. He thrust his penis inside my vagina from behind. He pulled my hair to put me through some pain.

He was simultaneously giving me pleasure by stroking his long and thick penis inside my love hole. I was shrieking with the pain while he vigorously kept exfoliating my brains out. Taking that a step further, he started pushing me down on the mattress by holding down my shoulder and neck.

He put all his efforts into pushing me down while the intensity of his fucking further increased. I started moaning loudly. But he kept his hand over my mouth while he continued drilling my love hole. I could feel his penis almost hitting the deep ends of my vagina.

He was using all his might in ravaging my vagina, and I absolutely loved every moment of it. Suddenly, he further increased his speed of tearing apart my pussy with his dick, and it felt to me as if he was about to cum. He pulled my hair more tightly as I started shrieking at the top of my voice.

This time I wanted us to cum together. In a bid to do that, I also started providing additional pelvic thrusts from my end as I moaned even louder. We both were lost in that fucking world and forgot everything else around us. He let out a loud shriek as he dropped his sperms deep inside my vagina.

He kept on stroking his dick in my pussy until the last drop of sperm was collected inside my vagina. I also cum a third time during this entire sex session. He finally let go of my hair and fell beside me on the bedsheet smeared with our body fluids.

My entire body was almost red, just as he wished. I could feel my pussy dripping with our fluids. We both heaved sighs of relief. But I knew that it was just the beginning of the night for him.

It didn't end there, and many more fuck sessions followed that night and the one week I was in Chandigarh.

15. The Trek

A few of my colleagues from the office planned to go on a trek to Kheerganga and asked me to join. I thought about experiencing something new and adventurous. So, I agreed to accompany them. The day before the departure, I packed my bag and got ready.

I met my colleagues at the Delhi ISBT Kashmere Gate. From there, we took an overnight bus to Manikaran (a place famous for its hot springs). We reached Manikaran at around 9 in the morning. We went to the famous Gurudwara to seek blessings and also bathed in the hot spring.

Many tourists were there as it was a weekend. But a tall, muscular, and handsome white guy caught my attention when he had a word with the guys in our group. After exploring and sightseeing around Manikaran, we decided to spend the night in Kasol.

Therefore, we moved to the Manikaran bus stop to catch a bus to Kasol. It was then when the guys in our group introduced us to the white man. Since he was traveling alone, they brought him along with them to keep him company.

The white guy named Adal (he was a German) introduced himself to all of us. I, too, shook hands with him. What caught my attention during the handshake were his ripped and veiny forearms.

The bus reached Kasol in an hour and dropped us a little far away from our cottage. We started walking towards our cottage.

It was uphill and isolated from the main market area, perfectly sitting in the woods. While walking, Adal came beside me and broke the ice.

He told me that he was an entrepreneur from Germany, 27 years old, and a fitness enthusiast. He loved traveling, and that was the reason he was there. He complimented my beauty and especially my long legs.

I told him about myself and also complimented him on his physique and good looks. It soon converted into healthy flirting, and we got comfortable.

We all rested a bit after reaching the cottage because we were tired. It was also going to be a bonfire night with dance, music, and drinks, of course. We had our dinner in the night and then sat around the bonfire. What followed was a lovely evening of people showcasing their singing, dancing, and other talents.

I also drank a little (I am an occasional drinker). Adal and the other guys smoked some joints. I was sitting beside Adal, and we were chatting and enjoying the bonfire. It went on for a couple of hours when Adal asked me to accompany him for a walk in the woods.

I was jumping inside. I agreed, and we both went for a walk in the woods holding each other's hands and doing some healthy flirting. After walking for some time, we heard some water streams nearby and went in that direction. We came across a small stream, not very deep, and I touched its waters.

It was very cold. Before I could even say something, Adal removed his tee and trousers. I was baffled when he asked me, "Care for a little swim session?" I couldn't help but admire his washboard abs, the good build chest, biceps, and triceps in the moonlight.

He was standing tall in front of me in underwear. He started flexing and showing off his sculpted body. Without caring a bit about the cold water, he jumped in the stream and invited me to join him. I tried to put some sense into him, but all in vain.

He was pestering me to join him, and he even sprinkled the cold water on me. The water was cold, but I was hot inside. I finally gave in, removed my top and shorts in front of him, and went down the stream towards Adal. Fuck! the water was very cold.

I went towards Adal in that stream and got hold of his arms. The water was very cold, indeed, and I was shivering. He placed his hands on my waist and our eyes locked for a few seconds. We both knew the fire igniting inside our bodies. He had beautiful blue eyes. He started to get closer to me by caressing my back.

We were standing very close in the stream when he asked me to take a dip. I was afraid coz the water was very cold. But he caught hold of me tightly, and we together took a dip. We were feeling each other's warm breaths on our bodies. He suddenly leaned towards me and gave a peck on my lips.

We looked at each other, and the very next moment, we had our lips locked in a deep passionate kiss. We started playing with each other's tongues, exchanging saliva in the process. I could feel his hands running all over me, fondling my boobs and rubbing my pussy area. I could feel his crotch getting hard.

Even I was exploring his hot body with my hands. He broke the kiss and went down on my boobs, and took one in his mouth over the bra. Due to the ice-cold water, my nipples were erect. He even bit my nipple. I was enjoying what he was doing to me.

I started feeling his big dick over his underwear, and he also started rubbing my pussy. Then, we heard some noises. We quickly came out, put on our clothes, and headed back straight to the cottage. I was happy at getting that little action. Since I was a bit tired, I immediately fell asleep thinking about Adal.

I lost track of time the next morning. One of my friends woke me up and told me to get ready quickly. We had to reach Barshaini in the already booked cabs from where the trek to Kheerganga begins.

The memories of last night's fun in the stream were still afresh in my mind. I was smiling, thinking of the moments I spent with Adal. I couldn't get enough of his sexy hot body. As planned, we reached Barshaini and began the trek to Kheerganga.

During the trek, Adal and I were continuously stealing glances at each other. I knew that that trek was going to be more adventurous and fun than I had thought. We all started the long trek together. But everyone got involved in their own small groups after some time.

Adal and I made our own small group. He smoked a joint and offered it to me too, which I declined. He asked me if I want to continue last night's fun. I was shy. But I answered in the affirmative and expressed my doubts about people who could spoil the fun.

He told me not to worry them and asked me to follow him, which I did. We reached a secluded place where he grabbed me and pushed me against a tree. He passionately locked his lips with mine and started feasting on my mouth. At the same time, his hands started fondling my sexy ass over the shorts.

I was feeling his washboard abs over the tee. I soon removed his tee and kissed all over his chest and abs. He removed my top and started sucking on my boobs over the bra.

After sucking on them for a while, he unbuttoned and unzipped my shorts and inserted his hand inside my panty, and started rubbing my pussy. He even inserted one or two fingers in my pussy and started fingering me while playing with my clitoris. I was sure then he was well experienced with girls.

I cum within a few minutes all over his fingers, but he still kept fingering. I never had cummed so soon. It was such an intense orgasm. The thrill of the surroundings speeds it up. But this man licked everything off his fingers. The scene of that German dude licking and tasting all my cum was so erotic.

Though I was a little skeptical, he asked me to return the favour.

We quickly exchanged positions. I unbuttoned and unzipped his 3/4ths and took out that long shaft from his underwear. It was hard and big already. I took it in my hands and started milking it.

I wanted to tease him a little before letting it taste my mouth. I started rubbing its tip and gave it a few kisses. He sensed I was teasing him and told me, "Bitch! You are going to pay for it." I laughed at his state and made a mocking pout.

Then, I took his dick in my mouth. It was hard and big, exactly how I like my dicks to be. He held my head and started fucking my mouth with his dick. He was moaning with pleasure. I felt slutty in that state in the jungle, blowing that guy who I had met no less than 24 hours ago.

I sensed he was close to his orgasm. I immediately removed his dick from my mouth and started using my hands. He came like a volcano. Soon, we both adjusted our clothes. We then resumed our trek as we had to reach the top before the sunset.

He told me that he was going to fuck me like crazy later in the night. I gave a peck on his cheek and told him that I couldn't wait to feel him inside me.

The trekking was a lovely experience, with the river Parvati flowing parallel. Adal and I were talking and flirting. I am sure if Adal had got any other chances there during the trek, he would have definitely groped me and kissed me. We finally reached Kheerganga, and it was a lovely experience.

We soon rattled in our tents, settled ourselves, and then we went for a hot water spring bath. It is separate for men and women. It was one relaxing hot bath. It made us forget all the exhaustion we had picked up along the way. After we were done bathing, we changed into something more comfortable.

I wore a top and shorts. We then visited the nearby cafeteria and ate something since we were famished. I was sitting next to Adal. Soon after we finished our meal, we moved towards our tents, where a bonfire was set up. We saw the perfect sunset from there and clicked many pics.

We then played some music and danced to our own tunes. I danced with Adal feeling his muscles and biceps. He was running his hands on my waist and back. Some people even got high on drinks and joints. Then, people started bidding farewell and went inside their tents after hours of fun.

I got inside my tent and zipped it from inside. I lay on my back and tried to get some sleep, but I couldn't. All the moments I spent with Adal were flashing before my eyes. I wanted to feel that hot body once again. I had developed strong feelings of lust for Adal.

I was a little wet thinking about him, and I started rubbing my pussy over my shorts. I heard someone calling my name outside. I quickly opened the tent and saw Adal standing outside. My happiness knew no bounds, and I quickly let him inside after confirming no one saw him coming.

He came inside, and I quickly zipped the tent again. I turned towards him when he locked his lips with mine and started sucking on my tongue. We were both running our hands over each other's back while sharing a passionate kiss, which went on for a few minutes.

Soon, he was all over me. I was sitting in his lap. He removed my top and started kissing and licking my neck and collar bone. Also, giving love bites on my shoulders. I was moaning softly. I also removed his t-shirt and bit his shoulders.

He started working his mouth on my boobs over the bra and bit my nipples. He made me lie down with my ass still in his lap. He took my right boob in his mouth and started pressing my left one over the fabric with his right hand. His left hand was supporting me. I couldn't help but moan lightly.

He then unhooked my bra from behind but didn't remove it. He just started sucking on my naked boobs while also pressing them. I was caressing his hair with my hands, pushing him more into my valleys. He increased the pace of sucking. I could feel his throbbing dick on my ass.

It was a bird asking for freedom from the cage. I thought of freeing it. We both sat on our knees and fit perfectly in that cosy tent. We got rid of our bottom wear and were only left in clothes covering just our privates. He, in his boxers and me, in my panties.

He had this huge tent in his boxers, which I placed my hands on and started stroking it over the undie. He was as fair as milk and started kissing me again when I pressed his balls. His hands were still working on my nipples and boobies. I slid down his underwear, and his dick sprang out.

It was huge and very fair. I touched its tip and took it in my palm. My palm couldn't contain its thickness. His dick was throbbing and was quite warm. I started stroking it gently at first, and then eventually, I increased my pace. We kissed all that while.

Then, I thought of making his dick taste my juicy lips and I leaned down and licked the precum covered big dick. I started sucking it. My mouth couldn't contain its girth and it kind of choked me. He then held my head and pushed the whole dick in my mouth, deep throating me.

But I didn't want to upset him. So, I continued sucking that monster dick even though I could hardly breathe. I sucked it for some time, and then I sucked his balls one by one. I guess he enjoyed his balls in my mouth. He was moaning in pleasure when I circled my tongue on his balls.

He made me lie down on my back, and he leaned over me and kissed me again. Making his way down to my belly through my cleavage all the way, kissing, licking, and sucking each part. He stopped at it and started playing with my navel.

He sucked it for some time and then moved further down towards my pussy. But he thought of teasing me. He held my right leg in his hands and started kissing it gently from toe to my inner thighs, sending shivers down my spine. He wanted to remove my panty in which I helped him fully by lifting my ass.

He brought his mouth close to my pussy and started blowing air. I couldn't take it any longer and lifted my ass to make him suck on my pussy. But he didn't budge and started smiling at me, teasing me all the more. I then held his head and pushed his mouth over my pussy.

He started kissing and licking and sucking it gently. He spread my legs wide apart and started playing with my clitoris. In between, he also licked the sensitive area of my inner thighs. I was there lying on the floor, enjoying the pain and pleasure.

While his tongue was working on pleasuring my pussy, his hands were all over my boobs, massaging them and his fingers twitching my nipples. He was licking at just the right places. He then opened my pussy lips with both his hands and slid his tongue inside my pussy walls.

It made me crazy. Never before had I been sucked like this. I started moving my ass to let his tongue more inside. He sucked for some time and then climbed over me again and started smooching me again.

Then, he slid one of his fingers in my pussy and started pleasuring me. I was moaning in pleasure and badly needed real action. He went down on me again and sucked my pussy till I came in his mouth. He licked my pussy clean while I was lying exhausted after an awesome orgasm.

We then lay in the tent. I was resting my head on his chest, feeling his hotness oozing body. But he was not done yet. His dick was still standing tall, saluting me. I, too, wanted to feel him inside me. I started caressing his dick, signaling him that I was ready.

He wasted no time and immediately went on top of me and positioned his dick on my pussy. I closed my eyes in excitement. He pushed his dick in my pussy. His dick was quite thick for my tight pussy. But after a few thrusts, it went all inside. Soon my pussy adjusted to its thickness, or it adjusted to the tightness.

All this while, Adal was slowly fucking me, kissing my lips, and sucking on my boobs. I was just scratching his back. I then signalled him to go fast since I was ready. He fucked me in that position for quite some time until we both came together.

We were exhausted after the tiring trek and lay in each other's arms. I woke up later in the night and found myself sleeping in Adal's arms. I woke him up. He opened his eyes stretching his hot body, and without saying a word, I started smooching him.

I asked him to leave before anyone else saw him with me in my tent. I unzipped the tent to check if the surroundings were clear. We both didn't want to depart and hugged each other in a tight embrace. But Adal thought of something and asked me to join him in the hot water bath.

I liked the idea. I also wanted to freshen up after the tiring fuck. We both put on our clothes and quickly reached the men's pool. Adal checked, and after confirming clear surroundings, we both went into the hot spring.

But we were not completely naked. I had my bra and panty on while Adal was wearing his boxers. Adal pulled me towards himself and started smooching me again while pressing my melons over the bra. I could feel his dick rising over my pussy.

His hands were running over my boobs over the bra and also rubbing my pussy. But we couldn't risk removing our inners there. At least I was conscious of such things. I was also rubbing his cock over his undie and also feeling that hot body full of muscles.

I sucked on his nipples, and we were in that spring for quite some time. We then got out of the spring and bid farewell for the night after a passionate French kiss.

We just met once more after the trek before we again got busy in our respective lives.

16. Football

It was a must-win game for our college football team. One of my friends was dating a guy on the team. So, a bunch of us girls decided to go support the team. The inter-college match would start at about 7 pm and we were there by 6:30pm. As the teams walked out, I noticed the captain of our football team.

I asked my friend. She told me that his name was Rahim and he was a senior to us. It had been a while since I found myself attracted to a guy. He was tall and fit and I kept my eyes on him throughout the game. A few minutes before the break, one of the girls spilled her drink on my top, making it wet.

I had no choice but to go clean it. For the same, I went inside. I don't know what I was thinking. I found the players' room open and I straight away went to the attached bathroom. I looked at myself in the mirror, admired myself a little and thought about Rahim.

Then, I reminded myself of the purpose of my coming there. I removed my top to clean it. It was then that the break was announced and Rahim and the other boys came inside the room. Rahim barged straight into the washroom. I was shocked at what happened.

Out of reflexes, I wanted to shout, but Rahim put one of his hands over my mouth and the other behind my back to shut me up. He signalled me to keep quiet since the other boys were in the room. All this happened in a jiffy. I was breathing very heavily.

My tits (caged only inside a black bra) were going up and down, which he could clearly see (or feel as well since he was close to me, so close that I could smell his sweat after the game). I couldn't help but notice and admire his big biceps.

Rahim (whispering), "Hey! I am Rahim, the team's captain and you need to keep quiet because all the boys are inside the room." I just nodded, and I am sure he was stealing glances at my cleavage. He slowly took his hands off me when he was sure that I would not shout any more.

He then suddenly announced to the whole squad, "Guys! My stomach is not well, and I might have to stay in for a while. Please manage yourselves. I am in a tough situation right now." This he said, faking pain in his voice. While he said this, I wore my top back. I hadn't cleaned it yet, but still, I wore it.

Rahim: - I have seen you somewhere! You study at my college. Right?

Me: - Yes, Rahim. I am Charmy, and I study in the same college as yours. I am in my third year.

Rahim: - Charmy, nice name.

Me: - Thank You.

This break time, the players use to change their clothes, sip water or energy drinks and shower to replenish themselves.

Rahim: - Look, I need to take a shower before the second half of the game begins and the boys are still outside. I am sorry, but I have no choice.

Saying this, he went below the shower and removed his vest and shorts, and started showering in just his underwear. The scene in front of my eyes was better than John Abraham showering in Dostana. My eyes were stuck on his muscular body.

My eyes went from his chest and biceps to those perfect abs and finally down to a bulge in his underwear. He caught me intently, looking at him without a blink. He then turned around while showering and gave me a glimpse of his well arched back.

I then came to know why he was the captain of the team. He was so hot, well built, and sexy. He turned towards me again. He looked into my eyes, still stuck on his well-chiselled body.

Rahim (winking): - Charmy, you should have a shower too. Look, the juice is still over your top. You came to clean it, right?

He was intelligent enough to observe everything. The tension in the atmosphere was increasing.

Me (still stealing glances at those abs): - No, Thanks. I think I will just clear the stain.

I tried to clean the top with water, but it was making my bra wet. Also, I was thrilled with a hot man bathing behind me. So, I thought of making good use of the opportunity and removed my top again, showing him my sexy gorgeous back covered with only the bra straps. I started washing my top with water.

Rahim: - What a view!

I heard him and immediately turned around to show him the perfect tits (caged in a bra) he might have ever seen in his life.

Me: - Did you say something?

Rahim: - Wow! You look hot.

He looked me in the eyes and showered praises on me, making me blush while I turned around again to wash my top. Our eyes met many times in the process while he was showering (with a huge hard-on). My perfect body acted as a catalyst, and his boner didn't go away.

I turned around and faced him while he was struggling to hide his boner. He then realized he couldn't go to the match with that boner. All of a sudden, he slid down his underwear till his knees while I closed my eyes.

Me: - Rahim, what are you doing?

Rahim: - Charmy, Open your eyes. Look what you have done to

me. I can't go to the match with this hard-on.

I opened my eyes and saw him holding his big dick. I was surprised at the size and couldn't take my eyes off the shaft.

Rahim: - Charmy, you have to help me. It is all because of you.

He started walking towards me. I was shocked at what he said, but I liked it. My eyes lit up at the thought of helping him. I, too, walked towards him and touched the head of his cock with my right hand. It was throbbing. I moved closer and touched the tip of his pulsating cock with one hand.

I rotated my palm around it, and with the other hand, I started feeling his chest and abs. I pushed him back gently. I stroked the dick for some time. But no, I knew such dicks can't just be controlled using hands. They needed my pink lips and my mouth.

I sat on my knees and took his stiff cock into my mouth and began sucking it. My warm mouth took the cock in a while, my tongue wrapped around the shaft. I made eye contact with Rahim while sucking his cock, which turned him all the more, and he tilted his head back in pleasure as he moved his pelvis.

He moved his hands on my head, caressing my hair. I was using my tongue as if licking a lollipop. I milked his cock using my mouth in that position for some time. He was enjoying every bit of it and also moaning lightly. My hands played with his balls, occasionally pressing them.

My mouth worked on the big shaft. I started sucking the tip of his cock, which made him go crazy. I sensed that he was on the verge. So, I took his dick out of my mouth, kissed its tip, and licked its side, making him twitch. Then, I used my magic hands on the piece of meat, giving it gentle strokes.

I took his ball in my mouth while giving him a handjob and blowing my hot breaths on the long shaft. He couldn't take it any longer and came out loads on the floor. I did my job pretty well and not to mention, on time. I got up with my head held high.

As soon as I got up, Rahim pulled me closer to him and tried to kiss me. But I immediately put my hand on his lips.

Rahim: - You know what, Charmy, I am still not done with you.

Saying this, he cleaned his dick, then wiped his body with a towel, and then wrapped it on his waist. He looked outside to see if everyone had left. He looked at me still in my bra and ogled at my tits and cleavage.

Rahim: - I think you can wear your top now. I have seen everything.

I immediately got conscious and quickly wore my top.

Rahim (As he put on his vest and then the underwear and shorts):- Shall we go to the ground? It's already getting late.

I nodded, and we walked out of the room towards the ground. But our eyes continued to meet each other throughout the match. I don't know what made it possible, but our team did win that match. Everyone started cheering and hugging each other at the win.

The organizers called it a day, and people soon started leaving the place. But I thought of congratulating Rahim on the big win and thank him for saving me from embarrassment. I walked towards him and saw him talking to a player. He saw me approaching and bid the player a goodbye.

Me: - Rahim, Congratulations! Thank you a big time for what you did for me back in the washroom. You saved me from such a big embarrassment.

Rahim: - And I can't thank you enough for what you did for me in the washroom. I think the credit for the win goes to you. And I am not going to accept just congratulations and thank you.

Rahim: - We have a party planned after this at a friend's house to celebrate the big win. I want you there. (He winks at me) I told you, I am not done with you yet. Your friend is coming too, to celebrate the victory of her boyfriend's team.

Me: - Alright, I will be there.

The very thought of it was exciting to me. We both parted ways smilingly, and I went back to my group and left for my place. From that moment on till the party, my mind was occupied with a hell of a lot of thoughts about Rahim. What would happen at the party, and how?

I reached my place, took a shower. I was thrilled inside, and the very thought of it was sending chills down my body. I chose a sexy outfit for the party – a halter top and denim. I deliberately wore a padded bra. I called up my friend with whom I had to go to the party, and we both left for the party.

I had made up my mind to have some fun. We finally reached the venue. It was a house party. I was thinking about those moments with Rahim nonstop. People were dancing, loud music and smoking and drinking. People were shouting and hooting to show their excitement at winning the match.

However, my eyes were looking for the person who was the sole reason I came to the party. While I was looking for Rahim, someone patted on my shoulder. I turned around to see Rahim holding two alcohol glasses. He was looking drop-dead gorgeous in that yellow shirt and denim showing off his muscled physique.

He hugged me lightly and kissed my shoulder. I wasn't expecting that at all.

Rahim: - Hello, Charmy! Let's have this drink. By the way, you are looking sexy. (He said, ogling at my tits.)

I took the glass from his hand and sipped a little. I am an occasional drinker.

Me: - You are also looking good, Rahim, but I prefer the shirt off.

Rahim: - Really? Even I prefer it off. But more than that, I would prefer your top off. (He said this while looking at my big tits in the padded bra.)

We started walking around the house, sipping that drink, both stealing glances at each other. We walked to the balcony, and there, Rahim started looking at me continuously.

Me: - What?

Rahim: - Charmy, Thanks for what you did in the washroom. Had you not done that, I wouldn't have gotten rid of the hard-on and maybe not have given my best in the match.

Me: - Well, you are welcome. But honestly speaking, I too enjoyed it a lot.

I said this giving a light punch on his abs.

Rahim: - Of course, you enjoyed it. Let me return the favour back.

My eyes lit up when he said this, but still, I faked.

Me: - What are you suggesting, Rahim?

Nobody could hear us in loud music. Rahim took my glass and placed it on a table. He held my hand and took me to a small room that looked like a storeroom. He pulled me inside, latched the door. He pinned me against an almirah, looked into my eyes, and finally placed his lips over mine.

I didn't resist at all, and I was waiting for this. I kissed him back and put my hands around his back. What followed was a deep passionate kiss. He pounced on me like a wild animal and kissed me while his hands explored my body and finally went to my ass. He squeezed my ass cheeks while kissing me.

Rahim: - You didn't let me kiss you in the bathroom. Now, I will.

Me: - Yes, kiss me. Fuck me.

We locked our lips again. Our tongues were fighting inside. We shared a deep passionate kiss. He moved back, looked at me from top to bottom, and again locked his lips with mine. Slowly, he went down, kissing my neck, collarbone, and shoulders while his hands groped my tits over the halter top.

Rahim: - I will show you what a real man looks like. I will make you feel what you have never felt to date.

I moaned with the pressing of my tits and twitching of my nipples. He then opened my halter top, removed it completely, and bounced back on my tits covered in a padded bra. He then opened my padded bra, which I helped him remove.

He took my right tit in his mouth and started sucking it while pressing the left with his hand.

Rahim: - Had I known they are this big, I would have definitely sucked on them in the bathroom itself. Better late than never.

He was sucking and pinching me hard, which made me moan in pain and pleasure. He groped my tits in both his hands and started blowing them.

Me: - Your mouth feels great on my boobs, Rahim. Suck them.

My words cast magic on him, and he started feasting on my melons again while I just caressed his hair in pleasure. He sucked my boobs till his mouth started hurting. He pinched my nipples, making me moan and shout. But the music outside was loud.

He made my boobies red and gave me a few hickeys as well. Then, he moved down, licked my navel and stomach while his hands still groped and pinched my melons. He then opened my denim and slid them down my knees.

He gave a peck on my pussy, and then got up and kissed me again on the lips. He bit my lips while starting to rub my pussy over my panty.

Rahim: - You are already wet, Charmy.

He was kissing and rubbing me simultaneously.

Me: - It's all because of you. You need to set it right.

I replied as I moaned. He moved down on me, held my waist with his hands, and started licking my inner thighs, sending me into heaven. He teasingly moved towards the wet spot, slid down my panties, and gave a lick. He started sucking it instantly as he couldn't wait anymore to return the pleasure.

Me: - Rahim that feels so good!

I enjoyed and moaned as he moved his tongue on my wet pussy

while pushing his mouth more in my pussy. He opened my pussy lips and licked the walls of my pussy with his tongue.

Rahim (chuckling): - You will come like a fountain. Just wait and watch.

Saying so, he bit my clitoris, and I moaned in pleasure. My moaning got intense and loud, and my legs started trembling as he continued sucking my pussy area. He inserted his fingers in my pussy and started finger fucking me. And then licked the area between pussy and ass.

I was spellbound, and that indeed was a first for me.

Rahim: - Your pussy tastes sweet and salty, Charmy.

He moved his tongue in circles around the clit while slowly fingering me deeply.

Me: - Rahim, I don't think I can hold on for long. I am gonna cum soon. You made me so horny for you.

He then completely took off my panties and denim but continued playing with my clit. I moaned in extreme pleasure.

Rahim: - I know you are close. I can feel your legs shiver.

Me: - Yes, Rahim. I wanna cum too bad. I can't take this anymore. Make me cum.

I moaned continuously as he worked his magic on my pussy. His fingers started moving in and out of my pussy very fast. After some time, I held his hair in my hands hard and moaned as my pussy oozed out its love juices. I finally had an orgasm, and I came harder than ever.

He finally took his fingers out of my pussy. I was panting, and it felt like I couldn't stand anymore. He then cleaned my pussy with a piece of cloth and moved up, and started kissing me passionately on the lips.

Rahim: - Enjoyed it? I returned your favor.

Me (panting): - My best orgasm to date.

I bit his earlobe and licked his ear. He started kissing me again and pressing my melons. I started getting my lost energy back and started reciprocating.

Rahim: - Well, that was just a trailer. You will love what's gonna happen next. He took off his shirt and denim and underwear and turned me around. He started rubbing his dick on my asshole. His hands grabbed my tits from behind while he kissed and licked my neck and shoulders.

Rahim: - Charmy, I am gonna fuck your brains out.

He whispered in my ears while still rubbing , playing with my boobs, and pinching the erect nipples. I nodded and moaned.

Me: - I would love that. Fuck me like it's the end of the world. I want this captain inside me now.

I said this taking his big hard dick in my fist.

Rahim: - Get ready for the pleasure of a lifetime. He positioned the dick on my pussy from behind and started rubbing it there. His hands couldn't get enough of my big tits.

Me: - No more teasing. Fuck me now. (I said sternly.) Just push it in. I want you very badly.

He then gave a thrust and pushed that hard meat's tip inside my wet pussy. It did the pain. But I endured it all and put my hands on the almirah as he pushed it deep inside my pussy after a few thrusts. He let it there for some time for my pussy to adjust and then began pounding me like crazy.

He pushed his cock deep inside my pussy and was increasing the pace and power with time. He started fucking me hard and fast while I moaned in pleasure.

Rahim: - Fuck, your pussy feels so tight.

He slapped my ass cheeks while fucking me. I let out a moan.

Me: - It's all yours.

I kept moaning, and he kept pounding me. My pussy had completely grasped his dick. With time, he increased his speed. He kept spanking my ass and pinching and pressing my boobies. Then, my asshole caught his attention. He started moving his hand around my asshole.

He started rubbing the area near my asshole, and my pleasure doubled.

Me: - Rahim, I am a virgin in the ass. My asshole is not ready for your thick cock.

Rahim: - It might not be ready for my lund but definitely ready for my finger.

He continued rubbing my asshole while fucking me and tried inserting his finger inside but couldn't get much success. My pussy was stretching and pulsating as he moved his dick in and out of my pussy.

Rahim: - Charmy, I am gonna cum inside your pussy. Your pussy is very tight. It's almost sucking my cock.

Me: - Yes, cum inside me. Ohh...Aaahhh...Fuck...Fuck...

He turned me around, inserted his dick in my pussy from the front. He began fucking again while his chest rubbed with my big boobs. He started fucking me wildly.

Rahim: - Aaahhh... Charmy, I am close.

With a loud moan and a deep thrust, he didn't stop and shot loads of his cum inside my walls. He cummed deep inside me, and I was moaning in pleasure.

Me: - Rahim, that was too good a fuck.

His dick slowly got out of my pussy, and I brought him close to me and started kissing him passionately for the lovely fuck and orgasm. He kissed me back, sucking my lips. I quickly switched sides and kissed him on the chest. I kissed his nipples, his abs, and his biceps.

Then, I turned him around and felt his sexy back and kissed every inch of it. I was feasting on his body.

Me: - I am still not done with you, Rahim. This is not over.

Rahim: - Sure, it's not. But now, we must get back to the party.

We kissed one last time before putting on our clothes and setting ourselves to head back to the party. I kissed his cheeks and pinched his nipples, and he too twitched my nipples. He opened the door and went outside. A few minutes later, I joined the party after applying a little makeup in the washroom.

Nobody suspected that this girl just had had an amazing sex session. But we had many more amazing sex sessions together before he graduated and landed a job in some other city.

17. Holi

This story goes back to March 2018 when I was in the last year of pursuing my degree. The Student Council of my college decided to have a grand celebration on Holi's occasion. For the same, they invited some other colleges to make the festival even bigger and more memorable.

It was basically a carnival for all the students to come together and enjoy a big party before graduating. I decided to go there as well with a couple of my friends. I got ready in the morning itself, wearing a white shirt and denim shorts. Underneath, I wore a white bra and black panties.

I was ready for a day full of fun and frolic and not to mention an unforgettable adventure that I didn't know then would happen. I tied my hair in a pony, and we left our abode to go to the celebration ground. When we got there, we saw students already playing with colours.

Then, someone called out my friend. As we turned, a group of 4-5 people came towards us. We got acquainted when my friend introduced them as her schoolmates. One of the guys who stood out from the group immediately caught my attention.

He was Akshay, a 6'2" tall and nicely build guy. His arms were shredded in that white tee he was wearing, giving him the torso of a Greek God. We wasted no time and started playing Holi with dry colours. The music was loud, and we grooved to a few songs.

The DJ was playing different Holi songs, and we were making

memories for a lifetime. I used green to colour all my friends. But for Akshay, I went for red for Akshay, which he also noticed. Even he applied some colour on my face and neck. I knew even he was into me.

I could clearly feel the same because he couldn't keep his eyes off me. After some time, the big announcement of water cannons being brought happened. We were more than happy playing with coloured water. So much so that we all got drenched in water, and our clothes took our body shapes.

My white shirt was almost transparent, revealing my white-coloured bra. Akshay's tee took his body's shape- the muscular chest and the perfect washboard abs were clearly visible. I felt my insides warming up. The DJ then played the song 'Balam Pichkari.'

We all started dancing and slipping in one another's arms without a care in the world. A few boys in the group began tearing one another's t-shirts, and Akshay was one of them. When they tore his t-shirt, I felt a tingling sensation inside my pussy.

His perfectly shaped body with a gym build chest and perfect washboard abs were tempting me. I tried not to stare, but I couldn't help myself, and I was totally checking him out. We girls were still stuck playing with water and colours (I so wish there were something like this for girls as well)

While applying colour on my friends, I moved towards Akshay. I started applying colour on his whole torso, trying to feel his upper body. His huge biceps made me drool, and he sensed that. When I was about to walk back, he playfully grabbed me from behind.

He started applying colour on my naked waist inside the shirt with the other. He wanted to avenge me for feeling his whole body and wanted to do the same. His hand went inside my shirt from below my waist. He applied colour just below my bra, and in doing so, he also brushed my boobs a couple of times.

It turned me on really good, so much so that I bit my lips in excitement. I didn't want anyone to see us. So, I went back to my group and resumed playing and dancing there. But my eyes were fixed continuously on Akshay. Then, we went for some juice and snacks.

We enjoyed the cultural event, which was a part of the Holi celebration. By this time, the guys had also worn new tees since they couldn't roam about bare-chested all day. A few spots on the ground were also converted into small mud pools to play Holi in the mud.

And when we came back, a few of my classmates picked me up and threw me in the mud pool. They started pouring the mud water on me, making me soak in mud from head to toe. A few moments later, even Akshay was thrown into the same pool by his friends.

I was happy someone was there to give me company. I got up feeling Akshay's veiny arms as an excuse. We got up from the mud pool and had to clean ourselves. I was looking for a place to do that. A friend of mine told me about the faculty washrooms (which were empty then) on the campus to clean myself.

I started walking towards the said place, and Akshay accompanied me, which I did not object to. I saw no soul inside the building and went straight inside the washroom. I didn't lock the door as there was no one, but I was surprised when Akshay got in.

Me: - Akshay, what are you doing here? Get out. Someone might see us.

Akshay still got in, grabbed me, and got me under the shower.

Akshay: - You had a lot of fun feeling me up in the field, and now, it's my turn to return the favour.

Me: - Akshay, not here. It's a fucking college. Someone might come anytime.

Akshay: - Nobody will come. Everyone is celebrating, and we have all the time in the world.

He pinned me against the wall from behind and started kissing my neck and unbuttoning my shirt. I let out a soft moan, and things started getting heating up really fast. The cold water from the shower was washing the mud off our clothes and bodies.

At times, he also spanked my ass. He was rubbing his cock over my ass, kind of dry humping me while pressing my melons over the white bra. He then removed my shirt and started smooching me from behind while his strong hands explored my upper body.

He brushed my boobs a couple of times, which sent shivers down my spine. He then turned me around. But seeing my doubts, he put his finger on my lips, asking me to shut up. I finally gave in and bit his finger. He started smooching me again.

Then, he moved down on me and kissed my cleavage and unhooked my bra from behind. My boobs were free, and he said, "Charmy, these are the best pair of boobs I have ever laid my eyes upon."

I removed his tee and started feeling his sexy body.

Me: - Akshay, you have such a sexy body.

I started feeling his torso while kissing him on the neck.

Akshay: - You too have the perfect body to make any man long for you. When I saw you today, I knew I wanted you in my bed.

I kissed his left bicep and bit it.

Me: - Oh! I love these biceps.

Akshay: - They are all yours. Play with them as much as you want.

It was enough to make me blush and turn red. while kissing my lips. I was feeling his abs with my hands and getting aroused by his touch. I started getting wet down there, and he passionately moved to my navel and played with it a bit before getting to the main area.

Things were getting really steamy between us, and we could

not keep our hands off each other. He got up again and guided my hand to the bulge in his trousers. I started feeling his huge dick. He started kissing, licking, and sucking my nipple with his mouth while one of his hands began pinching the other one.

It was a great combination of pain and pleasure. I unbuttoned and unzipped his trousers and started pressing with his balls over the underwear, and that was like gasoline on the fire for him. He went wild and started moaning. He too unbuttoned my shorts and rubbed my pussy over the panty.

As we were about to reach ecstasy, we heard some voices outside and quickly put on our wet clothes. I looked outside, and there were a couple of people in the hallway. I waited for a few seconds and moved out, and Akshay followed after a few minutes.

We got back to the ground and started playing Holi again with the others but couldn't keep our eyes off each other. We were constantly exchanging naughty smiles with each other. I knew that that wouldn't stop there, and we were in for some serious action that day.

I faked a headache and bid my goodbyes to the group, and Akshay offered me a ride home. He knew I was faking it and wanted to see how the rest of the evening goes for both of us.

The next moment, we were walking towards his car with black tinted glasses. We got in, and without even asking me, he started driving towards his flat, which he shared with his friends.

Akshay: - How's your headache now? Do you need a massage?

Saying this, he placed his left hand on my thighs and started rubbing them while his right hand was on the steering wheel.

Me: - You must concentrate on the road, Akshay. We will have plenty of time at the flat, don't worry.

But he didn't stop and continued moving his hand towards my pussy. I stopped him and guided his hand over my boobs while I started rubbing his dick over the trousers.

Me: - Don't be so impatient. Let's feel each moment.

Akshay: - Charmy, I can't keep my hands off you even for a second. I want to pleasure you until you scream.

Me: - Why don't you let me take care of you till we get to the flat?

Saying this, I leaned over and unbuttoned and unzipped his trousers and lowered his underwear. His rock-hard cock flopped out. It was about eight inches. I grasped it firmly, squeezing and letting it go and repeat. My fingers ran down the length of his dick and stopped at his balls, which I squeezed hard.

He let out a moan. Akshay was finding it difficult, switching his gaze between the road and me fondling his balls. His cock started oozing a little precum, which I took on my finger and ran it over my pink lips before sucking it off seductively. I had become good at giving blowjobs.

I knelt down, flicking the head with my tongue. I sucked it all the way down until my lips touched the balls and the thick cock hit my back throat. I started sucking, licking, and deep throating his throbbing cock while one of my hands played with his tatte (balls).

I could feel a little pressure building up in his dick. I didn't want him to cum in the car. So, I teased him a little and switched my focus on his abs. I licked and kissed one by one after lifting the tee he was wearing. He also continued fondling my boobs and massaging my back.

We finally got inside his flat and immediately went under the shower. He then started unbuttoning my shirt while kissing me and removed it. Then, I was only in my bra and shorts, and he started pressing my boobs over the bra. I also removed his tee.

We kissed each other passionately while our hands explored each other's sexy bodies. He bit my earlobes, and it drove me crazy. I unbuttoned his trousers, and the monster dick was ready to come out, tearing his underwear. I started rubbing his dick over his undie.

He removed my bra and started to suck on my nipples. His hands unbuttoned my shorts, and one of his hands found its way to my pussy over the panty. We broke the proximity. In no time, we removed every piece of cloth covering us and were then stark naked in the shower and hungry for each other.

We took the body wash and started applying it to each other's body. He started with my neck and then moved down to my boobs, nipples, clean and waxed underarms, and waist and finally went to my thighs. He started rubbing my pussy with body wash, and it excited me to a whole new level.

I also started applying body wash on his abs, chest, back, big arms, and finally moved down to his erect dick. I wanted to take it in my pussy then and there, but we first washed with water. He smooched me again, and then he picked me up in his arms and took me to the bedroom.

He put me on the bed, spread my legs, and started licking my pussy. This made me roll my eyes and moan in pleasure. His hands were doing my boobs, and he was pinching my nipples with his fingers. I moaned loudly in pain and pleasure. It got unbearable when he started sucking my clit while also inserting a finger in my pussy.

I pushed his head more in my pussy and wrapped my legs around him. He licked my pussy for some minutes, making me long for his dick in my pussy. He sensed that and placed the dick tip on my pussy, rubbed it there, and while smooching, he gave his first thrust.

I gasped for some breath when his dick went inside me, but I bore it all, and he kept going. His hands fondling my boobs and his dick getting deep inside me tearing my pussy walls. My legs were wrapped around his waist, and my hands were scratching his back in extreme pleasure.

He started sucking my boobs really hard and increased his pace while I began to moan in pleasure. I wanted him to fuck my brains out, and that was exactly what was happening. He rubbed his muscled chest on my boobs and started kissing and licking my neck.

I was moaning in pleasure and wanted his cum deep inside me, but he had different plans. He asked me to ride him, and I obliged. I laid on the top of his torso and positioned his dick on my pussy entrance. I wanted him to feel the same pleasure like me.

I rested my hands on his chest and twitched his nipples. Then, I started moving my ass, and his dick was going in and out of my pussy while my boobs bounced up and down. He cupped my boobs with both his hands and started moaning too. I increased my pace and started screaming his name while riding him.

We both were on edge. He wanted to get on top as we were close. He came over me again, pounding my pussy like there was no tomorrow. I was constantly biting my lips, and he had his hands all over my boobs. I asked him to increase the pace as I was about to cum, and he started thrusting with full force.

I couldn't hold it anymore and had a lovely orgasm. Around the same time, he also unloaded his cum deep inside my pussy. He lay on me, exhausted as our juices mixed and flowed out of my love hole. We stayed like that for a while, and while he rested on the bed beside me, I started feeling his body again.

I couldn't keep my hands off my Greek God. I sucked his nipples and gave love bites on his neck. His abs were inviting me to lick them, which I did.

Then, he got a call from his friends asking about his whereabouts and that they were on their way back. We got dressed, and he offered me a ride to my home. On the way, we enjoyed each other again, and he dropped me off, promising some action soon.

18. The Concert

Tired of my boring daily life and workload, I got really pissed off and wanted some time off for myself. I just wanted to have some fun so I could completely forget about work and spare a couple of hours just for myself.

I heard of a music concert and food night being organized in my city that coming weekend. I immediately called my friends, and they were ready for it too. It was on Saturday, and the day finally arrived after much waiting.

I dressed up in a modern attire (an all-black one-piece sleeveless dress which stopped right above my knees) and started working on myself. I wanted to make every eye turn. So, I put on some light makeup with a red lipstick, which I hoped somebody would eat in the night.

I took some time to get ready, and my friends were already calling me. I finally arrived at the concert and saw my friends waiting for me. My eyes were looking for a hot guy with whom I could spend the night.

The three of us were dressed in what pleases your eyes (of course, we were not naked), exposing the right curves at the right places. As we were heading inside, I noticed a group of three guys standing at the gate. It looked like they were waiting for someone.

One of the three guys in a black shirt and black wayfarers looked right into my eyes. We shared a rather short stare, but it was just enough to spark up our thoughts about each other.

Soon we all headed inside and acquired our seats. The concert was an extravaganza of some bands and solo performances, which I enjoyed to the fullest. It was then that I wanted to grab some juice and snacks. I headed out towards the drinks section and bought some juice for myself and my friends.

But I couldn't find any snacks there. As I turned, my eyes fell on the guy I had seen earlier at the gate, and he was carrying some snacks. I immediately went up to him to ask him where he got the snacks. He told me about it and even accompanied me.

During that time, we talked a little about ourselves, got introduced, and talked about how good the concert was. We gelled up (or we can say we were expecting the same thing from each other, which made us gel up). He was Abeer.

He was an open guy, and he was maintaining his physique pretty well (which, by the way, is the first thing I notice about any guy). He was tall and handsome and had made a good gym body. Also, he had put on a good perfume (I love when guys smell good. It shows that they are aware of being noticed).

We went back in and, along with the concert, enjoyed our delicacies. I was really flattered by that guy I met some minutes ago and started dreaming already. I was turning around, again and again, to look at him. He, too, was responding likewise.

Finally, the concert ended. My friends and I were chatting when he walked up to us to say a 'Hi.' My friends didn't interrupt much and left after making an excuse. He asked me if he could drop me off. I was literally waiting for this, and I immediately replied in the affirmative.

It wasn't a very long drive, and he took me to my place. As we were sitting in his car outside my building, he asked me about my weekend plans. I told him that I had no plans. I asked him if he would like to have a cup of coffee. It seemed like he was waiting for that and immediately agreed.

I was so excited. Just the thought of him doing me was making me wet. I am sure my panty was wet already. We went inside my house, and I asked him to wait until I changed (into something even more hot and sexy). I changed into just a sleeveless top and yoga shorts. His face brightened, seeing me like that.

When I was making coffee, I suddenly felt two cold hands running on my stomach and fingers playing with my navel. He was exploring my navel from behind, and I was enjoying it. My body was shivering, and I started panting and closed my eyes.

Just then, he planted a hot peck on my collar bone. I could feel his breaths on my shoulders. I couldn't resist anymore, my body couldn't hold back, and I gave in to his actions.

I turned around for a kiss, my hands running through his hair and also feeling his back. We kissed, and the kiss was getting more intense by each second. Soon, we were licking each other's tongue and sucking the lips. I was pulling him closer to me and wanted us to merge into the same body.

His hands were continuously massaging my hips and slapping them gently. I felt those little spanks on my ass. Seemed like he loved my round 34 ass. He cupped my ass and took me in his arms, and I instantly wrapped my legs around his waist.

The kiss was so passionate that when we broke it, we were both trying to catch some breath. I guided him as he carried me to my bedroom. He threw me on the bed. He unbuttoned his shirt to give me a view of his well-sculpted body.

He then turned me around on the bed and started kissing my neck and collarbone from behind and caressing my navel. He then worked his way inside my top. (I wasn't wearing a bra) and cupped my tits. I let out a loud moan when he pinched my nipples real hard.

"My Queen," he said, and I could feel his cock on my asshole. We were completely absorbed in lust. I was letting him work his way with my body. I was trying to recover and process what was happening. But lust had taken over me completely.

He took off my top and unbuttoned his shirt completely, which I removed while feeling that sexy body. We were both then naked from the top. I pulled him over me on the bed and started kissing him. He went down on me kissing my cheeks, ears and earlobes, neck and collarbone, cleavage.

He finally stopped at my boobs, which he kissed, licked, and sucked to his complete satisfaction. Then, he moved further down on my belly. He started circling his tongue around my navel and also blowing air around it. I jumped in ecstasy because it made me go nuts.

He went further down and removed my shorts. (I wasn't wearing a panty inside). He licked a little around my pussy area. My pussy had already oozed some love juices. He came up to kiss me again, but this time, his hands were exploring my pussy with rubbing it and, at times, finger fucking it.

I looked into his eyes and said, "Fuck Me, Abeer." But he had other plans. He wanted me to long for it. I was already on the verge due to the long foreplay. He laid down beside me on the bed and asked me to help him. I understood and immediately positioned myself near his crotch.

I then removed his denim and, along with it, his underwear. His cock sprang up, and I immediately took it in my hands and started stroking it. I played with his balls. He asked me to use my mouth, and I complied. I took the huge piece of meat in my mouth and started milking it.

I deep throated his cock and then took it out and repeated the process while playing with his balls and also feeling those abs and chest. I pinched his nipples, making him moan, and then, my mouth started paining. So, I asked him to do me.

He came over me and positioned . He gave a huge push and let his cock slide in my pussy in one go. Had he not been kissing me, I would have moaned like crazy. The dick filled my hole completely, stretching my walls and hitting me deep inside.

The room was filled with our moans and an ecstatic smell. Our bodies moved in synchronism, feeling all the pleasure. He kept pushing his cock deeper into my pussy and increased the pace. He quickly rolled on the bed, and I was on his torso with his dick still inside me.

I was panting, but my body wanted more of that. He started massaging my melons while moving his ass, continuing to fuck me. I started moving my ass to match the rhythm. Me moving made my boobs bounce. He pulled me towards him in that position and started smooching me, not leaving my tits.

He was holding my waist and moving his ass to slide his dick in and out of my pussy. I was enjoying every moment of it. I felt my orgasm building up, and even he started moaning louder. I knew he was on the brink of cumming too. We kept fucking in that position.

When I was about to cum, he immediately rolled over again and came over me. He started thrusting with full force. I enjoyed it, and soon, I couldn't take it anymore and had my first orgasm with this man. But he wasn't done yet and continued pounding my pussy.

He then got up and brought me towards the edge of the bed. He kept a few pillows below my ass and kept my legs on his shoulders. I was too tired to do anything. In that position, he started circling his dick on my asshole. He then held my waist, put his dick on my pussy again, and easily slid inside.

He started fucking me in that position. I was in much pleasure and didn't want him to stop. After a good fuck, he finally ejaculated all his cum inside me with a loud moan. He came out loads. I was very tired but also satisfied. My weekend plans were a success.

He then collapsed beside me on the bed and said, "That was intense." I was too tired to clean the pussy, oozing our love juices. I lay on his chest and could just say, "My King."

I don't know when I slept with him naked. I don't know what else happened that night. I woke up the next morning to find him sitting on the chair in front of me and extending a cup of coffee towards me, saying, "You forgot about the coffee yesterday."

I took the cup from his hands, smiling that he got much more than just coffee. As soon as we finished the coffee, he said, "Shall we?" We ended up fucking twice more that day before he finally left for his home.

19. The Sangeet

Last December it was my friend's wedding in Delhi. The wedding and the Sangeet were to take place in a hotel, and all the arrangements had already been made. On the morning of her sangeet (a function before the wedding day in Indian marriages), I reached the venue with some other common friends.

Here, in the hotel lobby, I met the protagonist of the story-Akshay. He was continuously ogling me, but that was nothing new to me in Delhi. I was used to being ogled at by men of all age groups. He showed us to our rooms while his eyes were stuck on my boobs.

What followed was a day full of food, gossips, laughter, and chit chats. Finally, it was Sangeet time, and we all went to our rooms to get ready. I didn't want to lose such a chance to display my oozing hotness in a sexy dress (off-shoulder blouse and a long skirt), which I bought especially for the Sangeet night.

I thought of being a good bridesmaid and go check on the bride. As fate would have it, I entered the wrong room. I looked around, but there was no one. I heard the shower running.

Thinking it to be my friend inside the shower, I shouted, "Niki, you are impossible. Still in the shower? You must be ready by now and look at you. Now, make it quick. I am waiting outside."

But I was shell shocked when Akshay stepped out of the bathroom with just a towel wrapped around his waist (He had deliberately wrapped it below his waist), revealing his hot gym build torso. Water was dripping from his hair onto his hairless, well-waxed chest.

This time, it was me who was continuously ogling at his washboard abs. He could clearly notice me noticing him. It was very difficult for me to take my eyes away from him. He started walking towards me, but I still composed myself.

He moved closer to me on the pretext of picking up his robe hanging behind me while blowing hot air on my neck and shoulder. He said, "You were saying something?" All I could say was, "I thought it's Niki's room. I am sorry." And I ran back to my room, all embarrassed.

Now, let me tell you all about Akshay. He was one tall, good looking and hot guy. One who can make girls go weak in their knees, and I was no exception. He was a fitness freak with a rigorous workout schedule.

The washboard abs, chiseled physique, broad biceps, and triceps were the result of hitting the gym and following a diet plan. It was after I got laid under him that I realized that he was also the proud owner of a big thick dick able to satisfy any girl.

But guess what, here he was after me. Guess I am one lucky girl to have such hot guys in my life. I thank God each day for the same.

Finally, it was time for the Sangeet ceremony. It was then when a girl from the groom's side told me about Akshay being the groom's cousin. And, it was tough to say which side rocked in terms of outfits because everyone was looking gorgeous.

Boys in tuxedos or sherwanis and girls in sarees, gowns, and sexy lehengas not caring a bit about the cold weather. Even I chose a sexy off-shoulder blouse (it showed a bit of my cleavage and was tight enough to reveal my assets) and a floor-length skirt showing my perfect hourglass figure.

It was one musical night with a lot of performances from both sides. All of us danced our hearts out. After all, it was our friend's wedding. Soon the party songs changed to a few romantic numbers for the couple. Akshay came in an all-black tuxedo looking drop-dead gorgeous and asked me for a dance.

It would have been rude if I had refused. As soon as I agreed to dance with him, he placed his hands on my bare waist. I placed my hands on his shoulders, and we started grooving to the music. I could feel his big hands touching my stomach and my back.

He even played with my navel smiling broadly at me. But I remembered the room incident and was literally blushing. Breaking the ice, he said, "That's a lovely perfume you are wearing!" The music was loud, and all I could do was to thank him.

We were dancing close, and I could feel his warm breaths on my shoulder. It was sending shivers down my spine. It was after the dance that we both wanted to eat something since we were famished. We strolled a few places there and ate some food.

He didn't leave any chance to touch my bare waist from behind while also cracking a few double meaning jokes. I was completely aware of what was going in his mind, but I was enjoying the touch and the talks alike.

Suddenly he said, "Your boyfriend must be very lucky to get into the pants of such a hot girl. I wish I could get into her skirt tonight." I was shocked (and excited inside) at his open confession that I turned back. That was when I bumped into a lady who ended up spilling her juice all over my blouse.

But what's done can't be undone. She apologized, and then, Akshay offered to help. He took me to the same room where I saw him topless. I did some drama of cleaning the blouse with some tissues, but it was all in vain. The drama was good enough for him to feel my 34s while pressing them a little.

My nipples started to get erect. I was enjoying the groping and pressing when he asked me to remove my blouse so he could clean it. Another shocker for me! I was skeptical, but he came close to me from the front side and started to unzip my blouse from the back.

It was like he could read my mind. Within no time, I was standing in a padded strapless bra in front of him, and he was giving me a broad smile.

Akshay, "How about settling the evening score?"

Me, "What score?"

Akshay, "Come on! You saw me topless today evening. I guess it's my turn."

I was standing in the bra and long skirt in front of him, and he had that satisfactory grin on his face. In an attempt to hide, I turned around, but he hugged me from behind. I could feel his hot breaths on my naked shoulders and my neck. He was kissing and licking my neck and my shoulder.

I was so easily giving in. I could even feel his dick in my ass crack. He moved towards my face and gave a kiss on my cheek from behind and licked my ear and bit my earlobe. I let out a small moan. His hands were exploring my navel and my stomach and not to mention my boobs.

He turned me around, and my blouse and his tux were lying on the bed. He started kissing my lips. It was one passionate smooch before it turned into a wild lip sucking competition. His tongue was in my mouth, fighting with mine. One of his hands was doing my boobs, and the other was spanking and pressing my ass.

He unhooked my bra, and my bare boobs became his playing ground. He immediately took one in his mouth and started biting my nipples. It made me moan, and the other boob was in his hand. He was twitching the nipple and pinching it. It was pain and pleasure for me at the same time, and I loved it.

But I had nothing for my hands and mouth. So, I pushed him away from me and quickly unbuttoned his shirt and removed it, and threw it away on the bed. Now, Akshay was just in his trousers and was topless. I had seen him that evening, but I didn't know it then that he would soon be entering my panties.

I was just in a long skirt, completely naked from the top. We were kissing wildly while our hands were all over each other's body, exploring each part. Then, I pushed him on the bed and threw myself over him. Firstly, kissing his hot waxed chest and sucking his nipples with circling them using my tongue.

I made my way down to his torso and licked and kissed his abs. All this while, my hands were playing with his dick over the trousers. Then, I was sucking on his navel. With my hands, I removed the belt he was wearing and unbuttoned and unzipped his trousers.

His underwear was concealing the meat I wanted in my mouth without any delay. But he thought of teasing me and flipped me over, and then, he was eating my navel while playing with my melons and my hands caressing his hair. He soon moved down to my feet and licked them one by one.

I was on cloud nine. I couldn't handle the pleasure, and my pussy was already flowing juices. He started to lick his way up inside my skirt. When he couldn't go more inside, he came out of my skirt and removed it swiftly. And he went back to my inner thighs, kissing them all over while I was moaning.

Soon, we were in 69 positions, and I was on top of him. The only pieces of clothing covering us were off. His tongue had already started working its magic on my already wet pussy, and I didn't want to disappoint him. I had that huge meat inside my mouth, and I loved it.

My mouth couldn't contain its length and girth. I licked and sucked his big tatte (balls) and also took them in my mouth one by one. His huge dick was all mine to play. The way he was so swiftly working on my pussy was the result of the pleasure I was giving him.

Soon, his cock grew harder, and I could feel his veins growing in my mouth. He started sucking on my pussy rapidly. And biting the clitoris and also swiftly moving his fingers in and out of my deep choot(vagina). I knew he was on the verge of an orgasm.

So I took his dick out of my mouth and started giving him a handjob, and he soon sprang up huge loads of cum. Even I came inside his mouth, and he was not hesitant about licking my pussy all clean. I have never been a huge cum fan. I don't drink cum. But we both satisfied each other.

It was evident when he said, "Charmy! Your pussy smells magical, and its taste is out of the world." But we both knew that we were not done. We had the whole night and also for the coming few days. The fire was still on, and it was not going to douse any time soon.

We laid there on the bed for some time, cuddling and feeling each other after having lovely orgasms. Then I went to the washroom to clean myself. I was completely naked, and Akshay watched me walk. When I came out, he tried kissing me, but I pushed him away and asked him to go clean himself first.

He hurriedly went inside to clean himself up. When he came out, I was on the bed, inviting him to do me. He wasted no time and jumped on the bed. He started smooching me while pressing my melons and massaging my clit. My hands couldn't get enough of feeling that sexy muscled back and the long cock.

So, I was kind of giving him a hand job. Soon, the tool was in its full glory and was hard. He climbed on me and positioned my legs in missionary over his shoulders, kissed me on the lips while rubbing his dick over my pussy. Soon he thrust the head in my tight pussy.

The feeling of a dick inside my pussy made me moan in pleasure, which aroused him all the more. Within the next few strokes, his 8-9 inches was completely inside me, destroying my pussy walls. My pussy had like completely absorbed his cock inside. I was moaning with pain and pleasure.

My legs were on his shoulders, and he was sucking on my neck, and my hands were on his neck and back. My pussy soon adjusted to the lund (dick). I adjusted my legs, and he was completely over me. We both started to move in sync. I dug my nails in his back due to the extreme pleasure.

He started pounding my pussy like crazy with wild strokes. I could feel him going deep inside. My moans grew a little louder. My legs locked his waist so I could feel him more. Had someone been there outside the room, he would have definitely guessed what was transpiring inside that room.

We went mad with the amazing fuck we were having. It felt amazing. I was missing my friend's Sangeet for that dick, but it was all worth it. Akshay wanted to fuck me in doggy. So, he went down on me, gave my pussy a nice lick, and tried inserting his finger in my asshole.

But I asked him sternly to not even think about it. I wanted more of that meat in my pussy. So, he turned me around and made me lie down on my knees and inserted his cock tip in my pussy from behind. I clenched the bedsheet in my hands firmly because I knew the pleasure was going to be extreme.

Akshay held my waist with both his hands and, in one go, pushed the 8" monster in my choot (pussy) from behind. My boobs were swinging like crazy in that position. He continued in that position for some minutes, and I could feel an orgasm building inside me.

Even his thrusts were getting fast and deep. He also started moaning a little louder. I decided to take the front seat, and we again changed position to cowgirl. I was riding him after coming on top of him and inserting that dick into my pussy while feeling those abs and chest.

My bouncing boobs were held by him in both his hands. He, along with pressing them, was also twitching my nipples. He also started pushing his dick, and our movements were in perfect sync with each other. We couldn't hold it any longer. We both cummed together while fucking.

He filled my pussy with his love juices. Our juices mixed together and came flowing out of my pussy. He finally took his cock out of it after ramming it. I fell on his torso after the fuck, and we kissed passionately. It was then when somebody knocked on the door asking for Akshay.

Akshay told her that he was feeling a little unwell and would be there in a few minutes. We then cleaned ourselves again and got ready for the lovely night that was to follow. We went back in the function as if nothing had happened.

The oldies were about to retire for the night. It was only the youngsters who were to remain there for a night full of fun and frolic.

20. Lockdown 2

With nationwide lockdown being announced in March, all the gyms, offices, schools, colleges, and other institutions closed. I was left in my flat with a couple of other flat-mates.

I missed hitting the gym because I didn't want to lose my cock erecting figure. So, I decided to do some regular warm-up exercises and some yoga on the building terrace. I put on a sports bra, loose top, panty and shorts and went to the terrace to do my much-needed workout.

It was around 9:00 in the night, and I didn't see anyone around in the moonlight. I felt and enjoyed the cool breeze for some time. I liked that the terrace was empty and I could enjoy it all by myself. I spread my yoga mat and after a few warm-up exercises, I did some regular yoga asanas for the next 30-40 minutes.

The time must be around 10 and I again looked around, but there was no one. So, I thought of doing some planks. I took off my loose top, positioned myself on the yoga mat and started doing some planks. I had done 10-12 planks when I heard a heavy male voice, "Good but not perfect."

I was startled, but I immediately realized there was someone else on the terrace. I quickly composed myself and wore my top and looked behind. "Excuse me!" I spoke. I could see a tall figure of about 6 feet standing in front of me but at a little distance. "The posture can be improved a little bit," he said.

I could clearly understand that he wasn't talking about the plank posture but my body posture. "Do you generally give your free advice to people?" I asked. Coming closer, he said, "Generally, I don't. But saw some scope of improvement here and I thought I could help."

He came closer, and I could clearly see his sharp-featured face. "Zayed," he said, introducing himself forwarding his hand for a handshake. "Charmy," I said, shaking his hand. He held my hand firmly. "I looked around a few minutes ago and you weren't here," I asked him.

He replied that he was there since the time I came there. I clearly wasn't expecting this and I said, "Well! You could have told me."

"How could I? I would have then missed the opportunity to see such a hot girl doing planks in her sports bra," he said, looking at my boobs. I was shocked at his audacity, but I kept my calm since that was nothing new in Delhi. He asked me if I was gonna complete my exercise or not.

To which I replied that I was done exercising for the day. But the truth was that I didn't want to exercise in front of him. I forgot to tell you about Zayed. Big and tall that he was, he was wearing a tank top and shorts. I could clearly see his veiny arms and legs due to the rigorous workout schedule, which I guessed.

His biceps could clearly be seen in the moonlight. He seemed to be one fitness freak, spending an ample amount of time in the gym. Sensing that Zayed had no plans to leave the rooftop any time soon, I decided to go back to my abode. I started walking towards the stairs when I heard him again.

"Well! That didn't look like much of a workout. Anyway, you can see for yourself what an actual workout looks like. Coz, I am going to do a hardcore workout up here." I turned back, making his plan a success (though I was kind of getting his intentions of seducing me through his body)

I decided to play along and said, "Alright! I will stay here, cool down from my workout and watch what your actual workout looks like." And, in the next 20-25 minutes, I saw him doing all those crunches, sit-ups, and push-ups. I was not wrong to guess he was indeed a fitness freak.

I was browsing on my phone and at the same time, I was keeping an eye on how Zayed was working out. I could clearly see his muscles getting warmed up when he said, "You know I can see you checking me out. Maybe you can join me in the workout."

He came near me, gave me a nice grin, removed his tank top, and started wiping his body with it. He asked me how it was for a view. For a moment, I went weak in the knees. I saw the sweat going down from his neck through his rock hard chest to the washboard abs.

He came closer to me to show off his toned body. Now, I was really checking him out so much so that I noticed the bulge in his shorts. I started to imagine the length and girth of the piece of meat inside his shorts. The aroma of his sweat was already giving a tingling sensation to my pussy.

I decided to play along. I removed my top and walked back to my yoga mat and started doing some planks. Zayed was checking out my ass. He kept continuously staring at me while I was working out my planks. He came closer, held my stomach with both his hands (it sent a chill down my spine)

He lifted me a bit to correct my posture. "There's nothing wrong with my posture," I said. He smiled and commented, "You don't know, but I am a personal trainer. I know that you are doing it wrong." Now, lust had taken over both of us, and we both knew what we wanted.

I was lying on the yoga mat facing him. He was almost lying on me (not touching me) in a push-up position. He did a few push-ups, during which he deliberately touched his chest with my boobs and his abs with my stomach to seduce me. I gave in and pushed him towards me and planted a kiss on his lips.

He was waiting for this and started kissing me back passionately. He then helped me get up, and I ended up feeling his abs and chest. Believe me, it felt as good as it looked. He pinned me against one of the walls there and planted his lips on mine. I was quick to respond.

We both were now completely engrossed in the deep smooch with our tongues in action. He then made me wrap my legs around him while we continued kissing. I was feeling his sexy gym build rock hard muscled back with both my hands.

He was supporting me with one hand and with the other, fondling my melons. I loved the feel of his muscled body pushing into mine, and I felt his chest and abs. His cock was hard enough to be felt by my pussy. We broke the kiss, and he tried removing my bra.

But I told him that the terrace wasn't the place for the action. He tried convincing me, but I stayed adamant. We decided to go to his place since it was empty. I quickly put on my top. The very next moment, he was walking behind me with his cock in my ass crack over the shorts.

His hands were feeling my stomach and melons. We got in a lift, and Zayed was quick enough to start smooching after pressing the button. In no time, we reached his place. He quickly closed the door and as he pinned me against the wall.

I could feel his dick pressing against my then wet pussy. I was much turned on. He carried me to his bed, kissing me all along the way, and I kept grinding on his dick. Placing me on his bed, Zayed removed my top and sports bra in almost no time and said, "Wow! Such lovely big boobs."

I was happy he liked them. He started licking and kissing my nipples with his mouth, and his hands were at work too with my boobies and my pussy. Wrapping his tongue around my nipples and moving it in circles, he was giving me the pleasure of the world.

I was thrusting his face more and more into my boobs, caressing his hair. I started moaning his name in pleasure. My hands took the liberty of going down his shorts towards the rock-hard meat I was interested in. He went down me and slid one of his hands inside my shorts. He started feeling my clit over the panty.

He kept moving his fingers in circles, exciting me more. At the same time, kissing my silky-smooth legs while I clenched the bedsheet in my fists. He then licked and drank juices from my pussy by moving the panty and shorts a little down.

He then pulled my panty down using his teeth, getting a clear view of my tight wet pussy. I then started pushing his tongue deep into my pussy. I could feel my juices flow, and he was more than happy to lick and drink all of them. After a tongue fuck, he made his way up again.

He kissed me on my lips, making me taste my own cum. I decided to return the pleasure, and we quickly switched places. Now I was on top of him. His legs were off the bed and the body on it. I removed his shorts along with the boxers, and a big dick about 8-9 inches long sprang up in front of me.

It was of good girth, and I knew I was gonna have a good time. Without wasting any time, I took it in my mouth, tasting his pre-cum. I lubricated it with my spit and started milking it while my hands played with his big tatte (balls). God, it grew more monstrous and wasn't fitting my mouth.

I stroked it for some time and then I licked and sucked his balls one by one. I started going upwards, kissing and licking the washboard abs one by one. I went through his chest, which I licked and kissed until my satisfaction – his nipples, his biceps, his neck, his ears. I didn't leave a place where I didn't lick and kiss.

I climbed over him and gently placed his cock over my pussy and said, "Fuck me like it's the end of the world." Zayed knew what I wanted, and he, too, wanted the same. He came on top of me while we completely laid on the bed and started smooching me.

He then went down, kissing my neck, my lobes (my weak points), and then he stopped at my boobs. He couldn't get enough of them and started teasing me again. Then, finally, through the cleavage and stomach, he reached my pussy. He gave it a lick and then started sucking my clit while his fingers were at work with my pussy.

I kept moaning and screaming his name in pleasure as he kept making his tongue go in circles on my clit. His long fingers were going in and out of my already leaking pussy. He increased the pace, and I asked him to fuck me hard. Guess he was waiting to hear just that.

He then got on top of me in missionary style and placed the tip of his cock on my pussy. He pushed the tip in, and I let out a loud moan coz his dick was thick. But I was ready, and he slowly thrust it deeper into my pussy. "Fuck! Charmy, you are very tight," he exclaimed.

He kept kissing me as he completely penetrated his dick into my pussy. Our hands were firmly clenched into each other. Each thrust made me feel like his monster cock was going deeper and deeper. When it was completely in, I wrapped my legs around him.

What followed was a long session of push and pulls. I could feel his throbbing cock enter my tight pussy and give me so much pleasure. I could feel my pussy dripping wet each time he entered. I enjoyed it so so much. In between, he asked me to ride him. So, I decided to take the initiative and got on top of him.

I licked my hand and held his cock and guided it into my pussy and started riding it like there was no tomorrow. While I was riding him, he used his hands to hold my boobs and massage them and occasionally pulled me to kiss my lips hard. He held my ass and squeezed and spanked it in between.

I increased the pace of riding. He used his fingers to touch my clit and rub it harder while I was riding him. We switched positions again. We kept fucking, and he slowly increased the pace and kept going in and out of my pussy. I was in heaven with all the pleasure I thought I was going to miss in the lockdown.

I was coming closer to the climax and kept moaning his name. Even he was about to cum and asked me where I wanted his cum. I told him to cum outside. He further increased his pace, and I scratched his back in utter excitement. He bit my nipples hard as his balls built up the cum.

I think we both came together. He took his dick out and sprayed all the cum on my pussy, some on my boobs. We both collapsed on the bed, tired of the long amazing fuck. After some time of lying down on the bed, exhausted. We decided to take a shower together coz of the fuck and workout.

And guess what? We ended up having sex in the shower. We came back in the bed and slept naked in each other's arms. We woke up to a day full of sex. While we were fucking the next night, I saw a silhouette outside the bedroom to which I just ignored.

We enjoyed the short stay we had there during the lockdown. After that, we both went to our hometowns. I am still waiting to get his monster cock back in my pussy.

21. The Gym

Once I had to travel to Bengaluru for a conference. Unfortunately, I arrived on a wet and gloomy day in the city. It had been raining heavily on and off since the morning. But that didn't mean business wasn't going on as usual in that busy city. I hailed a cab from the airport.

It finally pulled outside the lobby of what was quite an extravagantly lavish hotel. As I stepped out of the cab, I could see a few staring eyes. I was used to being stared at for my looks. I am taller than an average girl and that day, I was wearing skin fit blue jeans and a white shirt.

I had my bag in one hand and my jacket in the other. The cab driver got out of the car and pulled my other bags out of the boot of the cab. As I was rustling through my bag for my wallet, the cab driver was checking me out. The shirt revealed quite a bit of my cleavage.

I do have fairly large boobs as well which are more than enough to arouse any man. I paid the fare and proceeded into the hotel. It excited me that I was the kind of girl who could make heads turn as she walks by. It wasn't any different that day as I walked through the lobby to the reception to check-in.

While the receptionist was checking me in, he signalled the bellboy to carry my luggage. The young man came swiftly and stood by as the check-in was taking a bit of time. While waiting, he couldn't help but stare at my curvaceous figure. His eyes were transfixed at my butt.

As soon as I was checked in, the bellboy showed me my room and carried my luggage. As soon as he left the room, I opened up the curtains to let some light into the room. I looked at the view from the window and noticed the gym at the hotel. There was barely anyone in the gym at that moment.

I was feeling a bit tired from all the traveling. So, I decided to take a nap and maybe hit the gym later if I felt like it. I turned off the lights and I observed that the windows were less of windows and more like a full-length glass wall. There would be plenty of light if I left the curtains open.

After changing into a comfortable t-shirt, I sat at the edge of the bed. I took off my sneakers and lied down on the bed. In no time at all, I fell asleep. About an hour or so, I woke up suddenly from a dream.

I was thinking to myself, "Why did I have to wake up now? That big pile of sexy hunk was about to fuck me good and boy he did have a nice dick." Then, I was wet and horny and awake. I got up and went to the washroom to clean myself. I wore the jeans again and came back and sat at the edge of the bed.

I looked at the mirror on my front. I adjusted my hair for a bit and headed over to the windows to close the curtains. I noticed that a guy was standing at the balcony outside the gym and he was talking on the phone with someone. All of a sudden, I got a naughty and mischievous idea.

I started talking to myself in my mind, "This guy is taller than me like at least half a foot or maybe more. And oh my God, look at those arms and legs. He works out a lot. I bet he is ripped under that t-shirt of his. I bet he has a huge dick too."

Just looking at how hot he was as well as all those thoughts made me all the wetter and hornier. I finally decided to have some fun. I left the curtains as they were. I knew that if I turned around and walked over to turn the lights on, he'd check out my ass. It was getting dark outside.

As soon as I turned the lights on, he could see clearly into my room. I walked over to the windows, looked at the view, turned around and slowly took off my t-shirt. I had a red push up bra on and it made my breasts look bigger. I unbuttoned my jeans, pulled down the zipper and turned around.

Slowly I pulled down my jeans and he could see that I was wearing matching red lace panties. I took off my jeans completely and threw them onto a sofa lying nearby. Then I adjusted my panties around my waist and along my butt cheeks. I walked over to the bed, laid down and spread my legs.

He now had a full view of my body. I started to slowly touch myself imagining they were his hands running all over my body. I was rubbing my pussy over my panties with one hand whilst squeezing my boobs with the other. I even didn't know is he was watching me or not but at least I was thinking so.

I got up and placed myself at the edge of the bed. I took off my bra and started playing with my nipples. They were erect and I had never been so horny before coz I had never done such a thing before. It had been a long time since someone had fucked me really good.

I slid my hand inside my panties and started playing with my clit. I was breathing heavily and letting out soft moans from being aroused so much. My panties started oozing juices and had a big wet spot. I took my hand out of my panties and sucked on my fingers.

I was tasting my pussy juices, slowly and seductively as if I were sucking a big fat dick. I looked outside the window and saw that he was watching me play with myself. He hadn't figured out that I knew that he was watching me. I got up, took off my panties and dropped them on the floor beside me.

After that, I sat at the edge of the bed, closed my eyes and started to finger my pussy slowly. I was playing with my boobs with my other hand. I could feel the orgasm building up and so, I started rubbing my clit as well. I looked up to see if he was still watching but he had disappeared.

Seeing that he had disappeared, I didn't feel like doing it anymore. I ordered some room service and went to take a bath. I was done with my bath by the time the room service arrived. After I had my dinner, I took out my laptop and started watching some porn.

While I was watching, I heard a knock on my door. I closed my laptop and went over to see who was knocking on my door so late at night. I looked through the peephole and saw that it was the guy from the gym balcony. I felt scared, nervous and excited at the same time.

I opened the door and there he was standing in his shorts and t-shirt giving me a naughty and cheeky smile. "Hey there! Mind if I come in?" He walked as though I had invited him in even before I could respond. "I enjoyed that little show you put on earlier."

"What show? I have no idea what you are talking about," I replied.
"Sure you do. The one where you took off all your clothes and played with yourself."

I acted as if I was astonished but I still blushed and bit my lips and took a step back. He took a few steps towards me and whilst walking towards me, he took off his t-shirt and also dropped his shorts. "Tonight. You and me. Whatever you want." It sure was an offer that he would fuck me all night long if I wanted it.

I was excited yet terrified because looking down at his crotch inside his underwear, I could see a massive bulge. I bit my lips and looked back up into his eyes. His hands proceeded to pull down his briefs. I grabbed his hands and stopped him and looked him in the eyes.

He placed his hands on my neck, leaned forward and started kissed me passionately. My silence and lack of any resistance were in a way the approval he was looking for. Things started to get hotter as he started running his hands all over me and then started kissing my neck.

It felt good when his hands were playing with my boobs and grabbing and spanking my ass. I also started rubbing his dick over his briefs and it felt huge and he wasn't even hard. It sent shivers down my spine. I pushed him against the wall and took off my tee and he couldn't stop staring at my bra caged boobs.

"Take them off," I said eyeing at his crotch. He dropped his briefs on the floor. His dick must've been at least 8 inches and it wasn't even hard. It was just hanging there like a beast that had just woken up. I couldn't stop staring and my hand was already on my shorts rubbing my clit.

I was licking my lips and biting them as I looked into his eyes. He did the same and started to slowly rub his dick. We were both jerking off staring at each other. He walked over towards me, lifted me and threw me on the bed. He pulled down my shorts swiftly and went down on me.

He started licking my clit over my panties and occasionally sucking on it. On top of that, he was fingering me over my panty that it almost got me on the edge. It wasn't going to be long before he would make me cum. I grabbed his hair in one hand while the other hand clenched onto the sheets.

My legs started to tremble and shake as he kept on fingering me and sucking my clit until I had a huge orgasm. He came up, kissed me and I tasted my pussy juices. He pulled me up and made me sit on the edge of the bed. I was staring at an 8+ inch dick. I couldn't wait to see how it would feel in my tight pussy.

I looked up at him and gave him a naughty slutty smile. I grabbed his dick, lifted it and started teasing his massive hanging balls. I licked and sucked on them and even tried putting them both in my mouth. I slowly stroked his dick while playing with his balls.

What turned me on, even more, was the way he kept eye contact with me as I played with his dick. I could feel his dick grow more as I stroked it. I couldn't wait any longer and started sucking his dick. I took it in my mouth and his long thick dick was hitting my throat.

In a few more minutes of some sloppy sucking and deep throating his dick, I had gotten him fully hard. It was an unbelievable 9-inch hard dick staring back at me. It was very thick and the thought of it fucking my pussy and maybe even my ass made me terrified and excited at the same time.

He was ready to fuck me. He pulled me up and lifted me. I wrapped my arms around his neck. He lowered me on to his dick. He was in control and teased me by rubbing my clit with the head of his dick. He was driving me crazy. I wanted his dick so bad that I begged for it.

I grabbed his dick with one hand, stroked it slowly, looked him in the eye and said, "I want you inside me right now. No more teasing please." I closed my eyes and kissed him passionately. He lowered me down on his dick and it felt like he was ripping my insides apart.

I took a deep breath. My heart started to race. My hands clenched firmly on his back. My eyes were rolling and the only words out of my mouth were "Fuck, fuck, fuck!" At that moment, I knew if he could last long enough, then I was about to have the best sex of my life.

I leaned forward and nibbled on his ear, bit his neck. I scratched his back and ran my hands through his hair. He slowly lifted me and down till I was able to take his dick in fully. I leaned back and looked him in the eyes. He grabbed onto me firmly and started to pound my pussy.

I was moaning loudly; my legs were shaking and my toes started to curl as each thrust pushed me closer and closer to another orgasm. "Don't stop. Keep going. I'm gonna cum soon." He more than happily obliged and kept fucking me till I came hard on his dick.

As soon as I cummed, he pulled out his dick and put me down on the bed and started to rub my clit. It felt like I was riding a wave of orgasms. The way he was playing with my clit felt like another one was building up. In no time I came hard again.

He sat down at the edge of the bed and pulled me closer. I climbed on top of him on the floor and pushed him onto his back. I straddled him and teased his dick with my pussy. I kissed him and whispered in his ear, "My turn. I wanna empty your balls. I know you've been trying hard not to cum."

I straightened up and placed my hands on his chest. I lowered myself onto his hard dick, gasping as it filled me up. "I'm gonna make you cum like never before." I started to ride his dick slowly at first, gradually increasing the pace in a rhythmic up and down, back and forth motion.

I felt his dick getting harder and starting to throb as I rode him. My pussy was gripping onto his dick tighter and tighter. He tried to grab onto my waist to slow me down but I grabbed his hands and kept riding him faster. His facial expressions were making it clear that he was about to cum soon.

I got off him, got on my knees and started to suck his dick, focusing on the head. He sat up and looked me in the eyes with a fierce expression of passion and pure carnal lust. He had given me full control over his orgasm. I cupped his balls with one hand while stroking his dick with the other and sucking on the head.

I felt his balls getting tighter as he got closer. "Oh god! That feels so good. I'm gonna cum now. Fuck!" He cums a mouthful. It was more than I was expecting. It was so much that I had cum dripping down the side of lips onto my boobs and even on the floor. I looked up to him as I spit the cum.

"Well, looks like you haven't had cummed in a while." He gave me a sheepish grin and replied, "About a week or so." He was still hard and from the looks on his face, he wasn't done yet. He wanted to go again. He stood up, made me get up too and grabbed me by my neck and pushed me against the wall.

"I wanna fuck your ass," he said looking at me with a ravaging look. "I bet you do. But that's not happening today." I replied with a smirk and grabbed his cock and started stroking. His hands ran down my body slowly until they reached my pussy. We were both jerking off each other while making out.

He threw me onto the bed face first and spanked my ass. His big fat dick lay on my ass. I was shivering with goosebumps. Was he going to just shove it up to my ass without any warning despite me refusing him? It was a scary yet exciting feeling.

Suddenly I felt a warm blob of spit land on my ass and trickle down to my pussy. He was fingering my tight ass and stretching it up with spit as lube. I stretched my hand from underneath and grabbed his dick and played with the head while he was playing with my ass.

He placed his dick on my ass, teased me for a bit but then proceeded to my pussy and pushed it in slowly. It felt so big, hitting like that from behind that I winced and pushed him away. He grabbed hold of my hand and stopped me from stopping him. I let out a cry as he slowly pushed it in.

He grabbed my waist, leaned forward and asked me to look at him. He kissed me passionately and played with my boobs all the while his dick was in my pussy and I could feel it throbbing. I broke the kiss and nodded at him. He leaned back, grabbed my waist and started thrusting slowly.

It had been so long since someone with such a huge dick had fucked me so good that I had almost forgotten the feeling. I was breathing heavily with the sheets clenched firmly in my fists. His balls were smacking against my pussy with each thrust. He asked me to play with my pussy and I obliged.

I was getting closer to another orgasm and he started to fuck me faster and deeper. And in no time, I came cumming on the sheets with him still inside me. He slowly pulled out and my legs were shaking like I had the chills. He spanked my ass gently and pulled me up after I had stopped shaking.

He told me to stand by the windows. He spread my legs and pushed my face against the windows. He leaned in and whispered in my ear "I'm gonna fuck you till you can't walk straight." That got me hornier than before and begging for more. He slid his dick in my pussy in one quick and deep thrust.

It made me gasp and scream. "Oh my God!" He grabbed me firmly by my waist to stop me from squirming. I knew this was it. He was gonna fuck me hard till we both came. He started with a slow deep thrust in, making me squirm and wiggle my ass.

Slowly he increased the pace but kept a nice rhythm keeping me on the edge building up to an intense orgasm. As I got closer my pussy gripped tighter and tighter on his dick. He kept pounding my pussy hard till I came hard. My legs were shaking, back was arched and toes curled.

He didn't slow down after I came as he was right on the edge. He kept on going and the intensity with which he was fucking brought on another wave of orgasm, like having one right after the other. It was then I felt him cum inside my pussy as I was having an orgasm.

He kissed me and as he pulled out, I could feel a huge load of cum slowly drip out of my pussy and down my leg. But we weren't both done yet. As long as I stayed in the hotel, whenever we had time, we had wild passionate sex. He even fucked me inside the steam room of the gym.

22. Lift

That fateful night, I was returning to my building from a pub. It was quite late. I had had an amazing night with all types of fun and frolic and drinking and dancing. I was feeling extremely tired.

I knew I would go to bed as soon as I enter my bedroom. But destiny had some other plans for me that night. I entered the lift of my building which would take me on my floor. I saw that a young, hot, tall, fair and handsome man who I suppose was just returning from a rigorous gym session.

He was wearing gym shorts and gym vest revealing his big broad arms and well-developed muscles. Though I was tired, I couldn't help but notice him. I even noticed him noticing me. How couldn't he? I was wearing a yellow crop top and white short shorts revealing an ample body of mine.

I pressed the button of my floor. We had hardly gone up by 2-3 floors when the lift suddenly came to a halt. I thought it must be a usual 2–3-minute lift error. But it turned out to be something that would take long to be repaired. The sexy stranger with me in the lift used the landline in the lift to inform the security.

They came and checked what they could. Since it was night, the repairmen were all gone and would take time to come there. In about 15-20 minutes, we both knew that we were stuck and had no other option but to stay there calm and composed till the help arrived.

The muscled man broke the ice between us. "Hey! Krishna," he said to which I replied, "Hi! Charmy." He then asked me if I was returning from a party to which I replied in the affirmative. I asked him if he was returning from a workout session and I was correct too.

We called the security again and were told that we needed to wait until the help arrived. We were both very tired of our respective chores but couldn't help what was happening. Being a hot summer night, the temperature inside the lift was soaring and we couldn't handle the same.

We chit-chatted with each other to kill some time but to no avail. The hot atmosphere inside was another problem. All of a sudden, Krishna removed his gym vest and started wiping his body with it. I was spellbound seeing his hot well-chiseled body. I could see a good gym build body.

He was the owner of a broad muscular hairless chest, big broad biceps, and triceps. I could count 1, 2, 3, 4, 5, 6 six big abs. He had a completely waxed chest with no sign of any hair. then he turned his back towards me oblivious of me noticing him and continuing his wiping.

I was mesmerized to see a rock-hard muscled back. He noticed me checking him out. "Checking me out?" he winked and asked. "Checking you in," I winked back and replied. He then suggested me to remove my top to get rid of the growing hotness inside and flexed his muscles.

I was skeptical about removing my top and being just in a bra in front of Krishna (who was a stranger to me some minutes ago) But then I gave it a thought and immediately removed my top. Now, just a black bra was covering my 34 sized melons. I was standing before him in just that black bra and white shorts.

"Wow!" he exclaimed. I felt extremely proud of my assets and blushed a little. I pretended that it was very hot and started blowing my body with my top. By this time, I had made up my mind to feel that hot body. But little did I know what else I was gonna feel that night in that stranded lift.

We chit chatted again for another few minutes. But this time, shamelessly eyeing each other's body. "34 or 36," he asked. I was shell shocked at his audacity but kept my calm and asked him, "What do you think?" He was cleverer than me.

He replied, "I can't tell exactly. I need to use my hands to know the exact size." I couldn't reply immediately but then I asked him, "5 or 6?" (I meant to ask his cock size in inches.) He didn't reply anything to this to which I mockingly asked, "Smaller than 5?"

This hit him badly and he removed his shorts and was then standing tall in front of me in his brown underwear. "9," he said and pointed towards his hard cock growing inside his undie. I looked at his meat and to be honest, it seemed quite big in his undie.

By this time, we both knew what we wanted. I just thought something sexy and pretended to open the button of my shorts. "Krishna, Help me with this button. It's not opening and it's very hot," I said. He immediately understood what I meant and what I wanted.

He came very close to me and put his strong hands on my waist and felt my belly. Then he sat down and placed his hands on my shorts and opened its button and unzipped it. Without even me saying, he brought my shorts down to my feet all the way feeling my hot long sexy smooth legs.

He got up and we were standing very close to each other feeling each other's breath. "Come on Krishna, tell me my size," I said. That was an open invitation to him to feel my boobs. He wasted no time and immediately groped both my boobs and started pressing them hard while I started to feel in heaven.

He pretended as if he was doing it to measure my size. I had closed my eyes when he said, "I don't think I can know the exact size with this bra on." I just smirked at his witty nature and immediately turned around for him to open my bra hooks. He was very sharp and swift.

In almost no time, he had separated the bra from my body in which I helped him fully. With me facing the lift wall, he mauled my boobs from behind and started licking and kissing and sucking my hot sexy bareback. Then, he turned me around and I could clearly see the lust in his eyes.

We both joined our lips and what followed was a deep and long french kiss with us exchanging our saliva and our tongues feeling each other. We were kissing like crazy. After we had enough of the lip kissing, he started licking my face- eyes, nose, cheeks, forehead, ears and earlobes (my weak points)- he left nothing.

He then switched towards my neck and shoulders and armpits. All this while, he was continuously pressing my boobs. I was feeling in heaven and my pussy was flowing its love juices. He then licked and kissed and sucked my boobs to his complete satisfaction. Even biting my nipples hard in between.

I couldn't resist all the joy I was getting in that stranded lift. He went further down and removed my wet panty. He licked clean my juicy pussy and inserted one of his fingers inside. It pained a little but I tolerated it all and I didn't want him to stop.

I buried his mouth in my pussy and he too was perfectly sucking it. I knew I wanted something else for my kitty and immediately pushed him. It was my turn to return the pleasure and I made him get up and gave him a kiss on his cheeks.

My hands were feeling his hot chiseled body while my mouth was at another job of licking his face. I kissed his broad shoulders, his well-built chest, and his nipples. Then I went down and kissed and licked and sucked his abs one by one. I went up again and kissed his biceps and triceps.

His cock had grown to its full size and I knew it had to be taken out of that cage. I sat on my knees and removed his undie and the complexioned monster cock stood tall before me. I didn't wait much before putting it in my mouth. I started playing with his balls and milking his cock.

It wasn't fitting in my mouth and was choking me. I sucked it till my mouth started paining. Now, it was action time. We both got up and started kissing each other's lips. He positioned his cock on my pussy and slowly inserted it in my pussy. My pussy walls were broadened with that thick long cock.

It pained me but I knew of the pleasure about to come and I tolerated it all. Slowly, it made its place in my pussy and when this was done. He started stroking his dick. We were kissing and he was pounding my pussy. The position in that lift wasn't very comfortable and it was very hot.

But we were both enjoying to the fullest and having the best time. His hands were mauling my boobs, his lips were pleasuring my face and his tool was pleasuring my pussy. What more could I have asked for? With him fucking my hot tight pussy.

We were kissing and making minimal noise and my hands were feeling his sexy back with my nails dug deep. After a few minutes of this continuous stroking, we both were about to cum. But we continued fucking until we both cummed together. His cock was still in my wet pussy.

We were both panting with the hot fuck we just had in that extreme hot temperature of the lift. But we were both completely satisfied. Many more things followed that night in that lift till it got repaired in the morning.

23. Exchange Student

I woke up and ate breakfast. Then took a bath and wore a black bra to cover my big soft breasts and a black panty and a one-piece floral dress. Then I took the bus to college. As soon as I entered the class, I saw a big black dude sitting on the front bench. He was so massive that he almost looked like a man. He might be at least 6 feet tall and very well built. I could see his big biceps and abs from his tight blue t-shirt. None of my friends knew who he was and why he was there.

Then the teacher came to announce that we had an exchange student from a foreign university. Apparently, our college had some tie-up with that foreign university. After 4-5 days, he took the middle bench and was sitting right next to me. I could closely see how big he was.

In some ways, you can say he was the perfect man – the way men should be. All the guys from my class looked like kids in front of him. And that day, he said 'Hi' to me and we talked for some time. He told me he was there for around 1 month. After that, we exchanged 'Hellos' every single day.

I remember there was a day when I wore a very sexy dress at the college. It was a red floral crop top just covering my breasts and a very tight sheer yoga pant. Anybody could see the shape of my breasts as I was wearing a push up that day and could see my ass cheeks separated.

My soft plump ass would shake with every step and my flat

stomach was mesmerizing. The coolest part was when I entered the room, I saw every guy staring at me. That big guy had his jaw dropped. When I sat next to him, he whispered to me, "Gal! that's a hell of booty you got there and you are such a head turner babe."

I was flattered but when I looked at him, I saw a huge bulge in his pant. It was so huge that I had never seen anything like it before. I was shocked and tried to look away. But every time my eyes would come back there only. It was very hard to focus on the board that day.

The weirdest thing was that he was enjoying it and he started flirting with me a lot from that day onwards. He would compliment me every single day and tried to find ways to touch me. All he needed was an excuse to touch my hands, shoulders, waist and sometimes even ass.

Few more days passed and one day he was way too touchy and was flirting a lot. He was sitting with me that day. I was wearing a short skirt and a sleeveless top deep neck from behind. He complimented my dress.

He said, "Gal! you have got a thin tall body, massive tits, an ass to die for and a lean waist. Your ass is so soft and big and I can sense its warmth. You deserve better than shits in the name of boys you have here. You deserve black men who can worship your body the way you deserve."

I was shocked by the words he used and I just replied, "What the hell are you saying?" to which he came up with, "Girl, Congo guys have the biggest dicks. I can assure you that you won't even feel these Indian dicks once you taste mine." I was intrigued and asked how big he was. He said, "9 inches."

I didn't believe what he said. He said, "I can prove it to you, gal." I couldn't think of anything and I said, "Liar," and ran away. I had to watch black porn all night to control my urges. 2-3 days after this incident, I saw him on the basketball court.

He was wearing a tee and shorts and was all covered in sweat after some games. His tee had taken the shape of his body. I could see his big chest and abs trying to make way through that near the wet tee. I was observing him from a distance. Then he moved to the backside of the court and stood there.

I followed him and was looking at him wanting to see what he was up to. My heart was beating mountains and his body was all pumped up because of the game. He stood there and opened his bag and took off his tee. I could see every cut of the muscles on his back.

He was black and completely ripped. I prayed that he turned so that I could ogle at his abs. His hands were moving in such a flow that all I could think of was to bite his biceps. And then finally he turned and my jaw dropped when I saw those abs. They were so manly and hard like stone and chest all pumped up.

I won't lie but I did feel a tingling in my pussy just by staring at his manly body. I was so lost in his abs that I forgot where I was standing. Then he turned his face and saw me. He fucking saw me standing there staring at his topless body with one hand on my breast.

I swear I don't know when my hand moved to my big melon breast. I had to run away because it got too awkward. 2 more days passed. I was wearing a thin grey top which was taking the shape of my body and shorts at the bottom. I didn't realize that my top was taking a very nice shape of my breasts so much like two big balls floating separately.

That black beast of a man was giving very lustful looks to me like he was going to eat me. I decided to leave early that day. When I was in the hallway, he came from nowhere, took me inside a room and pinned me against the wall. He grabbed both my hands with his one hand and pinned them over my head.

I was very scared what he was gonna do and my heart was pumping like a canon. He smirked at me and said, "You look hot today babe. I saw you looking at me the other day. Liked what you saw?" I couldn't say anything and he said, "Maybe. I will let you feel my body today. I know that you want it. You can thank me later."

And all I could think of was what if someone saw us. Then he leaned over me and came really close and pulled up his tank top. Woah! Those abs were still that intact and I started getting wet again by being that close to that muscular body. He then came even closer.

His face so close to mine as if our lips were about to touch. I could smell the fragrance of his big body. He took my hand and put it on his chest. As hard as I tried to control myself, I couldn't control my hands. I was touching all over his chest and abs and feeling his body.

I was dripping wet down and my nipples were getting hard. My top was perfectly in the shape of my boobs. My nipples were poking out and boobs were like a grey paint had been coated over them. He fucking turned me on. He was into my brain and then he got back, gave me a wicked smile and left.

I was like, "Dude seriously! You got under my skin, made me horny in the hallway of the college and then just left." I ran home in guilt. I had to finger 3 times that night to get it out of my system. Then, it was nothing for the next 3-4 days and I was craving for him.

I would think about him and finger remembering his touch on my body. I would squeeze my boobs while fingering. I couldn't take it anymore. His silence was killing me. I wanted him to grope me like that again. I started to wear shorter clothes to get his attention but still, he wouldn't care.

One day I wore a very deep neck yellow top with tight black sheer yoga pants to the college. I intentionally bounced my ass as I walked because I was wearing a thong. And I got his attention. I was getting goosebumps. After the first class was over, I intentionally got up and went out.

As I was walking, I turned and gave him a wicked smile. And as I expected, he followed me. I was nervous about what I was doing and what was gonna happen. I was walking down the hallway while bouncing my ass. My ass cheeks were shuffling and then he held my hand and I stopped.

I was scared but happy from inside. He turned me around and touched my hair and said, "I know what game you are playing as I am the champion of it." I gave him a sinister smile and said, "Let's see how much of a good player you actually are." He smiled at me and said, "You are gonna regret it."

He lifted me up and put me on his shoulders like I was nothing but just a toy to him. He opened the men's room door and took me inside it. I was in awe and needed a moment to cope up with what just happened then. I was kinda scared and embarrassed to be brought inside men's toilet like that.

But I was enjoying it. I had never been to men's toilet before. I had an idea what was gonna happen next. It was gonna be the kinkiest thing I had ever done and that too with a big sexy beast who was raw muscles. I was just handling what happened to me when he suddenly threw me inside one of the toilet cubicles.

There were three toilet cubicles. I was handling myself somehow in the extreme left one which had the pissing booths next to it. He gave me a grim smile like he had achieved something. While on the other hand, I was shocked about my situation. I didn't expect that we would end up in the toilet, men's toilet.

He then closed the door of the cubicle and said, "Gal! You are gonna love it. I told you I got a 9 inches meat down there. If you still don't believe me, the proof is in front of you. Just grab the meat you deserve." I somehow handled myself and sat on the toilet seat.

My boobs were almost wide open coz of the deep neck top. Being in a men's room like that was making my pussy wet. I was berating the hot smell of men present all over in the atmosphere. I said, "Yeah, I will get the proof." and unbuttoned his pants. I could feel the bulge in his pants.

He was standing in front of me like a proud lion and touching my head like I was his pet bitch. I then unzipped his pants and dragged them down. He was pampering my head and moving his hand through my black-brown straight silky hair.

I was looking up straight in his eyes. May be trying to show him that I would be the perfect bitch for him. His boxers were so tight over his dick and balls like they were gonna rip off. I could already see how thick his dick was. My mouth was watering and my hands were shaking.

I gulped and then grabbed his ass and removed his boxers in one go. His dick jumped out of it and sat on my forehead. Woah! it was as big as 5 inches but it wasn't completely hard. Yet it was bigger than all of my exes. I couldn't believe it was so thick but still soft.

I looked in his eyes with my lips just one inch away from his dick. I was craving for it and said, "It's not 9 inches. I knew you were lying." Maybe I said that so that he could ask me to take care of it to see its actual size which he did. He said, "Girl! It's not hard and it needs a hand and a mouth. Then you will see how big and thick I am."

My brain suggested me to say no. But I don't know why I said, "Okay but I will just give you a few strokes and then it will be over. Nothing after that." He laughed saying, "You won't be able to stop yourself after that." I took his dick and politely moved it around my face like I wanted it to get inside my mouth some-how.

I started stroking and feeling that big dick with both my hands. With every stroke, it got bigger and bigger filling my hands more and more making me wetter. And he was just standing there with a prideful smile. It was already so thick that I needed both my hands to grab it.

I was so aroused by that dick as it had a very distinctive manly smell. It was driving me crazy so much so that I wanted it and I needed it. I had never seen a dick so manly which just by sight will make you its slave. It will command you to suck it. I was milking it faster.

That big black dick became more big and thick. The top part took such a shape that I just wanted to suck it while I stroked the whole dick. I was so lost in that dick that slowly I brought my soft cotton lips towards that enormous dick. Then I heard a sound.

He said, "It won't be enough to bring it in its true form just by stroking." I took it as an insult to my skills. I wasn't really trying and also, I really wanted to see it completely stiff. So, I thought a quick blowjob wouldn't hurt. Just a blowjob and it would end.

I said, "I will suck you for a few minutes. And that too only because I want to see how big you really are and then it will end. Okay?" He laughed and said, "We will see that, baby gal." I got on my knees and got a little closer to him. I took his dick and started shaking it vigorously.

I opened my mouth craving for his monster cock. I stroked it a little more and then touched my soft lips to the top of his dick. i moved my lips over it like I wanted to give him the best pleasure. Then I kept on stroking it and looked in his eyes. I was saying that I was gonna become a slut for him.

He was reading my expressions a little too well because he replied, "Do it, bitch. You know you want to." And like a proud bitch, I took his dick in my mouth while stroking it. My mouth was wide open – it was that thick. I could feel my lips getting all stretched out just by taking the top inside.

I knew I was gonna get ripped if I didn't stop then. Yet I kept on sucking his dick and trying to take more and more of it inside my mouth. I moved my soft hands over his dick. He was enjoying a tight soft mouth trying so hard to take his dick in and please him. I felt like my lips were gonna tear apart.

He was completely hard by then and that was driving me crazy giving me lewd thoughts. I wanted to take it, take it all and choke on it like a dirty slut. Then spit as much as I can on it and worship it by giving it the best blowjob. I wanted to be his whore and show him that this Indian girl gave that black monster the best head he can get.

And I was drooling over his dick sucking it, moving my head over it. My eyes were watery and my mascara had been ruined. He grabbed my hair and start fucking my mouth like a pussy. I was enjoying this humiliation. I grabbed his ass motivating him to fuck my mouth harder with more water coming from my eyes.

I was making weird gulping sounds. He too was panting coz of my tight mouth and soft lips. So, I took charge again and took the dick out, started licking it top to bottom and then bottom to top. Then I grabbed his balls. They were warm and I was amazed by the feel of those massive balls in my soft hands.

I wanted to eat them. I wrapped my tongue around his dick and started moving it all over it. I was so lost in playing with his balls that I didn't realize that it was a short break time. Suddenly, many guys started coming to the toilet and it was filled with them in a minute. They were pissing.

One was taking a dump in the next cubicle while others were just talking about teachers, classes, and girls. Even my name was brought up like how massive tits I had and how they all wanted to fuck me. And there I was listening to how my class boys wanted to fuck me and piss and dump sounds.

While I gave blowjob to this big ugly black hunk. He took off my top and threw it on the floor. His dick was tearing my mouth and filled my throat completely. I felt like my throat was just another pussy he wanted to fuck. Although I was choking I have to say that it was the best experience I had till that moment.

He was overpowering me. I wanted to show him that I was a good slut and could keep his dick in my tight throat a little longer. My nose and eyes were all wet and my pussy was dripping wet. While people were talking and peeing outside. I tried to make the least sound.

But I wanted to scream to show him how much his dick was making me wild. He grabbed my tits and licked and kissed and pressed them. Then I wrapped my soft 34 sized tits around his dick. I knew that those were the softest things his dick had ever touched.

So, I was wanking his dick with my boobs while I sucked his top. Now I wanted him to fuck me. My ass cheeks were wide open bouncing like footballs and my hands were on the toilet seat which I didn't care about anymore. He pulled and pinched my soft nipples.

Then grasped my waist moving his big hands over my soft body feeling it. I was stretching yoga pants even more. I didn't care if they were gonna slit off. I just wanted that dick inside me. We had no condoms there as it was unplanned. I was happy in my mind about this.

I moved my upper body even lower to give my ass an even better outline which he loved. He finally decided to fuck me and took his dick and slapped my ass with it, he was so tight. My ass was shaking inviting him to fuck me like a cheap slut.

I could feel guys putting their ears on the cubicle door as they knew that there was a girl inside. I grasped my waist and rubbed his dick over my pussy moving it up and down and moaning for the guys outside. Then he pushed and half of his dick went straight inside.

Omg! Gosh! I never felt that good and my pussy had never been filled like that before. I could feel his raw black dick in my pussy. I wanted it to molest my pussy, rip it apart, destroy it and widen it so that no Indian guy can ever use it again. I wanted him to use me.

Then he pulled it out, spat on my pussy and shove it all inside.

He filled my pussy completely. But still, a part of his cock was left behind. I could feel his hot big cock touching the end of my pussy. He growled as my pussy was really tight for him.

At that point, I was even enjoying the sound of guys pissing right next to me. He then pushed me away and sat on his knees and suddenly shoved his tongue inside my pussy. It was very quick and even his tongue was so deep that it made me scream a little.

He was licking the insides of my pussy while playing with my clit with his fingers. Then he moved his tongue over my clit while fingering me. He fingered me for a while and then again grabbed my soft plump ass. He stood right behind me. I moaned, "Please, give it to me."

This drove him crazy and he just took his dick and thrust it all inside me. I had to bite my own fingers to stop myself from screaming. He started pounding me really fast. His whole dick was going in and out. He was a pro. That massive dick was ripping my pussy. I was being used like a slut.

I could feel my insides of pussy being stretched along with his dick when he made moves. He was driving me insane. My pussy was wide open then I wouldn't even feel an Indian dick inside. Yet I was holding my legs wide to keep that ass curve for him so that he didn't get disappointed.

Pleasing him was my duty which was making me happy and satisfied. Then suddenly I could sense guys were moving out of the bathroom. I was happy coz then I could scream. My boobs were crushed inside his wide muscular chest. My body was moving up and down over his cock like I was a masturbation tool.

My hands were on his shoulder. Then I took my boobs and started feeding him as I wanted him to taste those soft milky white tits. He pounded me like a slut. His dick was touching my G spot and I knew I was going to cum the third time. I was screaming and moaning the whole time. He was like a bull fucking me.

I was feeding him my tits with one hand and with the other hand, I was playing with his balls. While he moved that fuck toy(myself) over his dick. I never felt like a slut before and I was enjoying it. I couldn't control and cummed all over his dick. I kissed him while my left boob was still in his mouth.

I was kissing him madly for satisfying me like that sucking his lower pure black lip. He tore off my pussy and I could feel the hole stretched out. It was like that was the time when I finally lost my virginity. He didn't stop and took me out of the cubicle.

He threw me on the floor of the bathroom just in front of the piss booths and put my thin legs on his shoulder. He went missionary on me. Pounding his massive 9-inch black cock inside this white Indian girl. Then taking it out all the way just to pound it again. I was rolling my eyes and my tongue was out.

I was dizzy and lost my wits. But he kept on pounding me like he didn't care what happened to me. He just wanted that tight pussy hole and he was owning it. I gave it to him myself. I was now his private slut whom he could fuck anywhere anytime. I wouldn't mind pleasing him.

He grabbed my boobs like he was gonna rip them apart while sucking on my boobs. His dick was reaching my womb. The slap sounds our bodies were making with every stroke was really loud. My tight pussy which had been destroyed by then was begging for more of his dick.

He was fucking me even faster. I felt he was gonna cum. Damn! That was the best sex I could imagine as I was being fucked by a black horse. His raw dick making way through my pussy finding the best place to cum. Although my pussy was ruined and wide open, it was worth it.

Then I understood how right it was – once you go black, you never go back. A part of me wanted him to cum inside as I wanted to feel his hot cum inside. He was pounding me even harder and I was screaming. He pulled my hair and bit my neck. Then I felt something really hot flowing inside me.

Fuck! That nigger came inside me and he wasn't stopping. He filled my womb with cum and it was dripping from my pussy. He took his dick out and wasn't done yet. He was still cumming. He stood up and poured the rest over my face. I had no idea what was going on.

But I wanted to taste his cum. I squeezed his dick to swallow as much as I could and lay there for a few minutes like a satisfied slut. I enjoyed it. It was the best sex I had. He adjusted his clothes and left me there like he didn't notice me. He needed to cum and he used my pussy for that and left.

I got back my wits after about 5 minutes and my lower body was aching badly. I couldn't move but somehow pulled my yoga pants up. There was cum all over the floor and my face. I found my clothes, wore them and got out of the toilet before someone saw me.

I looked back and I had a moment of regret as so much cum was wasted on the floor. I wanted to eat it. His cum was so thick and tasty – the best I had ever tasted. He filled my mouth and my womb and left.

24. Ex

The beginning is from Rakesh's point of view.

It was a Saturday night. I had gone to a pub just to gulp down some drinks and have some fun. It was just a few months ago that I had broken up with Charmy. I don't know why but I was missing her very much that night. It was around 10-10:30 in the night that I saw someone familiar at the bar.

I looked properly and it was none other than Charmy. She was looking so so elegant yet very sexy. She was wearing an off-shoulder one-piece black dress which was complimenting her smooth milky white skin. The dress was showing an ample amount of her cleavage and a large part of those milky thighs.

The feeling of missing her just went to skyrocket high as I had not seen her since our breakup day. But we didn't make any eye contacts. I thought she was ignoring me and so I followed her. She joined her friends on the dance floor. I was so happy to see her swaying her sexy body.

I also went to the dance floor and slowly made room near her and said, "Hey Charmy," with a big smile on my face. She smiled a little but didn't say anything and turned her face away. I tried to talk to her many times but she was ignoring me at the highest level.

This was hurting me as no ex had ever made me look like a fool in that way. So I went to the bar to have some more drinks. While having those drinks, I was continuously ogling at her body which was looking mesmerizing. I decided that I wanted her that night.

After finishing the drinks, I went to her again and this time I was more serious. I said, "I wanna talk Charmy. Can we please go somewhere quiet and talk?" She did not wanna talk to me and so again, she turned her face away. That happened a few more times and I started losing my patience.

Last time as soon as she turned her face away, I smacked her ass with my hand. Damn, it felt so good. I knew Charmy liked that kind of smashing and smacking of her ass. She turned with a furious face towards me and raised her hand to hit me. But I got hold of her hand. I took her outside the pub with less noise and nobody around.

I thought that would be the perfect place to talk to her. She was very angry and wanted to go to the bar again. But I didn't leave her hand and my grip was strong for her. She could not go so she had to wait. "What are you doing, Rakesh?" she asked me with a furious face. I went near her and gave her a small kiss on her lips.

She did not respond though she was surprised and liked it, I guess. "I just want to be with you again, Charmy, nothing else. This thought had been eating me for days. the moment I saw you, I knew what I need to do. I just wanna be with you. Remember our good old days. We used to have so much fun."

While saying this, I slowly made my hand to her tits. I gave them a squeeze and they were as firm and tight as earlier. She was angry with my act but she liked it. "We can't be together again Rakesh; you know we broke up. I don't want to have feelings for you again because, in the end, I only get hurt." She was pretty emotional on this one.

I did not expect that. I couldn't control and kissed her and she responded that time. It was so good to suck on those lips. But we parted our ways soon as anybody could come out or go inside the club. I told her, "Let's just enjoy tonight and let's see how it goes. I promise I will try to make it as memorable as possible."

She wasn't sure about this but gave me a nod. Then we went inside the club again. We directly went to the dance floor after gulping down a few drinks. The music was good with few lights and people were mostly drunk. So nobody knew what was happening around them.

While dancing, I slowly took her to one of the corners of a dance floor with nobody there. We started dancing again, this time with more intensity. Our hands were roaming around each other's body. I couldn't take my eyes off those beautiful tits which were literally popping out of that dress.

She knew that and said, "You can touch them if you like." I was on cloud nine hearing this. As soon as she said this, I turned her around and started playing with her tits over the dress. Half of the tits were literally hanging out of the dress. God, I missed them. I gave her neck a smooch and continued playing with them.

Now from Charmy's point of view.

I never expected that this would be happening with me that night. I was ready for some action and that was why I was wearing that short black dress. But never expected this with Rakesh. He was so good at playing with my tits which badly needed some hands on them.

I could feel a big bulge poking into my ass through his jeans. I slowly put my hand over it and started rubbing it. It was a nice big hard cock and as soon as I felt it, I knew I needed it inside me. The lioness inside me was awake then and I needed him at any cost.

He was busy playing with my tits, groping and mauling them and then he moved one of his hands to my thighs and soon inside the dress to my drenched panties. I was so wet with him playing with my body that my panties were drenched with juices.

He was slowly rubbing them while playing with my tits and kissing my neck and ears as well. I was really horny at that moment. I was rubbing his cock over the pants very hard. I needed him inside me right then and so I whispered in his ears, "I need you inside me, Rakesh!"

He looked at me, took hold of me and we went straight to the car parking lot. He pushed me into the car and started kissing me wildly. We both needed this and our places were a long way away. So he suggested that we should move to some hotel but I couldn't wait till then.

I asked him to fuck me in the car itself. He was surprised to see this sultry side of mine. We went inside the car and parked it in a corner where almost no cars were there. As soon as he did that, we pounced on each other. He adjusted the front seat so that he could lie down and I was on top of him.

I pounced on him like he was my prey and we started kissing again. I started unbuttoning his shirt and soon he was shirtless. That muscular body I was aching for was in front of me then. I started rubbing his chest and moving down licking his body up to his abdomen.

I soon removed his jeans and there was a huge bulge in his boxers. I started feeling it over the boxers and rubbing it. That made him crazy. While playing with my boobs, he unzipped my dress, making me semi-naked only in my bra and panties. My panties were so wet with my juices.

It only made both of us hornier. He was playing with my tits and pussy as I was busy playing with his cock over the boxers. I could feel and smell lots of precum and it was driving me crazy. He removed my panties. I removed his boxers and he directly inserted his big 8-inch rod in my wet pussy.

There was no need for any kind of lubrication since we both were very horny and wet. He inserted his cock and started fucking me. I did miss his cock and it was feeling so so good. He started sucking on my boobs, sucking one with his mouth while pressing the other one as he kept fucking me.

The hard cock was moving in and out of my pussy at such a fast rate that I was moaning loudly and taking his name, "Yes! Yes! Fuck me Rakesh! Fuck me harder!" My moans were very loud and to shut them, he kissed me. That was such a great moment.

He was kissing me while his hands were busy playing with my tits and he was fucking my pussy so hard. It was so slutty that we were having sex in his car. It was having so little space but we never felt uncomfortable or anything. We were busy enjoying the fuck and playing with each other.

It was 10 minutes of hard intense fuck and damn, it was so sexy. I was near cumming but he was going on at full speed. After a few strokes, he said he wanted to cum inside me. I too wanted to feel his hot cum inside my wet pussy. He started fucking me harder and harder.

I could feel the tension building up in his cock. We both knew that we were going to cum soon. And we did, with a loud moan, we both did cum. His cum inside my pussy was feeling so good. As we finished, I was still lying on top of him. We indulged in a long smooch and kissed each other like there was no tomorrow.

We checked and it was around 12.30 am. We decided to move to his place as I wanted more of that cock.

25. Muscled Man

I standing all alone on a dark road surrounded by jungle with heavy rain falling over my head. I was totally drenched in the rain. Also, I wasn't carrying an umbrella. I was regretting denying my friends' offer when they said that they would drop me off.

Thank God! I saw a car coming and I was hoping that it would give me a lift. You people must be wondering as to what actually happened. Well, allow me to clear your confusion. It was one of my friends' party and we all insisted on having it inside a farmhouse in a jungle.

At the party, I met a guy and we got into talking. We decided to go to his flat after the party and therefore, I declined my friends' lift offer. I was waiting after the party for the guy but couldn't find him. Out of insult and rage, I stormed out of there without thinking much and here was I all helpless.

As the car came closer, I went on the middle of the road waving and praying for it to stop and it did. I went towards it and found a guy in the driver's seat. I told him about my situation and he agreed to help me. I got in and he started driving. Seeing that I was drenched, he gave me a small towel to dry myself.

While taking it, I accidentally touched his wrist. Then I took the towel, dried myself a bit and looked at him. Scanning him carefully, I saw muscles popping out of his t-shirt. They were popping out from every part of his body. Sensing that I was eyeing him, he told me that he was a professional bodybuilder.

He was returning from a show which ended very late. While he said this, I couldn't really concentrate on his words as his well-sculptured body had me mesmerized and spellbound. With all this going on, the car took a turn and we found the road blocked by a tree.

It must have fallen due to the strong winds and the rain. We stopped there, thought for a bit and then took a small narrow road through the jungle. We had only gone about 2-3 km when we heard a boom noise. We found out that one of the rear tires was gone.

I was in the middle of a dense jungle with an unknown guy looking like a muscled dude inside a broken car with rain pouring heavily outside. We looked at each other and thought for some time. Then he asked me to wait inside the car while he would go and look for a house nearby to spend the night.

But I was scared and told him that I would go with him. Somehow, he convinced me to wait inside and then he disappeared into the jungle. I couldn't even call anybody for help as my mobile had shut down a long time ago. I don't know for how long did I wait but it felt like an eternity.

Then he came back all drenched in rain. He asked me if I could walk for a bit as he had found a hut nearby. I was more than happy to get out of the car. He took out a duffle bag of his car and we started walking. After walking for some time in the rain, I saw the hut he was talking about.

It was wooden made, a bit higher from the ground and there was a ladder. We climbed in the hut and found it just enough for us to spend the night.
As we waited there inside the hut for some time. The rain slowed down and soon, it was drizzling outside.

Both of us were totally drenched and needed to dry off ourselves. Oh! I forgot to tell you. I found out his name and it was Rakesh. He gave me the same towel he had given me in the car and asked me to dry off myself. He took his shirt off and squeezed it to dry it.

As both of us were cold, Rakesh started a fire in the firepit inside the hut. In that yellow bonfire light, I saw his full body stacked with muscles. It was glistening due to the reflection from the droplets of water. I was watching him closely lost in his body. Then suddenly he asked if I liked what I was seeing.

I couldn't respond in voice but just nodded my head up and down. Seeing that he smiled and said it was his turn to be impressed. I denied but he pulled me closer and put my right hand on his chest. Mesmerized, I started caressing his chest, biceps, and abs getting all horny and wet.

All of a sudden, he pushed me towards a wall, pinned me against it and brought his lips closer to mine. I could feel his warm breath on my face. As he tried going for a kiss, I pushed him back and at that snap. It was like he woke up from sleep.

Then apologized saying he wouldn't force me into anything. I would be lying if I say that I was okay. I was both scared and confused at that moment while still admiring his structure. He then stepped back to the fire and suggested me to remove my wet shirt as I might catch a cold.

For some time, I hesitated but he was right. So, I agreed and went to a corner and facing the wall. I undid the buttons. While taking the shirt off, turned my head slightly and saw him watching my sexy toned back as I was revealing it. Since there wasn't any other way.

I turned towards him hiding my boobs in the bra. I can say that Rakesh was really enjoying this view of a wet girl in a bra with her body parts glistening in the yellow light of the fire. As we were both feeling cold, we sat in front of the fire facing each other.

We were both seated when Rakesh complimented, "Those are some really nice boobs and of great size." Hearing that, I blushed. As we were feeling the warmth of the fire, my mind was exploding. What should we do next? I'm half naked, wet, sitting in front of a stranger who has a structure of a Greek God, in a bra.

His body is so hot plus he is looking at me right now and smiling which obviously means he likes me and my structure. I think I like him too and he did try to kiss me forcefully. Then he stepped back saying he wouldn't do anything by force. What is he exactly thinking?

Everything was making me very nervous and scared. Yet somehow, I was feeling thrilled and horny at the same time. While all this was going on in my mind, both of us were stealing glances at each other. Also, I was trying to dry off my shirt by holding it a bit close to the fire,

Suddenly I felt a tingling sensation in my boobs and it was only increasing. It was due to the wet bra. I felt very itchy around my boobs. I wanted to get out of that thing. But if I would have done that, Rakesh would have got a full view of my boobs. Well, there wasn't any other way and so I did what he said.

I went to the corner, removed my bra and itched myself and then squeezed the bra to dry it. While I was busy doing that, I think Rakesh was enjoying a sexy and beautiful view of my back with a side view of my boobs. Out of the blue, he asked smilingly, "Won't you let me feel your beautiful body, as I did to you?"

I looked at him surprised. He also suggested me to remove my shorts if I didn't wanna catch a cold coz they were wet too and water was dripping from them. I was really surprised by his boldness but I really liked it too. Without wasting any time, I put my bra back on and removed my shorts.

Then slowly walked back to my place in front of the fire. I stood in front of Rakesh just in my red bikini. Then I lay down on the hay there with my back towards the ceiling looking at him with a grin. I don't know when I made up my mind to have him inside me.

He understood my invitation. Just as he got up to come towards me, I stopped him and pointed at the jeans he was wearing. Seeing my gesture, he smiled and hastily took it off. Then walked slowly towards me, sat beside me and touched my back.

Although he had been sitting in front of the fire for nearly half an hour, his hands were still cold. When they touched my body, it sent a chill down my spine and I let out a very light moan. While feeling my back, he did something extraordinary. He started kissing my legs and then the whole back.

His actions were so pleasurable that I just shut my eyes lying there feeling his affection. Then he went one step further. He turned me over and started caressing my upper body like pressing my boobs over the bra and kissing my inner thighs. The rain became more violent with occasional lightning.

From my legs, he moved upwards kissing every part. Then he started kissing my stomach, followed by my cleavage, neck and then finally he was totally on top of me. He put his lips on my lips. As we were about to kiss, I heard loud thunder. Our lips touched each other and we kissed like there was no tomorrow.

As the mad kissing went on, I hugged him tightly. Clutching his hair with one hand and caressing his triceps and back with the other one. Feeling all the muscles while one of his hands grabbed me by my waist and the other one was pressing my boobs over the bra.

He then took my left boob out of the bra and rubbed on the nipple which literally made me go mad. He stopped kissing and started licking my neck with occasionally biting my ear. Then he went down, started sucking on my left boob giving small bites on the nipple.

He took out the right one and gave it a small kiss and moved towards the naval part and started kissing and licking on it. Going further down, he started kissing on my pussy over my panty in between giving a small finger rub on it while his other hand was caressing my boobs.

These pleasures had made me crazy being unable to cope up with them. I took charge and got on top of him giving him a deep smooch. I started returning the favor with caressing his whole body full of muscles and kissing them. I kissed his chest, biceps, 6 pack abs individually while flickering and playing with his nipples.

Later, I started kissing and licking them while my hands explored the best part of his body. The big tight bulge which my hand felt made me want it even more. I started rubbing it over his undies. I moved down towards his dick, kissed it over his undies.

I rubbed my face and my boobs over it and made it even harder for him to control. The tool looked as if it was about to tear apart his undies. I then gave him the wildest pleasure he could imagine. Finally, I gave in to my own desire. I removed his undies and his dick sprang out like a spring attached shaft.

It was dark brown, about eight and a half inches long. With veins full of raging blood making, it looks like a dick with muscles. Hard as a rock but butter smooth with a little drop of precum at its end. I couldn't resist anymore and started licking and kissing it vigorously.

After a while, I took it in my mouth sucking it as if it was the last one on the earth. All of a sudden, he gave a huge push gagging my throat and then took it out. I looked at Rakesh like a wild cat whose food got snatched from it. He pulled me back, took off my bra and threw it away and tore apart my panty.

Changing positions, he came on the top of me and sucked on my right boob while pinching the left nipple. Then went for the left one while pinching the right. My right hand clutched on to his dick constantly rubbing and feeling it. He sucked and bit my boobs till they were red and the nipples were sore.

He then gave me a lip kiss and moved towards my pussy. First gave a gentle kiss, sucked on the pussy lips, licked the clitoris driving me crazy for sex. Then he started sucking my pussy and licking it sending chills down my spine. While doing so, he also started entering his finger in and out.

I felt like I was about to explode when I had the wildest orgasm of my life. While I laid there with juices flowing out, he licked my pussy all clean. Then got up and brought his dick near my mouth. The smell was so intoxicating that couldn't control and started licking it again.

He then pushed it in my mouth. I gladly took it, made it dripping wet with saliva. He took it out, positioned himself in front of my pussy and with one big force he pushed all of it inside my pussy. Both the parts being greased beautifully, his dick went smoothly inside me and touched the end of my vagina.

He paused for a bit feeling the warmth and the tightness of my insides. Then started his movements. First, they were slow and long strokes, making me feel the structure of his muscular dick and driving me crazy. I was craving for it for an hour or so and finally, it was inside.

After a minute or so, his motion became faster. At that time, my sexual desire was the peak highest and wanting more of him, I urged, "Fuck me Rakesh. Fuck me more. Give it to me. Come on, you monster." These constant urges made him hornier. He started pounding my pussy all the more wildly.

Then he held my butt vertically in the air and started pounding it vigorously with all the stamina he had. The pleasure was so much that my words and moans became one. I felt like my insides were about to melt. And finally, I had the 2nd one, a huge orgasm.

He took his tool out and then again inserted his fingers. This time two of them and started a circular motion inside. It just made me moan even louder and the desire to have him inside me again just doubled. He then took them out, placed them near his lips and sucked off all juices from his fingers.

Licking them clean and then pulled me closer and smooched me again for long sucking my lips and tongue. While kissing, we exchanged our positions. I came on top of him, sat on his rock hard dick. It felt as if it went inside more than ever pushing the end wall.

Then I started moving up and down over him. While he got up a bit and took my right boob in his mouth sucking it while holding me with his left hand. My lust had taken over me completely. All I wanted was this man to devour me. In that position, I gave him my left boob to suck on, he did that gladly.

He then held my waist and started thrusting from downwards. Me jumping on him, he pounding me from downwards, it was heaven for me. After a while, we changed positions again. He came on top of me, pushed his tool inside and started destroying my insides.

I was mad and was crazily asking for more looking in his eyes with lust. We lip locked and sucked each other. He started giving long and powerful strokes and with each one, I felt as if my insides were about to be punctured. I held on to him with all my nails dug deep in his back.

The pain from that made him even crazier. So much so that he then lifted me up in the air. He stood firm as I wrapped my legs around his waist, with my one hand clutching his back and the other hand clutching his hair sucking his tongue. He started thrusting me, grabbing me with one hand.

Another one lifting my butt with one finger in my ass. He fucked my brains out like that for a while. I sensed his dick becoming harder and thicker than ever. My insides were about to melt sensing that we were both about to cum. He gave a final big thrust and we both came together.

I was moaning at my highest pitch which got lost in the heavy rain. The weather outside was cold but both of us were feeling hot, panting and sweating heavily. We both lay down on the hay there, with my head on his chest and arms around his sexy Greek body hugging him tightly.

It was not a stop to the fun-filled night that I experienced. The hut was a witness to the hard fuck that happened all night. All night, my moans must have been heard in the jungle.

26. College Fest

It was the last day of my college festival. The Grand Finale had just ended where they announced the winner of a college beauty pageant. I was waiting for my friend Anjali outside the makeup room. As I stood outside the door, Aryan Kumar walked past me.

I stared at him wide-eyed and could feel him tense and turn around. His blue eyes were sparkling. He flashed a smile and went inside. He was one of the hottest young models amongst the group of 3 from MTV Model Hunt. They had come to judge and mentor our participants.

As he passed by, I could see Anjali talking to the other 2 models – Rakesh and Aadam. They were good-looking themselves, but Aryan was a Greek God! Anjali was talking animatedly. I could see Aadam point his finger at me. As I went closer, I heard they were planning a night out and I was not up for it.

I told Anjali the same. While I said these words, I glanced at Aryan who was standing at a little distance from us. I could clearly see that he was gazing at my boobs that peeked out a bit from my maroon off the shoulder top. Anjali then took me aside.

Anjali: Charmy, come on babe! They are such hot models. We will have fun. You never know what might happen. I think Aadam is really into me. Please!

I still did not want to go but then Aryan came up to us and said in his deep voice, "Charmy. Why don't you join us, babe! You won't be disappointed." Flashing his killer smile, he convinced me for the plan. I don't know when I slept in the car.

Anjali told me later that Aryan kept touching me at the pretext of holding me while I was sleeping. As soon as we reached the farmhouse, I could sense something different about Anjali. Her face was flushed as if she had a long make out session. Aadam was holding her by the waist as we walked in.

Settling in the hall, Aryan went to get us a few beers. There were whiskey, tequila, and vodka as well but we decided to start off slow. We talked about the fest and the guys shared a couple of casting couch incidents they had in their industry.

By the time we were 2 beers down, Aadam and Anjali could not stop kissing each other! Her crop top was already pulled up a bit and Aadam started fidgeting with her pant. My face turned red. I decided to put this to a stop.

Me: Guys! Let's play 'Truth or Dare'. Anjali, bitch. You need to control yourself.

She just smirked at me while Rakesh got an empty bottle to get the game started. On the first turn, it was, unfortunately, my turn to choose. I decided to play safe and picked 'Truth'.

Aryan: Such a loser man! Alright. Let's make it spicy. What's your favourite sex position?

Me: Doggy style. Love it when the bodies make the sound against each other.

Maybe it was the alcohol, but I said too much. His eyes glinted as he spun the bottle again. Now it was Aadam's turn and he chose 'Dare'. Anjali immediately told him to remove his shirt which he happily did. She quickly gave his chest a bite before spinning the bottle again.

Aryan brought us some whiskey. But since I don't like it much, I poured myself some vodka and ice. It was now Aryan's turn. He chose to 'Dare' as well.
Rakesh spoke up before I had a chance. He told Aryan to dance. Now I was disappointed a bit since I missed my chance of doing something naughty.

But once he started dancing, I was taken aback. He kept staring at me while dancing. Slowly he opened his shirt, one button at a time. I had to stop myself from drooling as his body shone in the light. He had a waxed his chest which added to his sex appeal.

My pussy started feeling ticklish and I could not take my eyes off him. The bottle spun and it was my turn. The vodka kicked in and I picked 'Dare'. Aadam and Aryan were all topless now. While Rakesh wasn't in his complete senses since he consumed too much alcohol.

I bet Anjali must be waiting to fuck Aadam. But it was my 'Dare'. Before anybody could say anything, Anjali thought of playing cupid. She told me that Aryan would suck off the beer that will be poured on my navel. She quickly came near me and asked me to lie down on the floor and instructed Aryan. She pulled down my top such that my bra could be seen.

Anjali: Come on Aryan. Go for it.

And she started pouring beer on my stomach. As soon as it touched me, it made me shiver. Aryan didn't wait for a second. He quickly started drinking every drop that was being poured on my stomach. I can still feel the pleasure of his mouth. He was sucking my whole belly.

His tongue was working its magic on my navel. But Anjali didn't play fair and deliberately poured some beer on my top and my boobs. Angrily, I got up and went to the washroom to clean myself up. I had no other option and therefore, I removed my wet bra. I came out wearing only the top which was wet.

As soon as I came out, I could see Aryan hungrily looking at my white boobs from the semi-transparent top. I looked around and saw Rakesh dozing. Aryan pointed at the bedroom. I could hear loud moans from inside. I realized what was going on between Anjali and Aadam.

I decided to move away from the sexually charged atmosphere. I went to the kitchen to fetch a glass of water since any other drink would have made my mind dizzy. As I opened the tap, I could feel surrounded by someone. It didn't take me long to figure out it was Aryan.

He kissed my bare neck. Short, sweet pecks across my neckline. I could feel his cock from behind pushing against my ass crack. He felt huge even from the outside. Alcohol, his stubble grazing my skin, his breath. My pussy had it's own mind as it secreted juices.

I knew what I exactly wanted and needed that moment. I was too fascinated by him to say or do anything. While his hands worked their magic on my skin, I could feel my hands shiver.

I turned my face towards him and dropped the water on his body playfully. A hot model who could have got any girl in his bed was going crazy for me. The thought drove me crazy as I pulled him towards me. We kissed wildly in that position. I knew that night was going to be memorable.

Within no time, he removed my top and was pressing and kneading my boobs. He was circling my areolas with his fingers and his lips were working on my bare shoulders giving me love bites. He removed his jeans and underwear at one go and his cock stood up saluting me.

He undid my skirt before I could even protest. The very next moment, we were standing naked in front of each other. He picked me up in his muscular arms and placed me on the kitchen platform. Opening my legs wide apart, his lips found my dripping wet pussy.

He kissed my soft pussy lips and then gave a couple of bites. I was jumping and moving in excitement. My hands were on his head pushing his face deeper in my pussy. Then he started using his tongue. I let out a big moan. After a few minutes of sucking and licking my pussy like it's the last thing in the world, he found my clit.

He started making designs on it with his tongue. He knew the right places to lick, kiss and caress. I could feel my orgasm developing. All I could say was "Aahh, Aryan! Don't stop, don't ever stop that" before I released my juices and was breathless.

He cleaned my pussy juices while I was still resting on the cold granite.

He had not lost his hardness during that time. He stood in front of me and looked me in the eye. Lifting me off the platform, I wrapped my legs around his hips as he carried me across the room to the sofa. My breasts massaging his muscled chest.

He dropped me on the sofa, spread my legs and rubbed his cock against my pussy. His hardness made me wetter and in one push he went inside. My eyes popped out and I had to take a deep breath. He felt bigger after he went inside. He kept varying his pace as he started hitting the right places

Our bodies went 'thap, thap, thap.' as he pounded me, holding my legs apart. As he went deeper in my pussy, my legs folded. I welcomed him in my open arms. I could feel his sweat on my hands as I kissed him. He pulled out of me and came near my face. I took his cock in my mouth and started blowing him.

Swirling my tongue on his dick head, I stroked his balls with my other hand. I sucked him, spitting occasionally to lubricate it further. He throat-fucked me and I started gagging. Pulling out, he lay down on the couch and pulled my body towards him. I climbed on top.

Instead of facing him, I turned the other way. I pushed his cock inside my cunt and started grinding against him. I loved his feeling inside me as I increased my speed. As I rode him, he slipped a finger around and stroked my clit. Faster and faster as I drilled myself against his hard cock, he started moaning as well.

Smack. I got one tight slap on my ass that triggered a wave of orgasm inside me. I never knew this would excite me so much. I clenched his cock tighter inside my pussy. I could feel his dick shiver as he suddenly pulled out. He stroked himself and turned me around as he started fucking me doggy style.

"Your favourite, isn't it?" he growled in my ears as his cock went in and out of my pussy. "Ah, yes. Ah.Ah.Ah!" was all I could moan back in pleasure. He changed his angle a little so he could go in deeper and started hitting my G-spot. I could not control my voice as with every stroke, he hit my skin.

I was enjoying my pussy being fucked silly by this hot man! He held my hips as he finally got tired of fucking me and pulled me by the hair for the final rush of sex. One, two, three. Within 20 strokes he pulled himself out and started cumming all over my face and breasts.

I was red from the long fuck I got but a wave of happiness passed over me as I smiled at him.

27. Black Stud

I was so excited about that weekend! My favourite band was coming to a concert in Delhi. I just could not wait for the weekend to come. I and my girl gang of 4 had got ourselves passes for the event.

I had already planned my outfit for the night. I put on a red coloured halter top. It showed a bit of my size 34 breasts from the side along with a black leather skirt that stopped 2 inches above my knee. My legs were shining because of the chocolate wax I got done the previous day.

Since it was a concert, I also wore a couple of LED bands on my wrist. A deep dark red lipstick and loose hair completed my look for the night. I was all ready to dance the night away. I met my friends at the entrance of the venue – all of them looked stunning in their skirts/crop tops and shorts.

One of my friends got us a few funky hairbands with glowing devil horns. Damn, I already felt naughty donning them. Since it was just 6 pm, we decided to get ourselves a couple of beers before the main event kicked off. One beer led to another.

By the time the show started, we were a couple of pints down already plus had a pint each in our hands. The music started off slowly with the crowd still coming in. After an hour of pre-show, there was a 10-minute break. We were all sweaty after all the dancing and shouting and badly needed to quench our thirst.

As I went near the drinks stall, I could see a huge line. However, there were a few well-built guys who seemed to be Africans quite ahead in the queue. I decided to use my charm. I quickly walked up to one of them, put my hand on his arm and smiled at him.

I said, "Hey, can you buy me some beer please?" and handed him a 2000 rupee note. He just shrugged, excused himself and got an entire crate from the counter. Thanking him, I left. I and my friends chugged down a few pints and started dancing again as the music picked up the tempo.

I was swaying my head around, with my dark black hair flying in the air. The sweat drops building on my torso and neck. One of my friends slyly pulled out a tequila bottle from her bag and passed it around. After a couple of shots, all 5 of us started dancing a little more wildly.

The tequila was beginning to show its effect. By 8 pm, the main event started and the crowd went crazy. Listening to songs like 'Yellow' and 'Sky Full of Stars' live, my happiness knew no bounds. I wanted to have a closer look at the singers.

All around me, people were jumping, shouting and dancing making me feel hopelessly single. I turned around to see a muscular guy dancing in a group. On closer inspection, I concluded that it was the same guy who got me the beer. I leaned close to him.

I told him to raise me in the air as I wanted to have a closer look at my favorite singers. He didn't say anything but smiled a little. He picked me up like I was a tiny little doll in his veiny arms. He made me sit on his shoulders such that my legs were around his face.

I finally had a closer look at my favourite band's singers. I started swaying my arms and shouting with joy. The African guy was holding my thighs to keep me balanced on his shoulders. I also held his head for support sometimes. I was a little tipsy due to all the drinks that I had. But I was still in my complete senses.

I looked down to see the muscled man rubbing my milky soft

white thighs. His hands were not smooth. But I kind of liked the roughness as I could feel the warmth my pussy had started to gain already. The music got louder. The crowd along with me and the person I was sitting on were lost in the music.

We were shouting as loud as we could and dancing and enjoying to the fullest. This guy finally put me down. My friends pulled me again amongst themselves. I felt a little wet down after the guy's rubbing my thighs. But I couldn't do anything except to enjoy the concert with my friends around.

It was about 9:30 and the concert were close to its end. The crowd went crazy dancing. All the bodies were swinging their hips together when I felt a tall person standing right behind me. I looked behind and obviously, it was the same guy. I just smiled at him and started shouting and dancing again with all my energy.

I got my first surprise of the evening when the guy pressed my ass over my skirt. I was in full mood to break all barriers and enjoy what I was getting that night. So, I just kept smiling and doing what I was doing as he explored my soft ass cheeks over my skirt.

He then took his hands away and came quite close to me. I could feel his hard meat grinding against my back. Yes, my back as he was taller than me. He then placed both his hands on my naked waist. His big hands covered almost my entire belly.

Lifting me slightly, he pulled in so as to grind his cock in my ass crack over my skirt. I really liked this move of his. I was swinging my hips against his rod over and over. He turned me around such that we were facing each other. The dancing was still going on.

Our bodies were grinding against each other. He suddenly whispered in my ear in a gruff voice, "Hey, you want to get out of here for some time and come back?" His voice sent shivers down my spine. It was exciting me beyond my imagination to see a well-built black stud who was rock hard all because of me.

I just smiled at him which obviously gave him a green signal. Then we started walking hand in hand. We sneaked our way through the crowd. All along, he was squeezing my ass and pulling my hands in front of his cock. We found a tiny secluded corner behind the tents.

That was enough to turn up our hormonal levels. He pulled me in his arms and started kissing me. As he forced his tongue inside, he found the zipper on my top at the back. He pulled it down exposing my breasts caged in my bra. My white skin shone in the darkness.

His palms roughly pulled my bra aside exposing my already sensitive nipples. He pinched one of them as he kissed my neck. Breathing faster, I gasped, "What's your name?" Christopher. Just one word as he put his mouth on my breast and started sucking it.

As he worked on my right breast with his mouth, his right hand was caressing my thigh. Stroking from the outside, he rubbed his palm on my inner thigh. I was already getting very wet by our make out. Suddenly, he clasped my already wet pussy in his palm.

My eyes popped out as he looked me in the eye and started rubbing my pussy. Standing so close, I could feel his hardness. He just rubbed his cock over my skirt while kissing. I could not take it anymore as I felt my breath becoming shallower. I shrieked as his thumb stroked my clitoris.

I had my first orgasm (I did not know that it was just the first of many that night). I had barely recovered from my orgasm when I felt the hardness in my hands. When I looked, I found that he had lowered his pants and his undies both at once. Trust me though it was not the biggest, it was the thickest penis I had ever seen.

His dick was covered in precum. I stroked him a bit but he kept pushing me down. So, I went on my knees. The grass hurt a bit but the big black cock looked appealing. I took it in my mouth.

It would not go beyond the first few inches. Christopher was thrusting against me and somehow, I took half of it in me.

Using my hands on his balls I started building up a tempo, alternating between sucking and licking him. Realizing it was getting late, I decided to use my favourite trick. I sucked him faster while pumping his cock using my hands. I stuck out my boobs against his thighs and suddenly bit him.

That drove Christopher over the edge and his cum shot in my mouth. Though I spat it out, some of it still spilled on my clothes. What surprised me was that he was still semi-erect after having an orgasm. So, we were done with our first session for the night (That moment I didn't know how many more sessions were to follow).

After Christopher' ejaculation, I didn't want to waste any more time. I just couldn't miss my favourite band's musical ending for anything. So, we both came back to the concert. On the way back, he kept insisting me to remove my completely wet panties. But I didn't coz my skirt was quite short.

The entire crowd could have seen me without my panties had somebody raised me high in the air again. Anyways, I didn't find any of my friends in the huge gathering. But I didn't pay much attention to them and started grooving to the final songs of the evening.

The evening was promising to be a really long and interesting!

28. Black Stud 2

Christopher went to the drinks' stall and got us some soft drinks. I had seen his monster cock. I knew just seeing and milking it wouldn't do. All started jumping, shouting and dancing again. I got my second surprise when I felt a hand inside my skirt going towards my inner thighs.

I instantly knew whose hand it was but I was in no mood to stop it from reaching its final destination. Yes, it did reach there. He startled me when he slid aside my panty and inserted his thick finger in my already wet pussy. I just couldn't resist that and shouted with all the more enthusiasm.

The speed of his fingerfucking me with his hard cock hitting my back again. He whispered in my ears, "I would love to fuck your tight pussy in my bed tonight. What say?" As he whispered these words in my ears, the last song just got over and fireworks started all around us. My pussy was bursting its own crackers.

I turned around, gave him a peck on his cheek. Thrusting my hips against his hard cock and biting his ears, I shouted, "Yes! I'd love that." He pulled me out from the crowd and took me to the car parking before it got crowded. I could see his bulge from his linen pants.

We jumped in his car and got out of the parking lot. Though his hotel was 15 minutes away, it felt longer. I messaged my friends that I would find my way back. I told them to not wait for me and head back. But I didn't waste this time and removed my wet panty in a sexy manner and threw it at his face.

He just smelled and licked it and with his left hand, started rubbing my pussy. I also took out his already hard cock out from the cage and stroked it while he drove. He looked at me with fire in his eyes. I knew from that look that he is going to fuck me hard. We made our way to the lift towards the 15th floor.

In the lift itself, he removed my top and started biting on my boobs over my bra. Heading into his room, we started kissing as my back pressed against the wall. I removed his t-shirt while his hands worked on my skirt's zipper. I could feel my wetness. As I pulled his pants down, his dick sprang out and seemed bigger than before.

I started stroking him and sucked his balls for a bit. He pulled me up and literally threw me on the bed and got on top of me. He placed his penis near my pussy and in one stroke tried pushing the whole fucking thing inside. It was too much for me and I screamed.

I was very tight for such a large, thick piece of meat. Even with my pussy juices, it took him a few minutes to fill me completely. He started thrusting deeper and harder with each stroke as his lips found my nipples. With his tongue stroking and biting my tits and his dick inside me.

He had found a perfect rhythm. I was moaning as every stroke hit me in places that I didn't know existed in me. My nails dug into his back. After nearly 15 minutes, he turned me over and started fucking me doggy style. His pelvis hit my ass and our bodies made sounds as he pounded me.

While he fucked me in that position, my tits were hanging in the air and slapping against each other. Out of the blue, he spanked me. Not once, not twice but at least 10 times. Every time I let out a sharp moan. Pulling out of me, he came near my breasts which were by then red.

"I want to fuck your tits," he said. I pushed my breasts together and he spat on them. He slowly slid between them and started thrusting and sliding his cock between my valley. I wanted to ride him now. Going on top, I tried taking his cock inside me. My pussy burnt by the amount of sex we had.

He started to match me stroke for stroke. As his pelvis thrust against my vagina, I could feel it stroking my clitoris. Harder and harder as he pumped, my orgasm started building up. He pulled my nipples sharply. That made me shriek as I started cumming tightening my vagina against his still hard penis.

Christopher didn't stop as wave after wave of orgasms hit me. Since he hadn't cum yet, he turned me around and started thrusting like a machine. He slapped my boobs and made them red. I didn't know. But as he started kissing me again, I could feel one more orgasm building inside me.

He picked up his pace and I knew he would cum soon. I spread my legs wider and he grabbed that opportunity. He took me in his arms and put me on the table. I put my legs up on his shoulders since I was very flexible due to my regular yoga practice.

His cock went more smoothly as our body fluids mixed with each other. With one final push, he pulled his cock out. And for the final surprise of the night, he pushed 3 fingers inside me and finger fucked me as fast as possible. I started cumming again.

Before I could even finish, he pushed me on my knees and had an orgasm all over my breasts. He spilled out a huge load and I had his jizz all over me. Satisfied, he smiled for the first time that night. His penis still wouldn't go down. However, his wicked smile showed me he had some other ideas.

With my ass on the table, he spread my legs and went down on me. I could feel his hot breath on my pussy as he spread my vagina and put his tongue on me. I was very sensitive due to having multiple orgasms. His tongue started working its magic on me.

I could feel his hands rubbing and pressing my thighs. Slowly he started caressing my inner thighs with his palms. His tongue glided across my pussy. He kissed me, licked me and randomly bit my labia. My head was spinning with pleasure. When he sucked my clitoris, I had to wrap my legs tightly around his head and hold the table.

The pleasure was unbearable. He was sucking my clitoris as his fingers opened up my vagina and went inside. He pushed a couple inside me while his lips and tongue worked on my clitoris. I was having a hard time focusing. I was going to cum very soon. Suddenly, he thrust his pinky finger near my asshole.

I screamed in joy as another orgasm hit me. I squirted very little on his face. He looked at me with his liquid covered face and stood up. I could see his erection but I wasn't prepared for what came next. He pulled my hand and took me near the window. I could see the lights of the city.

Pushing my back a little lower, he started pounding my pussy as I stood facing the city lights. My white skin had red marks all over it. I knew my body would collapse soon. My breasts were hitting the windows and soon he placed them in his rough palms. Pressing my breasts in both hands he fucked me from behind.

With every thrust, he went deeper. I could feel every inch inside me as he stroked. He started grunting and his voice became hoarse as a big orgasm built up in his balls. He pulled my hair in a pony and screwed me roughly. My pussy clenched against him. He could not control himself.

Load after a load of hot white cum filled me. I could feel his balls unloading the sticky fluid. After a couple of minutes, both of us collapsed on the floor. My pussy was leaking his cum and my body felt sore. I couldn't help but smile after such a long satisfactory fuck. Christopher had already closed his eyes and his cock finally slept for a while.

29. Wedding

It was a chilling winter night of January when I went to attend the marriage ceremony of a close friend. The function was in a distant place. I got my separate room booked in the same hotel.

Our gang of girls was super excited as this was the first marriage among our friends. So, it was 8 in the evening. I was ready in my room. But as the baraat hadn't come, I was resting in my room. I don't know when I started to read sex stories which undoubtedly made me a little horny.

Then there was a knock on the door. As the baraat had come, I had to go down then. I went down with all the others. I was near the stage and rituals were going on but my mind was occupied with lust and sex. As I was thinking all this, I saw a guy standing at a distance gazing at me.

No doubt I was looking super-hot in that saree which was a low waist. And hence exposing a good part of my waist with a deep neck blouse. And yes, I made sure I gave a good view of my cleavage. There was this guy looking at me when I was all in a lustful mood.

And yes, he was looking very charming and handsome in his black tuxedo. At first, I ignored him. But it seemed he got his eyes fixed on me as he was scanning every inch of my body. The truth is that I was enjoying the game. After a while, I and he started to look at each other every now and then.

This might have given him a green signal, as in no time, he came and stood beside me. I was looking straight when I felt a hand sliding over my butt. He literally moved his hand all over in slow motion. I was wet and this made me lustier. He did it a few more times.

Then he stood in front of me and started looking at me. I saw him right in his eyes and bit my lower lip. He did the same. His eyes were hungry and I was his prey for the night. I too was ready to be spoiled that night. But I wanted to have more fun. So, I slipped from the crowd.

While passing from his front, I slid my hand over this crotch. Then I moved towards the eatery counter to have something. While I was sitting on a chair, he came too close to me. His hard cock was just an inch away from my face. I was getting wetter. The fear of someone seeing this was doubling the excitement.

I was enjoying this new thing. He moved and went to have his food. While he was having his food, I went near and passed in a way that my boobs got rubbed with his back. I must tell you this was very fascinating and pleasurable. Then, that was enough. I wanted the real play to happen.

His eyes were on me. I slowly moved away from him. While going inside the hotel, I dropped a napkin with my room number written on it. I went to my room, left the door open and entered the restroom. I applied my imported perfume, got myself ready and came back in the room.

There he was, my hunter for the day, gazing at me as I stood by the wall looking at him. He walked up and came near me and started kissing me on my neck, face, lips, and shoulders. He kneeled down and started kissing on my belly. He was biting and licking it. I was enjoying it.

He started to unwrap my saree. He threw it away, unhooked my blouse and took off my petticoat. He knelt down and kept my leg on his shoulder and started to lick my whole leg from ankle to thigh. He started to lick in my inner thighs and my pussy was dripping. By then, my panty was completely wet.

He looked at it and smelled my pussy over my panty. That was so exciting moment. He lifted me in his arms and took me on the bed. I was lying there and he took off all his clothes. Wow, there was this monster with a heavy chest and build up arms. When he took off his briefs, there was this real drill, full-fledged tight and no less than 8 inches.

I got my eyes fixed at it as it was amazing. He took off my bra and panty in no time. He jumped over me and started to smooch me while pressing my melons. He started biting my boobs and my nipples. He was sucking them so hard that they got all red.

He was biting my boobs and pressing them hard enough for me to feel the pain. But I was enjoying it all to the core. Then, he went down to eat my pussy. I lifted my legs and kept them on his back. I held his hair and buried his face in my pussy. He was licking it and eating it and was drinking the juices.

I was living the moment. He might have got suffocated. He got up and took a long deep breath. Then, he wanted to take his revenge. I was in full mood to give him what he wanted. I made him lie down on the bed and came on top of him. I took his dick in my hand and started to lick it.

As it got all wet with my saliva, I took his whole dick inside and started to stroke it. I was looking him straight in his eyes and he was enjoying this. He wanted more as he took my hair in his hold and made me take all his dick in. It went deep and my lips were touching his balls.

I was coughing and saliva was dripping from my mouth and rolling down to his balls and thighs. Then, he made me lie down on the bed, separated my legs and started rubbing his dick on my pussy walls. That act was loveable. Meanwhile, he was biting my lips and nipples which were hard by his tempting acts.

While doing so, he pushed his dick inside my pussy in just one shot which made me shout like hell. Then we were unstoppable.

He was pumping his dick in and out with all his force and with every stroke. My whole body was thumping. My boobs were shaking like hell. He was pressing them with force.

I was bloody enjoying the fuck. We then got up and came in doggy position. Then he inserted his dick back in my pussy again from the back and started pumping my pussy. He fucked me for more than 20 more minutes. Then made me sit on my knees, started fucking my mouth.

At last, he dropped all his juices in my mouth. I was tired but then he started licking and kissing my body again and was hard again in no time. He fucked me twice more that night. Then we laid in each other's arms and I don't know when I fell asleep.

30. The Movie

I was in the house of a person I had met just a few hours before fully naked with him licking my pussy. This guy definitely knew some kind of magic.

The way he was licking my pussy made me moan just like a Pornstar and it seemed as if he knew the right places. He made me feel in heaven. Such was his passion. He was dominating me completely. He was making me moan at his will but he still had a charm which made me enjoy his licking.

He was licking me for the last 15 minutes. It made me lose patience so much so that I wanted to grab his big dick. I sensed my orgasm coming so I told him that I was on the verge of cumming after his 20 minutes of licking. Suddenly, I released my love juices on his face.

To my surprise, he swallowed all my cum and licked my pussy clean. He got up and perhaps sensed my agony. He took my hand and placed it over his large tool inside his underwear. I knew it was my turn to return the pleasure. I got down on my knees and slid his underwear down to reveal a thick and long cock.

He helped me by completely removing his underwear and asked me to spit on his dick, lubricate it and then stroke him. I did so and began stroking his dick which was rock hard at that instant. After a few strokes seemed monstrous black and shiny. I had to spit a lot to lubricate such a big shaft.

What followed was a long and continuing sex saga. I was getting bored that day. But not even in my wildest dreams had I imagined that I would be getting such a hot fuck. I didn't have anything much to do to keep me busy that day. So, I thought of going to watch a movie.

I asked a few friends but all of them refused, giving one reason or the other. I tried to sleep but something else was written in my fate. At last, I thought of going alone. So, I booked tickets of a random late night Hollywood movie. I thought I would go out, eat something good and enjoy the movie.

Never did I know I would get to enjoy in an altogether different manner. As planned, I put on some nice clothes. (I wore a black crop top over a black bra to hold my 34 sized boobies and a brown mini skirt over a black panty) and went to the cinema. I enjoyed a few delicacies as it was still time for the show to begin.

I was having a good time alone. I bought some popcorn and a soft drink and went for my movie date with myself. When I entered the theater, I was surprised. The theater wasn't completely empty. But there were very few people whom I didn't pay much attention to and just grabbed my seat.

They showed some trailers and advertisements before the movie. After some time, I noticed suddenly that someone was sitting beside me eating his popcorn and relishing his drink. Finally, the movie started and I must say that it was one hot movie with a lot of sex scenes. Some scenes were very erotic.

There were a few kissing scenes at the very start of the film. These scenes were kind of arousing the sex deprived girl in me. Suddenly I felt a hand on my naked thigh. (I was wearing a mini skirt). I was taken aback and looked beside to deduce that the guy beside me was in action.

I removed his hand from my thigh and continued watching my movie. Not much time had passed when I found him deliberately touching his elbows with my side boobs. This time, I gave him a stern look. He got back to his normal self. More sex scenes followed as the movie picked pace.

He suddenly asked me why I was not enjoying the movie to which I replied that I was indeed enjoying. He then showed me a few more couples there enjoying more than just the movie. He asked me if I would not like to have the same enjoyment. I didn't reply anything and continued to watch the movie.

But now, I couldn't concentrate on it. I was more interested in watching the people who came to watch the movie. I again felt a hand on my thigh but this time, I didn't put it away. I rather let it stay there. Of course, it didn't lay still there. After a while, it started showing movement towards my inner thighs.

I was surprised but I didn't want it to stop. I wanted it to continue. He took his hand deep inside where my pussy was and started to rub my pussy over my panty. I was enjoying this sexy rub. When I looked at him, he gave me a victorious smile and continued the rub.

I didn't know what was going on in the movie. I had my eyes closed in the excitement which I only opened once I felt his hand sliding away from my panty and rubbing my naked pussy. The thrill of a stranger rubbing my pussy and that too in a theater was sending a chill down my spine.

He rubbed it for some time and then began drilling his finger in my deep pussy. He was fingerfucking me now making me feel in heaven. He then went on to remove the armrest separating us and came more close to me. While still fingering my pussy, he got his other hand in action and started to press my melons.

I was in 7th heaven. He took out his fingers from my pussy and licked his fingers clean off my vaginal juices. He then brought his face closer to mine and placed his lips on mine. What followed was a deep and erotic French kiss with our tongues exploring each other's mouths.

He obviously knew how to kiss a girl and kept kissing me for some time. All this while taking his hands inside my top and pressing my boobs over my bra. With me fully cooperating with this man whose name even I didn't know. Alas! It was intermission time and the lights in the theatre were switched on.

We both departed away from each other's body and tried to be casual. I wasn't able to meet my eyes with his. Surprising! Isn't it? I was shying away from the man I was just so intimate with. I heard something. He asked me my name. When I looked at him, he looked very casual.

We exchanged a few greetings for namesake. We then thought of going out till the movie started again.

31. The Movie 2

In the first part of this story, I told you about how this man got to explore my body. He got to finger fuck my pussy, press my 34 sized melons and kiss my lovely lips. His name was Akshay. During the intermission time, we thought of going out. He started walking behind me while I was walking in front of him. He was walking very close to me, keeping one of his hands on my naked thighs (I was wearing a mini skirt). I could feel his cock in my ass crack. Oops, I forgot to tell you what he was wearing.

He was wearing a light-yellow shirt and white shorts. I was sure he wasn't wearing anything inside the shirt but it was difficult to guess if he was wearing anything inside his shorts. From the feel of his dick, I could guess that it was a powerful one.

We came out of the auditorium and we were both very horny after the foreplay in the theatre. He told me that I had very good-sized and hard melons and a round ass and that my pussy was very tight and that he would enjoy a lot fucking my tight pussy.

He suddenly pulled me inside the fire exit area where it was completely dark and no other person was around. He pinned me against the wall and started to deep kiss me on my lips. I was scared of someone coming and so, I couldn't fully cooperate with him but I also did not stop him from doing what he was doing.

He was kissing me on my lips with his tongue inside my mouth.

One of his hands was continuously pressing my 34 sized boobs over my bra and the other hand was rubbing my pussy over my pantie.

He suddenly did something I hadn't expected at all. He removed my black top all at once. I was only left in a black bra in front of him. He then swiftly unhooked my bra and removed it completely. I was all topless in front of this man who was a stranger to me a few hours ago.

He kissed my nipples one by one swiftly and asked me to wear back my top. I did as he instructed. He told me that, that way, he can enjoy my bare boobies in the second half of the movie!

He then put my bra inside his shorts and told me to take it from there when I need to wear it again. I blushed hearing that. We couldn't stay there in the fire exit area for long and therefore, we came out, bought some snacks and went back to the theatre.

The movie had already started and another hot bed scene was going on in the movie. I suppose we took a long time in the fire exit area. We then took our seats and soon enough, it was completely dark in the theatre.

Akshay was in action again. He started with caressing my naked thighs and he was getting me aroused as he took his hand towards my inner thighs near my pussy area.

With one hand, he was relishing the snacks we bought and with the other, he was relishing this snack of my pussy! He slid my pantie aside and inserted his finger in my pussy and started to fingerfuck my pussy again. I was on cloud nine again as my pussy started oozing out its love juices.

The next station was my boobs. He put the snacks on the seat next to him. I looked around. Some were busy watching the movie while some were busy making their 'own movie'. He suddenly lifted my top above my right boob and started to suck on my boob. His hand was pressing my left boob over my top. I was enjoying getting my boob sucked.

He then repeated the same procedure with my left boob. He sucked both my boobs to his complete satisfaction and at times, biting my nipples with his teeth and doubling my enjoyment. After he was done, he unhooked his shorts and unzipped them. He took my hand and placed it on his rod over his underwear. I could feel its heat even above the underwear. I also didn't shy away from taking out his cock from inside his underwear.

As I had anticipated, it was one thick and long piece of meat to completely satisfy the sexy deprived me. It was almost as thick as my wrist and about 8 inches in length. He placed his hand over my hand and my hand was holding his thick cock. I started to stroke his cock and give him a hand job. I even bent down and took its tip in my mouth but the position wasn't very comfortable and so, I let my hand do the job.

We watched the remaining movie with his hands either exploring my pussy or pressing my boobs and my hands enjoying his cock. We decided to go to his flat after the movie. As soon as the movie got over, we went out, booked a cab and started straight towards his flat. We couldn't do anything in the cab. So, we talked casually about ourselves.

We kept our patience till the time we reached his flat. As soon as we entered his flat, Akshay locked the door quickly and removed my top and started kissing me. He was acting like crazy as he pinned me against the wall and started licking my neck and my earlobes. My excitement almost tripled as these are the weak points of any girl.

He upped both my hands and licked and kissed my clean armpits and my smooth sexy skin. Continuing his licking and kissing my body, he went down to my deep navel and then towards my pussy. He removed my mini skirt and my pantie both at once. I helped him get rid of them completely. He removed my footwear and I was completely naked in front of this so-called stranger.

Then he went on to remove his white shorts and along with the shorts came my black bra (which he had removed in the fire exit area) leaving him only in a yellow shirt and underwear with a large bulge. He sat down on his knees and started to lick my pussy.

I continued milking his cock which was too huge to fit my tiny mouth but I was still swallowing as much of it as I could and enjoyed sucking his monstrous cock. He too had both his hands on my head and was pushing his cock inside my throat with every stroke. I felt like choking but I didn't give up.

Then I took his cock out of my mouth and started my operations on his heavy cum filled tatte (balls). I pressed one of his balls and gave him a mischievous smile as he let out a loud moan after which I licked his balls and then came back to giving him a blowjob. This time I only stopped after I had Akshay down.

I knew he was on the brink of releasing his juices but I had no plans to taste them (as I really don't like tasting cum even though I have heard it enhances a girl's beauty). But he didn't let his dick out of my mouth until he had completely released his cum due to which I had to swallow it half-heartedly.

We were both very horny and wanted the actual fuck but we thought of doing it with complete enjoyment. So, Akshay went to his kitchen and brought us some juice. We had the juice as we were both very thirsty after the kiss, lick and suck session. After this quick session, we had the energy to start again.

Akshay picked me up in his arms and took me to his bedroom. I came on top of him and unbuttoned his shirt. To my surprise, I saw what I always look for in a man. He was one hot guy with a muscular physique. I removed his shirt completely and was lost in his big biceps and triceps, masculine hairless chest and sexy big eight pack abs! It seemed as if he hit the gym regularly. On top of all, he had this monstrous huge black cock too.

I didn't shy at all from kissing and licking and sucking his masculine body. I started from his neck. I licked and kissed and sucked his neck, his earlobes, and all this while, he was caressing my naked sexy back. My mouth made its way to his biceps and triceps and then I licked his chest, sucked his nipples and kissed his eight pack abs one after the other finally reaching his huge piece of meat after enjoying his navel.

I again took his cock in my mouth and milked it for some time. Akshay took charge then and came on top of my back and kissed my sexy back. He tried to insert his finger in my ass but he couldn't because I was a virgin in the ass and it pained me a lot. He expressed his wish to open my ass one day to which I just asked him to just fuck my pussy for that day. Now was the time for the actual fuck to happen.

Akshay came on top of me, placed his cock on my clean, neat and well-shaved pussy (I always keep my pussy clean) and gave it a light push due to which the dickhead went inside my pussy. Then he completely laid over me and started kissing and biting my lips and gave another push leading to half his cock inside my already wet pussy.

After the third and the final push, his complete cock, tearing my pussy walls, was inside me. Though it pained me a lot and all I could feel was that my pussy was tightly wrapped around his cock (my pussy is very tight) but in anticipation of the pleasure I was going to experience, I forgot all the pain. Soon enough, Akshay started to fuck me hard.

His cock was going deep inside my pussy and the room was filled with our fuck noises. While Akshay was fucking me, he was constantly kissing my lips and my 34 sized hard hot boobs. He fucked me for some time and then we came in 69 position with me on top of him.

We gave each other the pleasure of milking a cock and of sucking a pussy. After this quick 69 session, I took charge and sat and positioned my pussy over his cock and started jumping on his cock. I must say that he had very good stamina. All the while I was jumping on his huge cock, he was playing with my boobies.

After I was tired of taking charge, we gave tit-fuck a try. Finally, he came on top of me again and started fucking me hard. We were both enjoying to the fullest and after a few more minutes of this sexy fucking, we both cummed together. I laid on top of this sexy man all motionless and exhausted.

He fucked me twice again that night and, in the morning, I went back to my room. We fucked many times after that sexy encounter and then he left for Germany for some work and never came back since then.

So, not even in my wildest dreams had I thought that a movie date with myself will bring such long-lasting pleasure for me. Next time you go for a movie alone, be careful. A sexy guy can fuck you and make you dance on his fingers.

32. Landlady's Son

I was in the third year of my college in Delhi when I had to shift to a new room. I wasn't alone. There were other girls with me with the same purpose.

We looked for a number of rooms and at last, finalized some rooms on a floor which we found perfect according to our criteria. The owner of the house was a widow lady aged 50-60 years. She had a daughter who was married and two sons. Her elder son was well settled in Dubai while her younger son was doing his Masters.

There were already three girls on the floor and the three of us joined them. Within a week, we all gelled up and were like a family. The landlady used the ground and the first floor. We were all mature girls and each one of us had had her share of enjoyment.

3-4 girls still had their boyfriends whom they enjoyed with on weekends. I was single during that time. Since CCTV cameras were installed in the house to watch over the negative activities of the girls, doing any such thing on the floor was a big NO.

I noticed that the landlady's son, Salman, always looked at me in a weird way. Initially, I ignored him but later, his gaze made me feel a bit excited.

Let me tell you all about Salman. Salman is a 6 feet tall, young and handsome boy. He is gym built with washboard abs, biceps, and triceps. He has a masculine chest and a rock hard back. His witty nature and sense of humour made me fall for him.

Whenever I used to go upstairs and come downstairs, he would stare at my 34 sized big round firm melons and my 34 sized big round tight ass. We never got the opportunity to talk to each other. There were just normal hi hello exchanges. Also, it was a long time since my pussy tasted a cock.

So, I also started to smile at his gazes. This gave him a green signal. Somehow, he also took my mobile number from his mother and started to send romantic messages to me. I didn't respond to all his messages but I enjoyed reading them. There was no vulgarity in those messages for a period of time.

One day, he messaged me to come downstairs since his mother wasn't in the house. But I refused as I could be caught in the cameras. To this, he replied that he will switch off the cameras. I had no excuse but I told him that it will just be a casual meeting and nothing else will happen to which he agreed.

So, I went downstairs on the ground floor. From there, he took me in his drawing room and offered me some juice and snacks. I was scared of his mother coming but he assured me that she won't come soon. He then started to appreciate my beauty to which I was just blushing.

The same day, he proposed to me to which I happily said yes. Nothing romantic happened that day but from that day onwards, the equation between us changed. It was now shifted more towards the sexual side. We got very few chances to meet but we exchanged a lot of messages. This brought us even closer.

He then started demanding lip kiss from me. I had no apprehensions but we didn't get any chance to meet. What happened one day was that my roommate went to her friend's house and Salman got to know this thing by our usual chats. Later in the night, there was a knock on my door.

I thought it must be some flatmate but to my surprise, it was Salman. I let him come inside and enquired about the cameras. He told me that he switched off the cameras before coming. This made me happy. He then lay on my bed while I was looking at him.

He reminded me of the kiss. I asked him to take it but he told me that he will take more than just a kiss. He stood up, came closer to me and brought his lips closer to mine. Our hearts were beating very fast since we were going to share our first kiss together. He then placed his lips over mine.

We shared a wild lip kiss with his tongue rolling into mine and my tongue rolling into his and our saliva's mixing a great French kiss. He then moved on to kissing my eyes, my cheeks, biting my earlobes and sucking my neck and all this while, his hands were trying to take my top off. During this time, he pressed my boobies.

I was also enjoying all this and also, my hands were exploring his gym built hardback. After this kissing session was over, he removed my top and his shirt. I was only left in a black bra in front of him while he was not wearing anything beneath his t-shirt. All I could see was his washboard six pack abs and well built hairless chest and biceps.

He had an excellent physique. He told me that he dreamt about sucking my melons since the day he heard my name Charmy. He started to suck my boobs over my bra while I was fully cooperating with him. All this was short lived since there was a knock on my door. My roommate had come back.

Salman quickly hid under the bed and left once my roomie went to the washroom. She destroyed our pleasure night. We both hated her for interrupting but nothing could be done. We again had no choice but to message. Now, our messages got more vulgar. He used to send me his shirtless pics and I would watch them.

I also sent him my topless pics. But we didn't share the pics of our main tools since we both wanted it to be a surprise on our special day. Though we hadn't anticipated this, that special day came soon. One night, his mother had to go over her sister's place since there was some problem there. Salman told me about this.

We thought of enjoying that very night. Somehow, I convinced my roommate that I was going to stay over at a friend's place, did some drama and came downstairs. Salman was waiting for me. He had already switched off all the cameras. As soon as I got in, he quickly closed all the doors and windows.

He came closer and we shared a deep French kiss. After the kiss, he removed my top and bra in one go and also removed his t-shirt. My boobs were lying bare in front of him. He took my left boob in his mouth as much as he could and pressed my right boob with his hand. Then he took the right one in his mouth and pressed the left one.

I was enjoying this boob sucking session but now, I also needed something to play and suck. I started fondling his shorts. I sat down on my knees and lowered his shorts and underwear in one go and his cock jumped right in front of me. It was fully erect and straight, neither black nor white but a pink head and quite long and thick.

I wasted no time and quickly took it in my mouth and started milking it. It wasn't fitting in my mouth till I swallowed it as much as I could. I also licked and sucked his heavy cum filled balls. He then made me lie down on the bed and removed my shorts and panty.

We came in 69 positions with he sucking and licking and biting my pussy and me sucking his tool. He also tried to insert his finger in my ass but I was a virgin in the ass, I felt it too painful and so he let go that finger. After we sucked to our satisfaction, I came on top of him to kiss his sexy abs, lick his chest and eat his biceps. He made me go weak in the knees with his looks.

Now was the time for the real job. He positioned his cock on my pussy and gave a push. It pained a little because I hadn't been fucked for months but after the next few pushes, his cock was completely inside my pussy. My pussy was tightly wrapped around his cock – such was its girth.

He started pounding my pussy like crazy. The whole room was filled with our fuck noises. I was enjoying to the fullest. The mixed feeling of pain and pleasure with him fucking my pussy, kissing my lips and fondling my boobs couldn't hold me and I cummed but he was still not done. He continued to fuck me until I got aroused again.

Then after a really hot and sexy fuck session, we both came together. We fucked three more times that night. And after that, until I stayed in that house, whenever we found an apartment place and time, we fucked hard.

33. Khabir

My fifth semester in college was going on and I had a boyfriend Rohit. We had done everything except for fucking though I was all ready for it. We had kissed each other and he had sucked my boobs multiple times in the college bathroom. What we used to do was that I would go to the washroom and he would come after me a few minutes later and I used to enjoy getting my boobs sucked by Rohit. Khabir was the best friend of Rohit.

Though we, me and Rohit, got many chances to fuck each other but Rohit wasn't ready to fuck me. I didn't know why. This attitude of him was not going down well with me. I wasn't a virgin and I badly needed a cock in my cunt. This led to some frequent fights between us. Khabir was my friend too and the three of us were quite close. Khabir proposed me too but by then, I had said yes to Rohit. Once, I and Rohit were in the flat of my friend where we were supposed to fuck. We did everything but when it came to the actual thing of inserting the cock in the cunt, he ran away. It agitated me.

The next few days I was not talking to him but he convinced me.

Let me tell you all about Khabir. Khabir is a gym going muscled, handsome and tall hunk. He is six feet tall, fair complexion and extremely good sense of humor. He is a well-built guy with six pack abs, biceps and triceps. He had the best physique in the whole college and girls were after him. His tool is also quite thick and long. So, I and Rohit were not able to fuck each other even after two months of being in a relationship. Like before, Rohit once told me to go to the college bathroom while he comes after me. I went to the college bathroom and started to wait for Rohit. After some time, a person came and he switched off the lights of the bathroom and started to unbutton my shirt. I thought it was Rohit.

I also started cooperating and he then removed my bra and started to suck my boobs. He pressed my boobs hard. We were making minimum noise and in between, he was also kissing my lips. He bit on my nipples and we enjoyed for some time and then he went. Before going, he handed me a chit. After setting my clothes and coming out of the bathroom, when I read that chit, I was shell shocked. It read that the person who enjoyed sucking my boobs wasn't Rohit but somebody else. I was in a shock but I composed myself. I couldn't let Rohit know about it. But this thing was upsetting me a lot. I wanted to share it with some-one. Khabir was the only person left. So, I told Khabir everything from the start about how Rohit was not ready to fuck me for no reason at all and how a random person enjoyed my 34 sized boobs. He gave me another shock that Rohit lacked in stamina and that's why he was not fucking me. I was quite tensed that day. Khabir assured me that he would try to find the guy who sucked my boobs.

Few days passed and I was trying to avoid Rohit as much as pos-sible. He also understood the reason why I was avoiding him. We kind of broke up. Now, Khabir was my only friend with whom I shared everything. We gelled quite well and we were quite frank.

I used to share everything with Khabir. Though I and Rohit started talking to each other but now, we were not sexually in-volved with each other. Few days after, I found a chip in my bag. It read,"I am the same person who sucked your boobs in the bathroom and I know that you also enjoyed me fondling your boobs and playing with your body and I also know that your boyfriend Rohit can no longer satisfy you. So, here I am with an offer for you. Tomorrow, go to the college bathroom at 12 sharp and we will have fun again. If you don't come tomorrow, I will never write to you again."

I was perplexed what to do. A side of me was screaming to not go and another side of me was asking me to forget all other things and enjoy what you are getting. I was feeling so confused that I didn't even tell Khabir about it fearing him forming a view about me. After hours of thinking, I finally decided to go.

At sharp 12, I went to the college washroom and started to wait for the stranger. Few minutes after, he came and without speaking anything, he started to kiss me on my lips. I asked who he was but he didn't respond and unbuttoned my shirt. He took my left boob out of my bra and started sucking it while he was pressing my right boob with his hand. He was a good sucker and I was thoroughly enjoying because he was biting a little on my boobs.

I again asked who he was but he told me SssHhh. He sucked my boobs to the fullest and before going, he handed over to me a chit which read, "Thanks for coming. I promise you that you will keep receiving this love from me frequently." So, our story began. He used to keep a chip in my bag and I would go to the bathroom to enjoy. One day, according to my plan, I picked my nail in his neck wanting to find out his identity. My trick worked and I was shocked to see that Khabir was with a bandage on his neck. He was behaving so normally. I decided to confront him but before me confronting him, he told me the complete truth about how he had always lust for me and how he had always wanted to be my boyfriend. He asked me if I didn't enjoy his job to which I had no answer. I finally had to let go all of this but when Khabir asked me for a relationship, I couldn't say no and our relationship started.

We again began our boob sucking sessions in the college washroom but now, the difference was that I also used to remove his t-shirt and then I used to suck and lick his nipples, armpits, back, biceps and his six-pack abs. We couldn't go down because of the fear of being caught but we did insert our hands. He used to insert his hand in my panty and I used to do the same in his underwear and to tell you, he had a nice one.

34. Khabir and Jack

In my previous story, I told you about how my Boyfriend Rohit's friend Khabir had sexy boob sucking sessions we had in our college bathroom. We had become kind of 'Friends with Benefits' or 'Fuck Buddies'. Wherever and whenever we found it suitable, we fucked. Khabir had been keeping me completely satisfied sexually. I had kind of fallen in love with his aura, his persona, his biceps, his triceps, his sexy body, his rock hard back, his good lengthed cock and most importantly his sexy six-pack abs. Well, this story is not about Khabir but his friend Jack.

To be honest, till date, I just had the cocks inserted into my pussy. I don't know why but yes; I was scared to get my ass rammed. Whenever Khabir fucked me, he always used to say that I have a sexy ass and that ass fucking gives 10 times the pleasure I get with pussy fucking but the fear I had in my mind always stopped me. Though I had heard about this pleasure of ass fucking from my friends but still I was not ready for this.

At times, Khabir also tried to insert his finger in my ass but it gave me immense pain to which I thought that if a single finger gives such pain, then a thick cock would completely ram my ass. One day when Khabir was fucking me, he started to insert his finger in my ass but again, it pained a lot and so, I asked him to stop but he told me that I would have to get my ass fucked but I refused him strictly. But what then happened was that Khabir's birthday was approaching. I had to give him some gift.

I made a mistake by asking him what he wanted from me on

his birthday. He told me that I won't be able to give him what he wanted. I told him that if the thing is well within my budget, then I will surely gift him that to which he replied that the thing had always been well within my budget. When I pushed him to tell what it was, he told me that he wanted to double penetrate me with his friend in the pussy and in the ass.

I was shell-shocked. Getting fucked by his friend was less shocking than getting fucked in the ass. I told him that I will not be able to gift him this but he started to emotionally talk to me into it. After 2-3 days of his persuading me to think of it, I, after thinking a lot, gave him a nod but on two conditions. One that first I will fuck his friend Jack alone so that I can get to know him and second that first I will get my ass fucked by any one of them and then only I will double fuck them on Khabir's birthday. After thinking for some time, Khabir gave a nod.

This was the first time I was about to get fucked by a stranger. Khabir showed me his pics and told me that he ran his own gym. Khabir had also told Jack about me giving a nod.

When Khabir told him that first I will fuck him alone, he jumped with joy. Inside, I was also thrilled. Khabir told me that the day after tomorrow, he would drop me in his flat so that I can get to know him or I can get to fuck him. My heartbeat increased. I hadn't even met him once and I was going to fuck him. I was thinking that if Jack runs his own gym, how sexy his body must be. Though Khabir showed me his pics and I could see that he had a very good physique with flawless washboard abs, huge biceps and triceps, well build chest and back. The cutest thing I found in him was his dimples which were so suiting his face. Also, Khabir told me that he has a nice sized cock i.e. good length and girth. I prepared myself for the day.

I completely waxed myself and to wear, I chose a mehroon coloured bra over which I wore a mehroon coloured top. Bottomside, I wore a mehroom coloured panty and a cream-coloured long skirt. Khabir took me in his flat on his bike. Jack opened the door and took us inside. Khabir made us familiar with each other and he made us clear the purpose of why I and Jack had gathered in his flat. Seeing it was the first meeting with Jack and that too for such a purpose, I wasn't even looking at Jack in the eye. Though I saw that he was very handsome and gym build. Soon Khabir left us alone. Jack got up and locked the door. My heartbeat increased and I was a bit nervous too. Jack came near me and asked me if I was ready to submit myself to him to which I just nodded.

He then asked me to look in his eyes. I looked into his eyes. He asked me if I am shying away from him. I told him that I am a little nervous since I am doing it with a stranger for the first time. We talked for some time about somethings, about Khabir etc and my shyness faded away. There was a kind of magic and a spellboundedness in Jack. He them asked me if we should proceed with the purpose, we had got together for to which I replied that we should. He then picked me in his stong arms and took me to his bedroom. It was a well-furnished bedroom with a nice smell. He told me that I am very beautiful and sexy and placed me on a sofa. He lifted my skirt till my knees and started to lick my thighs. I enjoyed his licking.

While he was licking with his mouth, his hands went deep inside my skirt over the panty and he was trying to slide my panty downside but since I was sitting, it wasn't happening. His mouth was also buried deep inside my inner thighs and I am sure he could see my wet panty also. He brought his face outside and told me that I have a hot pussy and that he was lucky enough that he was getting to fuck me. He asked me what the size of my boobs was to which I replied, "34" to which he said, "Yummy". He then set my hair with his hands and brought his face close to mine and we shared a deep French kiss with our tongues rolling inside each other's mouth. He said that it was amazing to kiss me. He then kissed my whole face. He then licked my earlobes too which are my weak points.

Till now, I was a little shy but by now, all my shyness had faded away and now, I also started to take initiatives. Jack then started to press my boobs over my top.

My boobs had become very hard due to all the foreplay. Jack then got up and removed his t-shirt. I was amazed to see his body. I had seen such body only in porn videos. I told him that he has an amazing body to which he replied that this body is mine now. He then kissed me again while fondling my boobs and I also used this opportunity to feel his sexy body with my hands. He then made me get up from the sofa and removed my top and slide down my skirt and completely removed it after picking me up. He told me that I have an amazing pair of boobs. Jack then placed his mouth on my bra covered left boob and his hand was pressing my right boob. He was pressing hard and I was letting out moans while at the same time pushing his mouth more in my boob. He then turned me around and kissed and licked my bare back from top to bottom. It sent a chill down my spine. I was oozing juices downside. After he was done with my back, he unhooked my bra and removed it. He smelled it first and then threw it away. He turned me around and kissed my nipples one by one. He then examined my boobs very carefully.

He then removed his jeans and was only left in an underwear while I was just wearing a panty. He then slapped my ass lightly and started to lick my naked boobs while his hands were pressing my nipples. I was letting out sexy moans. He kissed and licked my navel area around the stomach and coming downside, he removed my panty and started kissing my pussy. He drank all the wetness and licked it clean. I was pushing his mouth in my pussy. He seemed to be a professional in licking a pussy as he was giving me immense pleasure. He asked me to give him some kisses on his body. I was waiting for this. I then made him lie down on the bed while I got over him and kissed his sexy abs, I licked his chest and kissed his biceps, I sucked his nipples and then I turned him around on the bed and licked and kissed his rock hard back.

He was the man of my dreams. I slid down his underwear. To my surprise, he was really hard. He had a very good-sized cock and it was quite thick. First, I milked it with my hands and then I took it in my mouth. I was licking it. It wasn't fitting my mouth still I took it deep into my mouth. Jack then started mouthfucking me. I also licked his balls. I was getting the wet downside. When I told him to do the needful, he came over me on the bed, placed his cock on my pussy and pushed it all inside in one go. I let out a loud moan. Though I was habitual of getting fucked by Khabir's cock, still it pained me a little. He started to fuck my pussy really hard. He was giving deep thrusts. In and out, in and out the cock was going making sounds in the room. His hands were continuously pressing my boobs and he was kissing me while he was fucking me. His cock was tightened with my pussy lips and this was giving me immense pleasure. I was moaning and saying, " Jack! Fuck me hard. Aaaahhhhh Fuck me."

He was also enjoying and saying, "Ah Charmy! Your pussy is so tight. Ah!" After about 15 minutes, I had my orgasm while Jack was still fucking me. After about 5 minutes, Jack also cummed inside my pussy. He took his cock out and laid down beside me on the bed and asked me if I enjoyed to which I replied, "Yes." I asked him if he enjoyed to which he replied that he did enjoy but the real enjoyment will be when he will get to fuck my virgin ass and when he and Khabir will double fuck me. He requested me to let him inaugurate my ass instead of Khabir. I gave him no answer.

He then went into the kitchen and brought for me and himself a cup of coffee. We chatted while drinking the coffee and then, we were ready for the second session. He fucked me that day in various positions. He even licked my ass which I enjoyed a lot. My boobs also milked his cock. After all the fucking, we were very tired and we slept off. In the morning, he fucked me again before he dropped me in my room.

35. Jack

In my previous story, I told you about how Jack fucked me hard in the pussy in his flat and later he dropped me in my room on his bike. Since I was tired by all the fucking we had in the night and in the morning, I slept immediately.

I woke up around 2 in the afternoon and all I could think about was Jack. Flashes of how he gave me immense pleasure by sucking my tits and pussy and by fucking my pussy with his hard cock were the only things going on in my mind. I had forgotten all about what I promised Khabir – my Fuck Buddy.

To remind you, I had promised him that I will get a double fucked by him and his friend Jack on his birthday. To get familiar with Jack (since he was a stranger to me), I got fucked by him (with Khabir's approval) in his flat.

I checked my phone and there were many missed calls from Khabir. I called him and he asked me if I enjoyed the fuck night with his friend. I replied him in the affirmative. He jumped with joy and told me that one of my two conditions has been met and now, it is time to fulfill my second condition. He told me how excited he was to fuck my virgin ass.

He asked me when I am going to let him fuck my ass. I asked him to wait for some more days till the time I mentally prepare myself to get my ass rammed. He then told me that Jack called him and told him that I gave him a lot of pleasure and that I was the best girl he ever had sex with. I blushed hearing this from Khabir.

We cut the call and I again lay down thinking about my Jack. The view of his sexy abs, biceps and triceps, rock hard back and masculine chest was flashing before my eyes. I closed my eyes and thought about how he licked my ass and the feeling when he gave kisses on my neck and earlobes.

When I was thinking about all this, Jack called me up. I picked up his call and he asked me how I was. I told him that I was good. He asked me if I enjoyed the day before to which I replied in the affirmative. He then asked me if I would like to have the same fun today.

I wanted to say yes but I had promised Khabir that I will get fucked by Jack only for one night and then he will fuck my virgin ass and then they both will double penetrate me together. I told this to Jack. He asked me to not tell Khabir about it and that he will pick me up from my room.

He also asked me to wear a short top and a mini skirt. He disconnected the call and I lay down once again anticipating about what was about to come. I wore a yellow crop top with a purple padded bra inside and a white panty over which I wore a white mini skirt. I let my hair loose and got ready to get fucked once again by my dream man.

I kept waiting for him to come. Passing that time was very difficult. When he came near my house, he gave me a call and I went to the man of my dreams. This time, he had come in his car. I sat in the front seat beside the driver seat.

Coincidentally, he was also wearing a yellow shirt with top three buttons open, showing off his masculine chest and white shorts. Though we had fucked the whole night the day before, I still couldn't meet my eyes with him because there was a feeling inside me that I was cheating on Khabir.

He just came closer to my ear and told me that the previous night was the best fuck night he ever had and licked my earlobe. He started to drive the car while I was blushing. He asked me if I was comfortable. When I replied in a yes, he brought his hands over my thighs and started to massage my thighs.

I smiled a little which gave him a green signal. He pushed his hands deep inside my mini skirt near my panty and started to rub my vagina. This was giving me immense pleasure and I was letting out sexy moans. He certainly knew how to pleasure a girl.

Then he took away his hands and started to press my boobies over my top. He told me that I have very soft and fleshy boobs. He then shifted his focus toch driving and he guided my hand to his cock and said that it was going crazy for me. I pressed his cock a little and I was surprised by the amazing length and girth that it had.

I wanted to feel it all over once again. I unhooked and unzipped his shorts but to my bad luck, he was wearing an underwear. Not able to control myself, I just started to lick and suck his cock over the underwear while he was driving and also pressing my boobs. I stopped sucking the cock and unbuttoned his shirt completely and started to kiss my favorite part of his body.

I kissed and licked his chest, his sexy body, his nipples and his six-pack abs. He suddenly stopped the car on a stranded road and we started to smooch each other. We kissed wildly.

Then he went downside to my top and slide it up and started sucking my boobs over my bra can I ask him to be patient till the time we reach is room. He started to drive fast and stopped only once we reached the parking. We quickly reached his room and as soon as he locked the door, we started to French kiss as if there was no tomorrow.

He was also pressing my boobs very hard. I was also not behind in pressing his cock over his shorts. He quickly undressed me and he removed his clothes as well, positioned his cock on my pussy and let it go all inside in one go.

I let out a loud scream as I was not prepared for this. But since we were both very excited, we started the fuck. He was also pressing my boobs and kissing my mouth while I was getting aroused only by feeling his masculine back.

He was lying on top of me and his weight seemed good to me. Finally, we both cummed together and he then lay beside me on the bed. We were breathless and sweating. I switched on the AC.

He apologized for the quick fuck because he was very excited. All I could do was smile.

36. Goa

I am Akshay, a good-looking guy with decent physique and a good athlete around 5'10" around 28 years of age....
Charmy is 24 years old having a sexy figure of 34-26-34....and extremely sexy.

I was staying in Goa for few days on work in a premium hotel on beach....and Charmy was staying in a rented apartment as she was there on a study project from college.

We both are fitness freaks....and one fine Saturday morning we met on the beach.... well, here is how it happened....

I was on my morning jog on the beach and was wearing shorts and a sleeveless t-shirt. There I see a beautiful babe in hot pants and crop top doing some morning exercises and stretches. I couldn't take my eyes off her and kept on looking at her while jogging in her direction. After a few more laps and crossed her multiple times....and while I did check her out...I thought she also did quite subtly...

After her initial stretches she did jog for around 20 minutes...

At the end of my jog, I did a few stretches to relax myself and after that decided to open a conversation with her. I approached her and introduced myself as Akshay and told that am impressed with her fitness levels...(I had removed my Tee at that time since it was all sweaty). She blushed a bit and said thanks for praise.

Me: So done for today's exercises?

She: Yes...need a bath soon...
Me: Let's get hydrated – wanna join in for some juice?
She: I don't mind....

So we walk to a nearby cafe and order fresh juices and some light stuff to eat...

Me: So what's your name?
She: Charmy
Me: You don't seem to be from here
She: Yeah...am not from here. Here on a study project. What about you?
Me: Well am on an official tour and staying nearby in that 5-star resort.
She: Interesting....always wanted to check it out...
Me: Anytime you want – am here for a few weeks...Well you look like a model...ever took any assignments...

She: Yes...has done a few but not actively pursuing right now.
Me: Well you should explore it seriously....
She: At an opportune time....
Me: Are you alone here or you have some friends?
She: Am alone here, a few friends had come for project, they left last week after finishing their part....I am here for around 2 more weeks...
Me: Interesting...I hope this gives us good opportunity to spend some time together and join for morning exercises and parties in the evening if you like that.
She: I do love to party and have been missing it...great we crashed into each other...

Me: Let's exchange contact numbers if you don't mind....
She: Sure...give your number ....I will call back....
Me: there you go (I share my number with her)
She: and that is my number...
Me: What are you up to today
She: Saturday hai....full day I am free
Me: Then let us spend the day together...depends on you...

She: We can do that...but I need to get fresh...
Me: You can do that at the resort...it will be super comfy...and do you like swimming?

She: I looooveeee swimming....but my stuff is in my room....let me pick up some stuff...
Me: Sure – let's walk to your place then...

We walk together to her place and talk and enjoy each others company.
She was staying in a studio room type of a place and packs her stuff fast...and I reminded her to pick her swimsuit also and she packs a couple of them...

We walk back to resort and enter from beach side....

Me: Do you wanna swim now or you wanna relax..?
She: Swimming will be refreshing :)
Me: Just take these 2 swim deck chairs and order whatever you wanna (I call the waiter inform the room number and we give order for cocktails). While he gets the drinks I will just get my swimming trunk.
She: Sure...I will also go and change
Me: Great...looking forward to check you out.

I go and change into swimming trunk (a short one) and wear a new sleeveless tee and get back to the pool and see Charmy resting after a swim shower on the deck chair and a bigger surprise was she in a bikini....flaunting her hot figure...

Me: Charmy – you are hot!!!!!
She: Thanks, and you look great yourself...

I remove my tee and take the shower and tell her I am getting into the pool you can join in...

She: Sure you go in... let the drinks come – will come in then

Drinks arrive and she keeps our drinks next to the pool and enters the pool....
We pick our drinks and say cheers to our friendship

She is a great swimmer and we swim comfortably with each other. We stop in middle and have our drinks and chit chat a bit. We are getting quite comfortable with each other.

After around 45 mins of swimming, we come out and I lift her out of the pool and during the course feeling her soft skin.

She: You are naughty guy.... let's finish our drinks....I need to get fresh...

Me: Sure...you can get fresh in my room...

She: Obviously

She dries herself and picks her stuff and without wearing anything else starts walking with me in her 2-piece towards my room.

We get in and I lock it....

Me: Make yourself comfortable. Do you wanna shower or enjoy the bathtub...?

She: You have a bath tub here....I would love getting into a warm water bath...

Me: Let me set it up

I fill it with warm water and bath gel with foam coming up nicely...

Me: Well its ready

I put towels next to the tub...while she keeps her change of clothes on the bed and it's quite a hot stuff with a nice short dress

Me: Towels are next to the bathtub and bathrobe is also inside...do you want anything else..

She: Thanks, Akshay....I will go in and get freshened up...

Me: Well if you won't mind can I join you in the tub after you are inside?

She: You are getting naughty....

Me: Well you are tempting me to be....

She hmmmm...let me get in...then you can join in...
Me: Great...

She enters the bathroom and in a while, she enters the bathtub naked....

She: Akshay....if you wanna join...now is the time...

Me: Am coming in babe

I enter bathroom...and she mentions not to remove anything before entering and remove only after entering...n I do so...

We are well covered with foam...and our legs are next to each other and one leg of ours can feel the other's leg all through the length and thighs till the waist area...and I give her a grin and she blushes a bit...

Me: Babe...you are HOT

She: You are no less....and see we are already in one room, one bathroom and am in your tub...naked...

Me: Yeah and am loving it...

She moves her leg and feels my chest with her feet slowly...

Me: Now someone is tempted

She: Well what are we supposed to do in this state!!!

Me: You are right...now if I get out of control...you better play along...

She: It is game on....

I start to move my feet across her waist and move each of my legs around her sides with her legs coming in straight and you can guess well ending around where

She: Well it seems to be out of control already...
Me: It's just starting babe

She caresses me there during the using her feet and my feet are playing with her nipples...

I pull her and make her slide towards me and make her rest her back on my chest and my hands go around her waist and I kiss her neck slowly and she closes her eyes.
We play somewhat more inside the tub and then come out naked and hug each other after checking each other out.

She: Akshay – you are quite well built down there
Me: Thanks, babe....well it's yours....

We take a shower together and dry ourselves and come out...I move her clothes away from the bed to couch and she comes over and joins me on the bed and we get into a tight embrace and start making out (mind it...we are making out not making love yet)...

We kiss each other passionately while sitting facing each other with her legs around me....I pull her more close and start kissing her boobs slowly and suck her nipples and they rise further.

She makes me lie down and kisses me all over my body starting from the neck, shoulders, chest, and waist....and gives short kisses down there and takes in the head a bit and sucks it.

I turn her around and kiss her legs all the way up from toes to knee to thighs and moving up to paradise and give her a short massage with tongue there....

From there I move up and am on her and I start kissing her and she kisses me back with tongue inside each other's mouth and there I go and slowly angle my arrow perfectly towards the target and shoot it slowly and bang it hits the target slowly piercing through it and with target being a bit moist pricing is quite easy and it slowly goes in....when it is half way I stop it and move a bit around at that level and she enjoys and moans and has her first orgasm after a while...

Now I go in slowly and enter her completely. We start wild lovemaking and move with other slowly caressing each other completely....

And that's how our first encounter went.

37. Raj

I am 21 and I m a very beautiful girl with big eyes, fair colour and excellent figure. My breasts are well developed. I am such a girl that everyone's penis will get erect on seeing me and everyone desires to fuck me. I currently study in some college in Delhi. Many boys wanted to have relationship with me but I didn't pay attention to anyone. This story is of a year back. I was in the second year of college when my boyfriend Raj fucked me for the first time. I was a virgin then. Like other girls I also joined a gym where I met Raj.

The gym is in Delhi near my college campus. Though my friends used to talk about how their boyfriends fucked them and all, I had never been in this experience. Though I had some boy-friends and I was in relationship with them, I didn't even kiss anyone. Only Raj got the opportunity to explore my body completely first. I went to the gym for some days and then I began to lose interest as I used to get very much tired.

I told the owner about the same. He asked me to stay for some more days as he will employ a trainer for me and I agreed. Few days after he introduced me to Raj and when I met him for the first time, I couldn't get my eyes off him. He was in a vest and boxers. His well chiseled body made me awe struck. I was speechless. Let me tell u about Raj. He is a 6 feet extremely handsome guy and he was having excellent biceps and six pack abs.

He told me that he studies in Delhi as well as works in the gym. This way body is made and money is earned. He also told me that he wanted to have eight pack abs. Then began our training sessions. He used to train me and also, he told me about what to consume in my diet and what not. When he trained me, I constantly looked at him and I think he also noticed the same thing. He also began to show interest in me. I also started to lose my tiredness and I started enjoying gym. Raj used to touch my private parts.

He kept hand on my thighs sometimes he pressed my boobs etc. This continued for some months. One day he told me to go with him to the bathroom. I was hesitant initially but then I agreed. When I went with him, he closed the door. I was uncomfortable but he told me to calm down.

Then he removed his vest. I was scared out of hell. I liked him but this was not done. But to my surprise he just told me to see his 8 pack abs which he just finished making. I was highly relieved. I touched his abs and he hugged me. I too hugged him back. My breaths were very deep then. We came out and everything normalized. Then one day he proposed me for a relationship and I agreed happily. Then our relationship began.

We used to talk even after gym. Chat for long hours etc. We went for dinner movies etc. We went for hate story 2 once and then in the hot scenes he took my hand in his and kissed it. I was ok and didn't feel bad. After the movie while roaming in the park he wanted to kiss me . He was a man after all and I allowed him.

Then happened the first kiss of my life. He kissed my lips and I closed my eyes . I was completely lost. He put his tongue in my mouth and started sucking it I too did the same . His hands were on my waist and mine were around his body. Then after some minutes I realized I we r in public place and I removed my mouth from his. He apologized.

We began walking and while departing I kissed him again. This time I asked him to kiss me. Now kissing was a daily act. We used to go in bathroom and kiss for long. Then one day he asked me to show him my breasts. I wasn't comfortable and I left. He apologized and I forgave him.

When one day we were kissing he started pressing my boobs I started to enjoy. I fell in his trap. He asked me to remove my top. I agreed. He removed my top and I was only left with a black bra over my upper body. He was kissing my lips and pressing my boobs. I was in heaven. Then he started to kiss my boobs from the bra and also, he licked my armpits. He unzipped my bra and I was completely naked from upper body.

He continued sucking my boobs and I was moaning. All this was happening at his room as I had come to visit him. Then he removed his vest and I hugged him tight. I don't know what was happening to me but there was a sweet itching in my vagina. I also kissed his nipples armpits and full 8 pack abed body .I was enjoying to the fullest .My breasts were very hard and he was constantly pressing them and kissing them. He licked my complete body. I too kissed his navel. But then someone came and we had to stop.

I went back and realised what have I done. I discussed with my friends but they were normal. They told me that it is normal in any relationship. I didn't talk to him for a week. But then I also needed sex. The 8th day I called him and asked for an apology. He laughed and we again began to have fun. He kissed me and pressed my boobs and he used to suck my boobs after removing my bra. Everything was back to normal.

Then one day he told me that he wanted to have sex with me. I agreed. The problem was to find a place for sex. God helped us. And his floor mates went to a trip. I shaved off my pussy well and also got a new dress and went to his room at the decided time.

He opened the door. He was wearing vest and boxers. He told me that I was looking very beautiful and started kissing my lips. I too responded back and we deep French kissed. He closed the door and we kissed again. He then removed my top and started kissing my boobs he removed my bra too. For the first time I saw the bulge in his boxers his cock seemed too large I wanted to see it. I also removed his vest and started kissing his body. I licked his armpits nipples and whole body.

I was enjoying kissing his body. He also kissed at the back of my ear and neck. I was on heaven. He started kissing me again. He picked me up in his arms and we went to his bedroom. There we had some hard drink and the kissing session began again. This time he went to my jeans and started unzipping it. I couldn't resist. He completely removed my jeans and I was just left in a black panty.

He told me that I was looking very cute with just the panty and I smiled a little. He then started kissing my pussy over the panty. I was thinking how can one lick such a place. He then removed my panty too and I was completely naked before him. This was the first time I was completely naked in front of a man. I closed my eyes. He kept sucking my pussy until I cummed. I was on cloud nine. But he again aroused me by continuously kissing my pussy.

He then removed his boxers and was only left in a underwear. He asked me to remove his undies but I was hesitant. He them placed my hand on his cock and asked me to remove his undies. I was shy but I took off his underwear. He put my hand on his big cock and it was very hot. I still remember its touch. His cock was nearly 10 inches long and 3 and half inches in girth. I was wondering how will it go in my vagina.

I started playing with his cock and he told me take it in mouth. I was hesitant but, on his insistence, I licked it. Its salt taste influenced me. I took it in my mouth. He started mouth fucking me. I licked his balls. After some while I told him not to test my patience and put it in my vagina. He agreed and touched the top of the cock on my pussy but I was a virgin so it was difficult. So, he used some oil and spit and gave a push. I screamed. I told him to take it out but he didn't stop and he was catching me tightly that I couldn't even move.

He started kissing me. When my pain reduced, he gave another push. I felt as if I will die but he continued doing his work. I was feeling as if a knife was there in my pussy. He then gave his final push and 10-inch cock was in my pussy. I almost fainted. He continued fucking slowly and gradually I started enjoying too. The Air-conditioner was on but we both were sweating.

He increased his speed and I was enjoying. I kept telling him to fuck me harder and harder. He fucked me for half an hour and then he took out his cock and forcibly put it in my mouth and cummed all over my mouth and started kissing me. I was feeling like vomiting but then he and I cleaned all the cum together. The bed sheet was full of blood as I was a virgin.

He asked me whether I enjoyed and I just kissed his cock. He fucked me twice more that night and then he dropped me to my hostel. I am in love with his 10-inch big cock. I showed my friends his cock pic and his body and they are all jealous of me. I and Raj meet daily now and he kisses my lips sucks my boobs and fucks me hard with his 10-inch cock. Everybody in the gym also know that we are a couple and no one disturbs us.

Sometimes even in the gym bathroom he removes my bra and panty and licks my boobs and pussy. I also remove his vest and boxers and enjoy kissing his 10-inch cock. I am in love with his 8 pack abs and biceps and I once I even told him to remove his t shirt in public for me and he happily agreed and removed his t-shirt. I kissed him on the cheek and then we fucked at night. That night I gave him double pleasure. Now we fuck almost every day.

Once he told me that he wants to fuck my ass but I was frightened seeing his cock size. I refused but I again fell in his trap and that night I enjoyed having my tight ass sucked. Now I and Raj go to parties together movies etc.

Once he even fucked me in my hostel room and once in the gym. Now his urge for sex was increasing. It was a problem. Once he asked me to fuck in the park. And once he mouth fucked me in the mall bathroom. This was my story.

38. Raj 2

I told you how my boyfriend Raj fucked me hard with his 10-inch-long thick cock. About me, my colour is fair, eyes big and sexy figure. My figure is 34-24-34. Let me tell you a few things people asked me- pink nipples, excellent boobs etc.

After my virgin seal broken, I was a sex diva. I and Raj constantly enjoyed almost everywhere we met. We tried numerous positions and only a girl can understand the mixed feeling of pleasure and pain. Only a girl can understand the feeling when her boobs are pressed and sucked. It is always so much pleasurable that it can't be described in words. I and Raj went to gym daily.

By now, I had gained a good figure and also reduced some weight. Raj just used to work out to maintain his 8 packs and biceps and triceps. We also had a common friend Lohit in the gym who was also a trainer at the gym. He is that second person I had sex with. He was also a well-built guy with masculine body and colour fair and height 6 inches. He used to look at me lustfully and I noticed that.

I told Raj about the same but he didn't pay much attention because Lohit was his friend. Everyone at the gym knew that I and Raj are a couple. Once I and Raj went for the late-night show of a movie. I hope you understand why? Raj was in denims and shirt while I was wearing a shirt with a short denim. In between the movie, he started rubbing my thighs and I was aroused. I smiled a little and he continued his work. He took my hand and placed it on his cock which I pressed a little.

He started to unbutton my shirt and half unbuttoned it. My black bra was now visible. He started rubbing my breasts over my bra and even pressed my nipples. It was dark and I suppose no one noticed. I pressed his lund. He then took my boob out of bra and started sucking it. I was moaning a little. He brought his face close to my face and licking my ears told me to come in the washroom after him. He went and I followed him some minutes later.

I went into the lady's washroom and suddenly he pulled me in one of the doors and immediately planted kisses on my face. I asked him to be patient. He then completely unbuttoned my shirt and started to suck my nipples over the bra and he was pressing harder. I was moaning. He then went down and unbuttoned my shorts and started to remove my shorts but I stopped him and asked him to continue over the shorts.

He started licking my half visible black panty until I cummed. Guys my panty got all wet and squeeze. I then got up and unbuttoned his shirt and what I like the most in sex-nipples. I licked his nipples and sucked them. With Raj in my company, I always felt Lohit as I was having a superb boy with such muscled physique and big lund (cock). I kissed his body and had just started to unbuttoned his jeans when we heard a knock on the door. We quickly grabbed our clothes and went out of the washroom. Some were surprised seeing a cool dude in the washroom but I think they understood. By now, I had got over the factor Log Kya Kahenge(what will people say)

We were back in the Audi. He unbuttoned my shorts and started fingering me and then took out his cock. I started to play with my tool. I think a girl saw us doing that as she was pointing towards us. But I didn't care and continued sucking his cock. I was wearing half unbuttoned top and he was pressing my boobs and I was sucking his cock. Now, it was difficult to control.

So, we went back to his room in his car. Inside the car, I completely unbuttoned our shirts and I took out his cock and started giving him a blowjob. I kissed his body which always fascinated me and he was also pressing my boobs a little. Little because he was driving. We reached the room continued the fucking session. First of all, we completely removed the clothes and started kissing like long lost lovers.

He then sucked my boobs and pressed them hard. I let out a moan. I too kissed his nipples and armpits. After that he started to finger me. I think I was completely wet and I was moaning heavily. He started to fuck me and inserted his 10-inch cock all in once. I let out a loud scream and he continued to fuck me.

I was feeling pain but gradually it reduced and we both started enjoying until he cummed in my pussy and we laid on bed tired with he over me and my arms over his back nail biting it. We stayed in that position for some minutes. Then we had a deep French kiss and continued again.

I again sucked his cock and it was hard again. He then fucked me again. We then fucked 3 more times that night and he dropped me to my hostel and I slept being tired.

39. Lohit

I told you about Lohit in the last story. 6 feet height, excellent physique and of course good personality. He always fucked me with his eyes. Once Raj was not in the gym and I was doing normal exercises and all. I went to the washroom to freshen up and I had not opened the door that Lohit called me from behind and asked me to go with him. I asked him where but he told me to keep quiet and follow him. I obliged.

He took me in some store room and removed his vest and closed the door from inside. I forgot to tell you that he was wearing a vest and boxers while I was wearing a sports bra and shorts. He told me keep quiet. I understood what he wanted. I wanted to shout but he kept his hand on my mouth and quickly lowered my shorts. He picked me up with his hand still on my mouth and completely removed my shorts. I wanted to go out but he told me that I can go out but only in my panty. He then came nearer and removed my sports bra too. Now, I was only in a bra and panty in front of him. Black bra and panty.

He then showed me a video clip of me and Raj fucking hard and asked me to cooperate otherwise the video will go viral. I was shocked and puzzled. I was thinking how he got that video. Was Raj the black sheep or was there anything else that I didn't know? He told me that he wanted to sleep with me. I was helpless. He told me that the video was made by Raj and now Raj and he will double-fuck me.

He asked me to cooperate and enjoy otherwise....... I was shell shocked. I wanted to kill Raj for a moment. Lohit told me that I will be in heaven if I once get double fucked and will always demand two lunds (cocks) in future. I thought for a moment and then I surrendered. Then Lohit came near me after removing his boxers and started to kiss on my lips with his hands squeezing my boobs. He was shirtless and kissing my lips. He pressed my boobs very hard and was very rough in sex. He was eating my mouth. His tongue was in my mouth.

Then he spit in my mouth and continued kissing. I was helpless. But then I thought to enjoy too. He left my mouth and removed my bra hooks in a second. I was completely naked from upside. He started sucking my boobs and he also bit my nipples hard. I moaned but he continued. He then removed my panty too and I was completely naked now. He was still wearing his underwear and I was completely naked. My pussy was oozing juices out of excitement.

He then sat on his knees and licked all my juices and started sucking my pussy. I could clearly see the bulge in his undies. He bit my pussy, pressed my boobs and kissed my lips. He then asked me to remove his underwear with my mouth. I removed his undies with my mouth. He was having a good 9 inches long and 3 inches thick cock. He asked me to take it in mouth. I took the cock in my mouth and he started to mouth fuck me. He completely inserted his cock in my mouth and his balls hurt my face. He then breast fucked me.

Then I asked him to fuck me but he told me to have 69 first. I agreed. He lied on the floor and I lied on him. He started to suck my pussy and I started to lick his hot cock oops lund. He then came over me and aimed for a shot after placing his cock on my pussy. He pushed and the cock went inside easily due to Raj's 10-inch-long thick cock. He then started to fuck me. His hands were squeezing my breasts and his mouth was on my lips and boobs. The room was full of noises and I also kissed his nipples and armpits.

He fucked me and cummed in my pussy. He wanted to fuck again but I asked hin to let it go for some other time. He agreed. I started to wear my clothes but he took my bra and panty and I had to wear just sports bra and shorts. I also took his undies and we both deep kissed and left for the gym. He reminded me of the double fucking thinking of which I was shell scared.

He told me come to Raj's room tomorrow otherwise he would leak my video. I agreed but I was very scared. I never thought in my wildest dreams ever that Raj will deceive me like this. But also, there was a feeling of pleasure in getting double fucked. All the night went in thinking. I called Raj but he didn't receive any calls. I told my friends about the same but few told me that I was trapped but few asked me to enjoy to the fullest. I was scared as well as excited. I was not scared because I was going to be double fucked or that two men were going to rip my ass and pussy. I was just thinking that the pain that I will be going to encounter.

Whenever I thought about the same, I would remember how much it had pained when Raj had fucked my pussy. I was scared. The full night went in thinking this. I was not at all thinking that two men will be fucking me. I will be a prostitute or whore at all. I was fucked by both these men. So why not the two of them at the same time. The next day rose. I washed myself thoroughly cleaned my pussy and all. I am now waiting for what will happen next.

www.ingramcontent.com/pod-product-compliance
Lightning Source LLC
Chambersburg PA
CBHW070853160726
48004CB00003B/1055